"You still have ___ **he reminded her. "What does fake dating look like in this deal? Do I get to kiss you?"**

Her brows shot up and her gaze swept down his entire body in a way that added some sizzle to the crackle, and it sounded exactly like the beginning stages of a raging fire.

"You say that like it's a perk."

Her tone made him grin. "If it is, it goes both ways."

Her chuckle was silky. "Spoken like a man comfortable with his skill set. I do generally find confidence attractive, but don't worry. You're not my type."

"Same." *Liar.* She was everyone's type and he was probably going to spend the next forever doing a terrible job of resisting her. But he had to—she was literally his prime suspect. "So no kissing. Fine. But we have to make it believable. Plus I have to have free rein without raising eyebrows. Solution?"

"You have to move in here. Obviously." She stared him down. "After you pass a background check and I see official orders regarding my aunt's cause of death."

"Done."

Dear Reader,

Thank you for picking up *Undercover Sabotage*! I'm thrilled to welcome you to the sun-drenched hills of Texas wine country—where danger lurks between the vines and romance blooms despite all odds. This is the first book in a new, hopefully long-running series starring the Shadow Rangers, an elite special ops branch of the Texas Rangers that's totally off the books.

When I first imagined Samantha Wagner, I saw a woman whose entire identity was built around achievement and success. What happens when someone like that inherits a vineyard she knows nothing about? And what if that inheritance comes with a target on her back?

Enter Dean Carter, former Texas Ranger with uncompromising principles and a wounded heart. He's investigating a murder, she's his prime suspect and neither of them expects the attraction that ignites between them. Their journey explores what happens when two people with completely different worldviews find themselves drawn together while facing escalating danger.

I've always been fascinated by vineyards, the perfect blend of science and artistry, precision and patience. They're places of beauty that hide the incredibly hard work happening beneath the surface. What better setting for a story about two people discovering that love requires the same patience, care and sometimes—a deep dive?

Wishing you romance, suspense and perhaps a glass of your favorite wine as you turn these pages!

I love to hear from my readers. Find me at kacycross.com.

Kacy

UNDERCOVER SABOTAGE

KACY CROSS

ROMANTIC SUSPENSE

MIX
Paper | Supporting responsible forestry
FSC® C021394

**Harlequin®
ROMANTIC
SUSPENSE™**

Recycling programs for this product may not exist in your area.

ISBN-13: 978-1-335-47192-5

Undercover Sabotage

Copyright © 2026 by Kacy Cross

Harlequin Enterprises ULC
22 Adelaide St. West, 41st Floor
Toronto, Ontario M5H 4E3, Canada
www.Harlequin.com

HarperCollins Publishers
Macken House, 39/40 Mayor Street Upper,
Dublin 1, D01 C9W8, Ireland
www.HarperCollins.com

Printed in Lithuania

USA TODAY bestselling author **Kacy Cross** writes romance novels starring swoonworthy heroes and smart heroines. She lives in Texas, where she's seen bobcats and beavers near her house but sadly not one cowboy. She's raising two mini-ninjas alongside the love of her life, who cooks while she writes, which is her definition of a true hero. Come for the romance, stay for the happily-ever-after. She promises her books "will make you laugh, cry and swoon—cross my heart."

Books by Kacy Cross

Harlequin Romantic Suspense

The Shadow Rangers

Undercover Sabotage

The Secrets of Hidden Creek Ranch

Undercover Cowboy Protector
Bodyguard Rancher
Decoding Danger

The Coltons of New York

Colton's Yuletide Manhunt

The Coltons of Owl Creek

Colton's Secret Past

The Coltons of Arizona

Colton at Risk

The Coltons of Dark Canyon

Colton's Wilderness Rescue

Visit the Author Profile page
at Harlequin.com for more titles.

Chapter 1

The last thing Dean Carter expected to be doing after quitting his law enforcement job was responding to an invite to discuss another one. From his former mentor in the Texas Rangers, no less.

It was a testament to his respect for Joseph Strickland that Dean had even answered the phone in the first place. Wallowing in disillusionment didn't allow a lot of extra time for chitchat, let alone the hour's drive from Blanco to Kerrville.

What else did he have to do though? Run his fingers over the bullet scar near his ribs for the four millionth time? Besides, Strickland hadn't taken no for an answer, and honestly, he'd piqued Dean's curiosity with his cryptic job offer that came with zero details.

If he wanted to know, he had to get in his truck. With his dog, Alfred—nonnegotiable.

The blue heeler came instantly when called and hopped up into the Ford Raptor that Dean bought with the state's blood money. A happy-I-didn't-die present to himself. He liked the truck, but not the circumstances required to have enough in his bank account to pay cash without flinching.

"Wanna go to Kerrville?" he asked Alfred, who lolled out his tongue in response. Dean mostly took that as a yes, but they were still feeling each other out. "Normally, I'd say be on your best behavior since I guess this is a job interview, but I'm not really sure I want it, so just be yourself."

Advice he'd take to heart as well. And if Strickland didn't like guys who brought dogs to job interviews, oh, well. Dean had found Alfred in the last kennel at the shelter and they'd bonded instantly. The name had come with the dog, but he'd kept it. Alfred took care of Bruce Wayne faithfully and provided low-key companionship, so the name had a lot of good vibes wrapped up in it.

Relying on a dog instead of people—for anything—certainly got Dean's vote.

The Texas Hill Country unrolled beneath his tires as he headed west from Blanco, miles of rugged terrain with winding roads cutting through limestone cliffs. The blue sky above was streaked with high, thin clouds, which did nothing to dispel the heat this time of year. You couldn't buy a breeze from Waco to San Antonio after mid-June unless a hurricane blew up in the gulf, and then you just wanted to turn it off.

The pin drop Strickland texted him sat outside Kerrville, which lay a little too close to Bandera for his taste. Once upon a time, he'd have swung south and picked up Jake for lunch or hung out at his former partner's ranch for a few hours. Nowadays, the most energy Dean spent on Jake Dalton was deleting text messages from the traitor.

The GPS told him he'd arrived. Dean steered his truck onto the paved road barely visible between the thick pines and halted at the imposing gate to press the button on the speaker box. A twelve-foot brick wall painted the color of tree bark extended on both sides as far as he could see.

"Good afternoon, Mr. Carter. Mr. Strickland is expecting you." The disembodied voice floated from the speaker box, which went dead with a click before he could tell the guy, "No *mister* before Carter needed."

The gate yawned wide. Dean drove through it, the concrete

even beneath his tires. Freshly poured, then. Impressive grounds gave way to a circular drive, but the imposing house stole the show, an architectural masterpiece of glass and stucco rising up against the backdrop of hills.

Not one single part of this scene felt inviting, even though he'd clearly been expected.

Security cameras swiveled silently, tracking his every move as he parked in the circular drive behind a white Silverado, High Country edition. Looked like Strickland had come up in the world since parting ways with the Rangers.

"Stay in the car, Alfred," he instructed. The dog would be reasonably safe if Dean left the AC on with the engine running—and he planned to.

Gone were the days when he failed to secure a fast getaway.

Dean slid to the ground, his fingers brushing the scar on his abdomen absently. As he approached the door, Strickland himself opened it. Whatever windfall had led to this fortress hadn't afforded him a butler?

"Dean Carter." Strickland's voice carried easily across the distance. "You're a sight for sore eyes."

Something unfolded in Dean's chest, but it wasn't nearly enough to let him catch a full, unconstrained breath. Maybe a handful of people existed in the world who Dean would consider a friend. The jury was still out on whether Strickland fell in that category.

But it was nice to see a friendly face. "Strickland. Looking good."

Not a platitude. Joseph Strickland was pushing sixty but seemed to have found some magic formula to keep himself fit and strong. Only his silvering hair had changed, giving away the number of years in his mentor's rearview mirror.

They clasped hands and did the one-armed dude hug thing that seemed to be expected between two people who used to be close but hadn't seen each other in several years.

"You holding up?" Genuine concern bled from the older man's gray eyes.

It was a toss-up which dumpster fire Strickland meant to ask about, but Dean didn't feel like having the conversation required to clarify, so he covered all the bases in one shot. "I'm good."

Strickland raised his brows, but didn't press him on it. "Glad you came. I wasn't sure you would."

"Same." Strickland could draw his own conclusions from that.

His host lifted his hands to indicate the house and the grounds around him. "Pretty snazzy, right?"

It felt like a test, but Dean had no clue what Strickland expected him to say after inviting him to visit what amounted to a hidden stronghold that clearly hadn't been bought with a former Ranger's salary. "It's something, all right."

"A bit overwhelming, I realize. Let me show you something."

Strickland guided him down a long hallway that echoed as they crossed the expensive-looking tile on the floor. When they came to a closed door, Strickland stepped up to a panel on the right side and peered into it. A red line shot out and scanned his eyeball.

"Joseph Strickland. Access granted," the female voice announced from the panel.

The door slid open, retracting into the wall, revealing a cavernous room with a configuration that Dean recognized, having frequented gun ranges often in his career. But this was the first time he'd walked into one at a residence.

He blinked rapidly. Still a gun range.

Strickland unlocked a case to the left of the door with his thumbprint and took out a weapon, but not one that Dean had ever seen. The color of the metal reminded him of Silly Putty, which was an odd choice for a firearm. Until Strickland racked the slide and held it out as if he meant to fire at the wall.

The gun practically vanished in his hand. The color made

it imperceptible against his skin. That was a trick and a half. Immediately, half a dozen scenarios where that weapon would have saved lives sprang to Dean's mind.

Strickland had his attention.

Then he held out the weapon, nodding to indicate Dean should take it. His fingers closed over the grip. The metal even felt different.

"Step up to the line," Strickland offered. "See how it feels."

That was an invitation Dean would never refuse. He adjusted his stance at one of the bays, noting the lack of range officers, which presumably meant he could fire at will.

Taking aim, Dean squeezed the trigger. Nothing happened. He tried again. It was like the mechanism was locked, but when he examined the weapon again, he couldn't see any aftermarket release mechanism. Obviously, the gun's tech extended to more than its cloaking abilities.

"Did I fail the test?" he asked Strickland wryly, since his earlier assessment of what this was seemed to be accurate after all.

"Not at all. It was a demonstration." Strickland took the gun and stepped up, firing at the target three times in quick succession. The bullets left the chamber with high-pitched zings that indicated a silencer might be built in. "Biometric. Only I can fire it. Handy, right?"

Immeasurably. The wrong hands could never turn that weapon on its owner. He wanted one.

But its very presence raised the question: "You called me here to show me your fancy gun collection?"

Strickland smiled. "I needed you to be clear on the resources I have available to me now. It's part of the sales pitch."

Dean couldn't wait to hear it, then. "You get points for effectiveness."

Demonstration over, Strickland exited the gun range and led Dean to what must be his office. Warm leather-bound books lined rich mahogany shelves, while three enormous and sleek computer monitors blinked silently from their ceiling mounts above a massive oak desk. The surface was completely clear.

"Have a seat." Strickland gestured to one of the high-backed leather chairs facing his desk.

Dean settled into the left one closer to the door. Habit.

Instead of sitting behind the desk, Strickland took the other one, sitting at an angle, an unusual move likely meant to create a power balance. They were all friends here. Apparently.

Strickland leaned back, his steely gray eyes assessing Dean. "What have you been doing with yourself since you quit the Rangers?"

The question hit Dean like a sucker punch. Mostly because he couldn't answer it without sounding pathetic. "I got a dog. Rescue. He's taking a lot of my time."

Lies. Alfred had blended seamlessly into his life, which sort of ruined the intent—to give him something to do. So instead he spent a lot of his waking hours feeling restless or useless or angry or all three at once. Being a Ranger had given him purpose, and then one bullet had felled him like a two-hundred-year-old oak in a lightning storm.

That alone hadn't shattered his faith in the system he'd sworn to uphold. No, that had come later, when the filth who had pulled the trigger flashed some dollar bills around and escaped prison time.

Again, Strickland raised his brows as if starting to catch on that Dean held the truth very close to the vest. "And Jake? How's retirement treating him?"

Dean's jaw clenched. *Jake.* The final nail in Dean's coffin. Even after Ruiz went scot-free, Dean might have soldiered through. But then Jake had turned his back on the Rangers. On Dean. Because of a *woman*.

"Wouldn't know," Dean ground out. "Haven't talked to him."

Something flickered in Strickland's eyes: Understanding. Sympathy. Calculation. "It's not easy when the people we trust let us down. When the system we rely on to keep us safe fails. But sometimes, it opens doors to new opportunities."

There it was. The reason he was here. "Which is what exactly?"

"I'll answer that with a question of my own. Did you leave the Rangers because you'd put away all the bad guys?"

"Not even a little bit." The sentiment might have come out as a growl. "I have a feeling you already knew that."

Strickland nodded with a small smile. "I suspected. We're cut from the same cloth. I saw it when you joined the ranks all those years ago. We're warriors on a crusade for justice."

Yeah, Dean was that all right. It didn't sound like a compliment though. More like Dean was an idiot and a fool for not wising-up to how the system really worked way before now. "Fat lot of good it does to be an idealist in a world designed for the richest guy to win."

The small smile on Strickland's face widened. "That's why it's handy to have become one of those richest guys. I have more money than I can ever spend in a lifetime, so I've made it my business to ensure there's something standing in the way of the bad guys the system can't—or won't—stop. There are still people out there who care about things like right versus wrong. Justice. Truth. I think you're one of them. That's why you're here."

Dean scrubbed at his neck, trying to process the explosive concepts his former mentor had so casually thrown out. "That was a lot of words. Are you, like…some kind of vigilante now?"

"That would indicate I operate unsanctioned." Strickland watched him closely. "Nothing could be further from the truth. I'm well-connected. Well-funded. Elite. Selective. I want you to join me."

The laugh that bubbled up from Dean's throat had not one ounce of humor in it. "So, you're saying I can go back into a broken system. No thanks."

"It's not the same system. We operate outside it. I was personally asked by a high-ranking official in this state to head a shadow unit. It's a division of the Rangers. Wholly off the record. Few people know it exists. I get orders from the governor's office, but you work for *me*. Because I have powerful people's direct contact information, we get special privileges regular units can only dream of. Plus, we have private money. Mine. So I say how it's spent. You want to drive a Ferrari on assignment, make your case. You need military-grade equipment, it's in the closet on the south side of the war room."

"Do I get my own biometric firearm?" The request was out of his mouth before he could second-guess how eager it made him look.

But the demonstration had worked. Piqued his interest. Spelled out exactly how high-tech this operation was.

"Naturally." Strickland inclined his head.

The excitement in Dean's chest fizzled. It sounded too good to be true. And nothing worthwhile ever started out that way. "If I say no thanks, do you have to kill me?"

Strickland didn't crack a smile at the joke. "You're not going to refuse. You're the most black-and-white guy I've ever met, so I get that operating in the gray is an odd place for me to ask you to be. But you have something to give, something this state needs badly. Honor. Courage. A drive to ensure the bad guys are brought to justice. I'm offering you the means to do it your way, no longer hampered by the bounds of a rigid system that will always fail due to bureaucracy."

"Do I get a code name?" Like that was the most important question he could ask. But this was all so out of left field that he couldn't formulate a coherent thought other than, *Yes, please.*

He wanted this opportunity so badly he could taste it. And he scarcely knew what was being asked of him. But he was so tired of sitting around, and anything that came with cool technology sounded better than that.

"You want a code name, you earn one," Strickland said, steepling his hands. "From the team. Everyone here deserves to be on the team, by the way, on merit, not reputation."

That was the kicker right there. They needed to get a few things straight before anyone got the wrong idea. "I don't need a team. I work better alone."

At least then, he'd know from the outset he'd be walking into a situation without backup.

Strickland nodded. "Had a feeling you'd say that too. I get it. That's the beauty of working in the shadows. There are a lot fewer rules."

How few? Dean's gaze narrowed as his brain started clicking down a dark path. "If I say yes, can I have a shot at Ruiz?"

They stared at each other for a moment. Strickland blinked first. "We get our orders from the state. We don't go rogue and perform our own witch hunts. I want to say that straight out. The Shadow Rangers might operate in the gray, but at the end, we're dispensing justice."

Shadow Rangers—a fitting name, if a little on the cheesy side.

"Trust me, he's still wallowing in illegal activity." Dean cleared his throat. "Those are my terms."

Nodding, Strickland glanced at the set of computer monitors in the corner. "If he's dirty and slipping through the cracks, my contacts will know. Should be a slam dunk to get an authorized order."

With that promise secured, Dean had zero reason to say no. He didn't want to say no. Ruiz was the mother of all carrots, the baddest bad guy alive who deserved death by a thousand fire ants. But Dean would settle for a meeting with the slimeball in a place with no security cameras.

"Given your terms," Strickland continued, "I have my own. We'll call this an audition, of sorts. You see how you like the part, read a few lines, test out the props. I'll evaluate your performance and see if this is a good fit. We both weigh in at the end. What do you say?"

"The end of what?"

"Your first assignment."

Before Dean could respond, a sharp knock interrupted them. The door swung open, and two guys waltzed in, both carrying themselves with a certain confidence and authority that Dean recognized a mile away. They were both military or law enforcement. Retired, probably, given the reason Dean was here.

The similarities between them ended there.

The first one was all coiled energy and sharp edges. Sandy-blond hair, green eyes that missed nothing and a crooked grin that suggested he knew a secret you didn't. Behind him loomed a broad-shouldered man with jet-black hair and piercing gray eyes. His face was a mask. Cool. Detached. He gave off a vibe that said you didn't want to meet him in a dark alley.

"Tanner Callahan," Strickland said as he gestured to the blond. "We call him the Phantom. He can be anyone, anywhere. Vanish into the crowd. Poof. You never knew he was there."

"Carter," the guy said. "Your reputation precedes you."

Dean tipped his chin, but didn't get up to shake hands since obviously everyone had been briefed that he'd be coming by today. This was less a meet and greet and more an evaluation.

Fine. He had nothing to hide. And the eval went both ways.

"This is Beckett Granger. Information specialist." Strickland pointed at the hulking figure behind Callahan. "Aka Mr. Freeze."

Yeah, that jelled. Ice was already starting to form on Dean's extremities as Granger stared at him.

"You in?" Granger said by way of greeting, which told Dean everything he needed to know about the man. Few words. Do your job. Everything is cool, no pun intended. They'd get along.

"Looks like."

His soul loosened all at once. And with that, it was decided.

Dean was doing this. How could he not at least try it out for a shot at Ruiz?

An uncomfortable silence settled over the room as the three men sized each other up. Dean felt the weight of their gazes, searching for weakness, for any sign that he didn't belong. They'd be looking a long time.

Strickland cleared his throat, which did zero to break the tension. "Now that introductions are out of the way, let's get down to business."

He picked up a device and swiped across the screen with one finger. Motors whirred and dark shades sank down over all the windows. Simultaneously, a large screen descended from the ceiling, then an elderly woman's picture appeared in the center.

"This is Greta Wagner, of Wagner Wines, a 123-acre vineyard and processing facility near Fredericksburg. Three weeks ago, she was found dead of 'natural causes.'"

The air quotes were implied.

Dean leaned forward, his wilted investigative instincts kicking into high gear. "You don't believe the coroner report."

"Not given the circumstance," Strickland said with a nod. "She'd set up a living trust with her niece as the beneficiary. Samantha Wagner. Who dropped everything in Houston and moved to the vineyard immediately after learning of her inheritance."

"I haven't looked into the value of a winery lately," Dean said with heavy sarcasm. "But I'm guessing it's worth more than a couple of dollars."

"North end of ten million," Strickland said and leaned back.

Oh yeah. There was fire beneath this smoke.

Callahan let out a low whistle. "Is the niece single?"

"Yes." This from Granger, who apparently had already done some prelim research into the obvious prime suspect.

Strickland's lips quirked up into a half smile. "This case isn't as straightforward as it seems, or Greta's death wouldn't have been brushed under the coroner's carpet. That's why Dean is on point to turn over some rocks at Wagner Wines."

Dean felt a familiar thrill of anticipation rushing through his veins. This was what he lived for—used to live for. Was he really being given an opportunity to rain down justice on the heads of the wicked, but this time on his own terms? He could scarcely believe Strickland meant to offer this gig to *him*.

"What's the plan?" he asked, already mentally gearing up for the investigation.

Strickland's eyes glinted with approval. "Head to the vineyard, get close to Samantha Wagner. Find out what she knows, what she's hiding. Uncover the truth, your way. The team is here to provide support. As you need it."

Apparently, he could set his own rules here. He was used to working as part of a team, sure, but always within the structured hierarchy of the Rangers, which he never wanted to do again. This felt different. Looser. A better fit at this stage of his life. As if he could write his own ticket, serve justice instead of the letter of the law, with no repercussions. It was dizzying.

Strickland leaned forward, his gaze intense. "Just remember this is an audition. Show me what you're made of. I'll show you what having unlimited resources can do to help. Then we see what the future looks like."

He met Strickland's gaze, his jaw set. "When do I start?"

"Right now, if you want."

Dean held up a finger. "First, I have to feed my dog."

Chapter 2

The sun had barely crested the horizon, but Samantha Wagner already regretted her wardrobe choice. The silk blouse and designer jeans didn't do dirt well, and honestly, she hadn't used enough deodorant to combat the heat. She didn't *own* enough deodorant to combat this heat.

She trailed behind Jules Foster, the vineyard manager, with no shot at keeping up. The older woman moved with purposeful efficiency through the rows of vines as if she'd been born in the labyrinth and never got lost.

"What's on the agenda for this morning?" Samantha asked brightly, wincing as her confidence-boosting Alexander McQueen heels sank into the soft earth for the umpteenth time.

"Examining the vines." Jules barely spared her a glance as her weathered hands gently examined a cluster of leaves. "Looking for pests. Disease. Any sign of damage. Same as every morning. The vines need constant attention."

Samantha nodded, trying to look knowledgeable and probably failing miserably because her face most likely reflected her inner panic. They had to do this visual examination of *all* of the plants? Every day? Rows upon rows of grapevines marched away from her, their leaves rustling gently in the hot breeze as they stretched to the horizon for a million miles. Or 123 acres, to be precise, if she recalled from the dizzying amount of information dumped on her over the last couple of days.

This was her kingdom now. She had to get a handle on this stuff. Her life in Houston—gone. Burned to the ground. Not literally, but close enough, and not by her hand. Okay, she'd thrown a match onto the bridge, but only after Caitlyn Herrera, Betrayer of the First Order, had shoved her out onto it.

So, no problem. This was just her one shot at proving she could rebuild her life from the ashes, that was all. The winery belonged to her now, a shocking windfall that still didn't seem real.

"How long have you been working here?" Samantha called, attempting to make conversation, desperate to establish some kind of rapport with this woman who was now her employee.

Jules straightened, fixing Samantha with a hard stare. "Twenty-two years. Started as a field hand, worked my way up. Unlike some people who waltz in and take over."

The barb hit its mark, but Samantha maintained her smile. Easy, after facing down corporate sharks on the regular. "I know I have a lot to learn, but I'm committed to making this work. For Aunt Greta's legacy, and for everyone here at Wagner Wines."

Did that sound practiced? Because she had repeated it to her mirror, multiple times, still unable to quite process that she was now the Wagner of Wagner Wines, smack in the heart of the Napa of the south.

Jules snorted. "Legacy? Is that why you drove Ben away?"

Samantha blinked, caught off guard. "Who is Ben? I don't recall meeting anyone by that name."

"Ben Hawthorne. You know, the winery's general manager? The guy who's been running this place for the last decade." The look Jules gave her set off a chilly slosh in Samantha's stomach. "Oh, right, you didn't meet him because he quit the moment you showed up and announced you were planning to run things."

Oh. Well, that explained a few things. She'd been wondering why no one seemed to be in charge, which was why she'd jumped right into the deep end, excited—and okay, maybe a little desperate—to prove Greta had made a wise choice in be-stowing this honor upon her.

She hadn't meant to step on anyone's toes. "I didn't real-ize—"

"Realize what? That you completely disregarded the people who've poured their lives into this vineyard?" Jules shook her head, disgust swimming through her eyes. "Look, Ms. Wagner, this isn't some corporate playground where you can sweep in and start making changes. These vines? They're living things. They need care, attention and respect. Come back when you're ready to bleed over them, like the rest of us."

Samantha flinched. She opened her mouth to defend her-self, to explain that she didn't have a mode besides *leaving it all on the field*, but Jules was already moving on to the next row of vines.

"And for God's sake, change into some proper shoes," Jules called over her shoulder. "You're liable to break an ankle in those things."

Ugh. That had gone well.

As Jules disappeared into the vineyard, Samantha felt a crack fork through her confidence. She was out of her depth, facing a steep learning curve that suddenly seemed insurmountable if one manager had already quit and the other one hated her.

Why had she thought she could do this thing?

Because her great-aunt had *believed* in Samantha, that was why. Obviously, Greta Wagner had seen something in her. Un-derstood Samantha's fierce business acumen.

She'd listened to the lawyers explain terms she'd only heard in passing before—living trust, beneficiary, inheritance (that one had filtered through much faster than the others)—and realized she no longer had to sit at her desk in EchoForge's glass-and-steel skyscraper, bathed in humiliation and resent-ment as all her sales deals for the company's software solu-tions vanished.

She could run Wagner Wines.

As soon as she figured out how to marshal the employees.

She needed an affirmation. A…catchphrase. Something to help her focus and reframe her purpose here.

I own Wagner Wines. Boring.

No whining, just wine. Better, but not personal enough of a mantra to motivate her when the going got tough, and based on this morning, that was going to be a constant.

It had to be snappy, with a reminder that she was going to slay this fresh start. *Samantha the Vineyard Slayer.* Yes! That was totally it, a stellar combo of success and Buffy. It would even work as a T-shirt.

As she started envisioning the font, one of the vineyard employees approached, hat in hand, from the direction of the tank rooms. A handyman, if she recalled, but she hadn't interacted with him directly yet. His expression said he wasn't too excited about ending that streak.

"Ms. Wagner?"

"Yes," she answered with a touch too much cheer as she sorted through her brain for the guy's name. Matt? Mark? Dang, she wasn't going to come up with it. "What can I do for you?"

"There's a problem with the roof on the maintenance shed."

His tone wedged into her already frayed nerves. What? He didn't like her either? What was with all these vineyard people who didn't want to give her even a half of a second to make a first impression?

She crossed her arms and tried to infuse a friendly expression onto her face that conveyed authority and assurance. "Okay. What's the problem?"

"It's leaking. It needs to be replaced, but the roofing company can't come until a week from Thursday."

The tone had shifted from mild disdain to extreme annoyance. Clearly, this announcement was supposed to mean something to her, but she had no clue why a roofer's schedule had landed in her lap. "Do you need me to call them and ask for an earlier appointment?"

The handyman shifted from foot to foot as if he had things to do besides hashing this out with her. "They're booked. There are no earlier appointments."

Mike. That was his name. He stood there as if she had to fix this problem immediately or everyone's day would be cursed. Including hers. Though honestly, it felt like that ship had already sailed.

Okay, one step at a time.

"Is this a problem you would have normally brought to Ben? And you can't because he's gone?" Mike nodded. Progress. "And you want me to fix it?"

More nodding. Great. So this was how it worked around here. The handyman expected the person with Wagner in her name to be handy in his stead when he couldn't figure out how to do his job. Probably a fair trade in his head since she'd been the one to eliminate his normal go-to manager from the mix.

Squaring her shoulders, she nodded right back. "Show me the problem?"

Mike tucked his head down and led her to a shed, presumably the one with "maintenance" as its first name, one of the smallest buildings on the property. Everything else was enormous, including the house that sat several hundred yards from the commercial area, on the back half of the land past the vineyards. It was her house now. All eight thousand square feet, though one woman could not begin to fill the rooms with enough of anything to keep it from feeling like a mausoleum.

"It's the roof," Mike told her, jerking his head toward the offending area without an ounce of irony, which was its own kind of talent.

Since she'd been at Wagner Wines all of five minutes, this was obviously a test. One she would pass or die trying. A ladder leaned against one of the walls, so the math wasn't hard, here. If she wanted to understand what problem Mike expected her to fix, she had to climb up to see it.

Or he could just tell her. But given their do-si-do thus far, that was unlikely.

Fine. Jules's warning ringing in her ears, Samantha kicked off her stilettos and started putting her hands and feet to good use. Halfway up, she remembered that climbing ladders wasn't one of the activities at Body by Belinda, where she did Pilates three days a week back in Houston. This thing was really rickety and kind of swaying in a weird pattern, which also brought home the fact that four rungs up the ladder was pretty high off the ground. And so was the roof. Which she still hadn't reached yet.

Best part yet? Mike seemed to have vanished. How was she supposed to figure out the problem? Guess?

The next rung she stepped on groaned with an odd sort of splintering sound.

A male voice from behind her called out, "I'm looking for Ms. Wagner. I was told I could find her out here?"

As she turned her head to see who this new voice belonged to—and it was definitely not Mike since this male didn't automatically sound like he hated her and blamed her for ruining everything—the rung cracked.

The world tilted sideways as Samantha plummeted toward the ground. A scream ripped from her throat as she braced for impact.

But instead of hitting the hard ground, she hit something else. *Someone* else. Or rather his arms as he caught her expertly, the scent of citrus and something distinctly masculine filling her senses.

"Whoa, there," the deep voice rumbled, vibrating through her chest since it was snug up against his. "I'd say that's not the safest way to get down from a ladder."

Samantha locked gazes with her rescuer, who had intense

blue eyes the color of ocean water from the air. The rest of him defied description, since her brain had turned into mushed avocado the moment she'd absorbed the masterful artwork of his chiseled jawline and tousled dark hair made for a woman's fingers.

Hers specifically.

Would it be rude to run her fingers through it to see if it was as soft as it looked? She'd have to remove his hat, and that would be a shame because the battered Stetson looked mouthwatering on him. She swallowed.

"I…uh…" Samantha stammered. *Mayday. Brain not braining.* He was so close and so much and she was not at all used to a man's presence seeping into her bones. "I mean, thank you. Obviously. That could have been nasty."

He set her down gently, but kept a steadying hand on her elbow. "It's no problem. Are you all right? Any injuries?"

"Other than my pride?" she asked ruefully, and then did a quick inventory, noting her back felt like she'd hit an iron bar instead of his arms, which given the way he'd effortlessly held her weight, probably wasn't that fanciful of a description. "I'm fine. How are you?"

The stranger stepped back, scrubbing at his neck. "No worse for wear. Glad you're not hurt. I was in the right place at the right time."

"Looking for me, I guess. Hi," she responded with a goofy wave, her voice automatically lilting into this chirping register that made her sound stupid. "I'm Ms. Wagner. Samantha."

What was wrong with her? Yes, the guy was hot. So were a lot of other guys, and none of them made her feel the slightest bit flustered. Maybe it was his sheer size, easily topping her five-nine with enough left over that she could slide on her heels and still not be able to look him in the eye. And he'd clearly been cut from a mold that had then been smashed to smithereens soon thereafter, because she'd never seen a man in real life with shoulders and biceps like *that*.

Without fully thinking through how much more daft she could get in his presence, she held out her hand, which he shook graciously. The white-hot zing in her stomach nearly put her on her knees, which she did her best to cover since he didn't seem the slightest bit affected by her.

"Nice to meet you. Dean Carter," he replied, his lips quirking into a half smile that made her stomach do a little flip. "I'm here to ask you a few questions about your great-aunt, Greta Wagner."

Okay, that was not what she'd been expecting him to say. She took a minute to slide into her shoes, gaining a much-needed several inches. Now she could look at his chin without craning her neck. "Questions? Like what?"

Dean glanced at Mike, whom she'd frankly forgotten existed, as he wandered back from wherever he'd been, and then back at her, his expression sliding into something a little more guarded with the addition of extra ears. "Is there somewhere we could speak privately?"

Oh, sure, so her brain could completely desert her? He'd like that, wouldn't he? Actually, she didn't know what he'd like, and she needed to get her wits about her fast. "We can talk. But first I need to see about this roof."

Except the rung she'd been standing on had separated from the side, hanging uselessly against the aluminum frame. It would be really hard to skip that one safely.

Dean's eyes followed hers. "You're going to need a different ladder. I'd hate for you to fall again. Though, if you want, I'd be happy to stand here and catch you."

Samantha felt heat rush to her cheeks, a mix of embarrassment and something else she wasn't quite ready to name, but started with an *a* and ended with *ttraction*. Maybe more so because he hadn't said anything that sounded like *Leave the roof-*

fixing to us men or some other misogynistic nonsense. Huge points to Dean Carter for that.

"We don't have another ladder," Mike informed her flatly. "I have to go into town to buy a new one."

"Sounds like my part can wait, then," she suggested gleefully because spending even five minutes in Mr. Carter's company sounded a whole lot more fun that the roof repair party Mike had set up for her. "Would you like some iced tea?"

Dean nodded his assent and followed her toward the office she'd commandeered for herself in the back of the combo gift shop and wine-tasting area, which she'd assumed had been Greta's. Though now that she looked at it again with a fresh eye, it did have a masculine feel to it, probably because she'd stolen it from Ben, the missing general manager.

Firming her mouth, she snagged a couple of bottles of iced tea with lemon from the refrigerator near the door of her—Ben's—office, handing one to Dean as she swung around behind the behemoth of a desk. He waited until she'd taken a seat before sliding into his own guest chair.

A gentleman in delicious, subtle ways. She did like the way they grew their men out here in the Hill Country, especially when they came with a lot of extra features, like lips with a slight bad-boy pout and a tipped-back Stetson in a condition somewhere between lived-in and beat-up.

"You've got an hour," she said with a smile. "What questions would you like to ask me?"

Hopefully, she could answer them when she'd never even met Greta Wagner. Her great-aunt had been estranged from the family, or at least that was what Samantha had gathered when she'd started asking questions of her own.

"I'm investigating the circumstances surrounding your aunt's death." Dean let that comment unwind in the room as he kept his gaze trained on Samantha.

Too trained. Something jumped on her nerves, an odd sort

of niggle, clueing her in that Dean's presence here wasn't quite the lucky bonus she'd been framing it as. "Investigating? Are you a cop?"

That would explain his commanding presence, stellar reflexes and cut physique all right.

But Dean shook his head slowly. "Not exactly. I'm in the private sector."

The niggle got a little more insistent. "You're a private investigator? Okay. Someone hired you to look into my aunt's death? Why? She died of natural causes."

Dean's expression got a lot more shadowy. "We have reason to believe there might be more to it than that."

Her brows lifted as she stared him down. "What reasons? What are you dancing around? If you have something to say, Mr. Carter, spit it out."

He nodded once in acknowledgment of her straightforwardness. "It's possible Greta Wagner was murdered."

Samantha's world tilted on its axis again, only this time with no ladders in sight.

Chapter 3

Murdered.

The more Samantha repeated the word in her head, the less sense it made.

This cowboy/cop/rescuer/who-knew-what-all thought someone had *killed* Great-Aunt Greta? And he'd shown up to the vineyard without so much as a by-your-leave, throwing explosive words like *murder* around. It wasn't true. It couldn't be true, or they never would have given her the vineyard without an investigation. Right?

In full damage-control mode, Samantha leaped up and skirted the desk, slamming the door closed so nobody could accidentally—or on purpose—eavesdrop on this conversation.

"You can't say things like that," she hissed under her breath once she'd taken her seat again, now sorry she'd moved the computer monitor to the side to unblock her view.

Good Lord. What if someone had heard him?

"I have to say things like that," Dean said, his voice level. Because he didn't yet understand the disaster unfolding here. "This is an active investigation. I'm going to need to interview the staff, review the winery's financial rec—"

"Hold up there, partner," she said with an unamused laugh, flashing some jazz hands to demonstrate the point that he needed to slow his roll all the way down. "You can't talk to the staff. They…"

Hate me.

Which was going to come out pretty quickly the moment Dean Carter opened his mouth. The staff would probably line up to tell him how awful she was. Were they mad enough about Ben quitting to throw her under the bus?

Anything approaching a flutter or a goose bump with Dean's name on it got sloughed off in favor of the more expedient issue at hand. Someone thought Greta had been murdered. Maybe even here at the winery. And this guy was here to expose the killer.

What if it *was* true? She didn't know anything about the vineyard or her aunt's circumstances. Could someone have really killed her and then covered it up or something? Samantha should do everything in her power to expose the truth, if so.

"Ms. Wagner, it's important that I have access to the staff. And the financial records." Dean's gaze crackled with intensity that chilled her blood all at once. "Unless you'd like me to subpoena everything. Then I dig extra deep to see what you're trying to hide."

Her temple started throbbing as his meaning blared through her breastbone like a foghorn in the swirl of mist that had become her reality in the last few minutes. "You're not going to find anything hidden, Carter. No matter how deep you go."

He sat back, banking his weird intensity. "Then we don't have a problem. Let me do my investigation and prove you're not the perpetrator. I go home, no harm, no foul."

Blinking, Samantha stared at him. Oh, jeez. This actually *could* get worse. "You think *I* did it?"

Of course he did. Anyone with a brain would think that. Follow the money. Everyone knew that was how you found the mastermind of whatever thing you were trying to figure out.

Dean's lips lifted in a half smile, the same one that had seemed kind of flirty outside. Before she'd understood that he'd come here to bury her under an avalanche of suspicion.

"Did you?"

"No! Of course not." She frowned, trying to corral her racing thoughts. "I don't think anyone did it. She died of natural causes. That's what the lawyers said when they came to talk to me about my inheritance. Why in the world would you suddenly decide that's not the final word on the matter and show up here to upset the status quo I've been trying desperately to maintain?"

Yes, she did sound panicked, thank you very much. Dean Carter could not start nosing around, not now. Not when she still had so much to learn and so many obstacles in the way of success.

Besides, this was all a wild-goose chase. Who was this guy to question the cause of death that had already been issued?

"I can't share the details of my investigation," Dean said evenly. "Not while I'm in the middle of it. Safe to say, there's enough of a question about the manner of her death that it's in your best interest to let me prove you didn't do it."

Her eyelids fluttered closed. Direct hit. If she wanted this to go away, she had to let him investigate. If she let him investigate, the staff would glom on to the idea that she'd done it. Or at least been involved.

Worse, all of this meant he'd be *here*. On the property. Running around with those biceps and those eyes, distracting her from her mission to drink from the firehose called Owning a Winery.

Time for a recalibration. She opened her eyes. "You can't investigate. Do the subpoena thing. I'll stall it as long as I can."

She crossed her arms, staring him down, daring him to try her. He'd lose. These Alexander McQueens on her feet ranked second of all her shoes for their infusion of power and confidence. *Come at me, Dean Carter.*

He stood, rising over her like he'd materialized from the underworld. "Let me show you something."

"No to that too. I have a winery to run." *Learn* to run. A distinction he didn't need to know. He'd just add it to his already impressive arsenal of weapons aimed at her.

"I promise this is worth your while." His gaze swept her with a once-over. "And then I'll let you get back to work. Two minutes."

Warily, she stood, but only because she was starting to feel tiny as he towered over her.

Joke was on her. He still topped her by several inches and she did not like how weak in the knees it made her feel. "This better be good."

Without comment, Dean stepped back to allow her to pass him so she could lead the way out of the room. It was another subtle gentleman move. What was he like on a date, then?

She swept past him, head up. And then realized she didn't know where they were going. No problem for Mr. Carter. He joined her in the hall and put his electric fingers on her elbow to guide her, taking a discreet side door so they didn't have to waltz through the tasting room.

This was what he was like on a date, obviously. Considerate. Intense. Masculine. She practically shivered.

"Where are we going?" she asked, her tone dropping a touch in some kind of automatic reaction to the images swirling through her head. Which shouldn't be there but, oh well, no one had to know.

"Back to the shed," he responded as they rounded the main building.

The full sun hit her in the face like a two-by-four, slamming her with a wall of heat. Next time she inherited a vineyard, would it be too much to ask for it to happen in January?

Dean didn't even notice. He moved with purpose, no extraneous swishes, which she knew because she'd been watching how his body flowed through its motions.

He grabbed the ladder from where it leaned against the shed, easily picking it up and flipping it around on the ground, then pointed to the rung that had broken as he knelt near it. "See this?"

Not from her vantage point, no. And the stilettos weren't helping her balance any either. So much for these jeans. She dropped to her knees and peered around his shoulder, which seemed to double as a furnace, heating her torso where they were practically touching. "See what?"

"This rung didn't break randomly. It was cut. With a saw most likely."

Samantha forgot about the dance her skin was doing and leaned in closer. "What? How do you know th—"

Oh, well it was obvious now. The aluminum rung had a clean, diagonal cut running across its underside about three quarters of the thickness, the metal edges sharp and glinting in the sunlight. The rest of the aluminum had wrenched apart, curling in on itself as it weakened enough to snap under her weight.

A chill ran down her spine. What if Dean hadn't been there at exactly the right time? She would have hit the ground, as someone intended to happen. This had been done deliberately. But how would anyone have known she'd be climbing it?

Mike.

Mike had known, because he'd encouraged her to do it. Had Mike cut this ladder? It was a huge leap from disliking someone to potentially causing them harm.

But she didn't know the staff at Wagner Wines from Adam. Jules could have done it in hopes that Samantha would eventually climb the ladder. And maybe had set up a whole series of booby traps like this across the property, in case Samantha didn't fall right into the first snare the vineyard manager had set up.

Her skin went clammy despite the heat. Next time, Dean wouldn't be around to catch her.

"Okay, you've made your point," she murmured and shut her eyes for a beat, swaying as she climbed to her feet.

Instantly, Dean's fingers closed around her arm, steadying her. He seemed to have a sixth sense for when she would need him but managed to give her space the rest of the time. Nice trick.

Calla Riley, the manager of the tasting room and gift shop, strolled by from the employee parking lot in the back, a lunch sack in her hand. She nodded to them both, her gaze lingering on the spot where Dean's fingers still clutched her arm. Yes, he was standing too close and her face probably telegraphed how much she liked the way he smelled.

Great, now everyone would think she and Dean were dating, like she'd randomly invited him to show up at the winery and follow her around.

Her brain snapped onto that idea instantly. Why wouldn't she? If she was in a long-term relationship, it only made sense that her boyfriend would show up here after a few days.

"I changed my mind," she told him. "I'll let you poke around, but you can't tell anyone you're investigating."

Dean did that thing where he read her mind and figured out his sheer proximity had started making her head swim. He stepped back and resituated his hat. "How do you expect to explain my presence here, then?"

"Simple." She crossed her arms and tilted the axis once again. "You'll be playing the part of my boyfriend for the foreseeable future."

Dean waited for Samantha to clear the door to her tiny office before shutting it again. It would be fantastic if they'd managed to leave the mild insanity on the other side of the wall, but in close quarters, the crackle that filled all the spaces between the two of them got worse.

So, that was a thing. One he hadn't seen coming.

"What is this madness you're talking about, now?" he asked, crossing his arms in hopes that it would provide some kind of barrier against whatever was going on here, but he had the distinct feeling he'd only experienced the leading edge of the circus his life was about to become.

And Samantha would be playing the part of the ringmaster.

The very single Samantha, who looked nothing like the picture Strickland had shown him. Oh, she was a stunner all right, as he'd expected, but quite the opposite of the ice princess he'd geared up for.

Instead, he'd gotten an animated live wire who made sticking your finger in a light socket seem like the safer option.

Samantha whirled to face him, not opting to retreat behind the desk like he'd anticipated. "Which part is tripping you up?"

"The part where you mentioned that I would be your boyfriend."

"Not my real boyfriend," she said with a laugh. "Because that would be weird. We'll be pretending."

"Oh, well, that makes it less crazy," he shot back with heavy sarcasm. "Somehow we got off track. Let's start over. I need access to the winery and vineyards, particularly the staff, so I can investigate Greta's death. And then you say, 'Yes.' No other words."

"You're the one who's off track if you think I should willingly stop everything I'm doing so I can help you find evidence that will prove Greta was murdered when it's obvious I'm going to be the main suspect."

There it was. The stubborn tilt to Samantha's chin that had come out the first time she'd said no. This investigation was getting off to a *great* start.

Except this wasn't supposed to be a traditional investigation. He didn't do that anymore.

Everything he thought he'd known about what to do, how to act, who to *be* when on assignment slid away.

The job had changed. Maybe he should as well. After all, Strickland wanted an audition, maybe it wasn't so far off base to be contemplating playing a role to get the part he'd really come here to land: permanent member of the Shadow Rangers and a chance to right the wrongs with Ruiz's name stamped all over them.

"Okay." He raised his hands in surrender. "I get that you might not be too keen on an angle that might incriminate you. How is pretending that we're dating going to change that?"

Her gaze shifted, no longer staring him dead in the eye. In fact, she might even be avoiding making eye contact. His senses tingled.

"It will keep you out of the way," she told him bluntly. "Which is where I need you. Not underfoot."

His brows shot up as he absorbed that. "You must not date much if you think that's how it should be done."

"I date. All the time," she shot back instantly. "I just like men who are workaholics and cancel as much as I do."

So, not very much at all. Intriguing.

The problem being of course that he wasn't supposed to be intrigued by Samantha Wagner. What he was supposed to be doing was getting close to her. Skillfully extracting information from her about her aunt's death. Instead, he'd barged in here flashing his credentials that didn't exist, as if she would respond favorably to him throwing his weight around because catching a murderer should be at the top of everyone's list, not just his.

Dean cracked his neck. He could back slowly away and forget the idea of joining Strickland's team. Or dive into this circus.

"Let's say I agree to be your fake boyfriend," Dean said slowly, his gaze fastened tight on the woman who might or might not be a murderer. "What does that look like in your mind? How would I have access to question the staff?"

"You can't question the staff," she countered, a panicked expression replacing her stubborn one. "They can't know about the investigation. I'll help you. Ask me anything you need to. I'll give you unrestricted access to all of my aunt's things, accounting statements, whatever you want to see in exchange for doing this my way."

"And your way is the fake dating route?"

She nodded, still looking very much like a deer that had

bolted onto the road before realizing there was a semi bearing down on her. Something had spooked her. Because she had something to hide? Did she think she had a shot at keeping him from finding it with this fake boyfriend routine?

All at once, he couldn't *not* do this. Call it curiosity. Gut instinct. A strange desire to do the unorthodox, strictly to see if it got him style points with Strickland. All of the above.

"You still haven't answered my question," he reminded her. "What does fake dating look like in this deal? Do I get to kiss you?"

Her brows shot up and her gaze swept down his entire body in a way that added some sizzle to the crackle, and it sounded exactly like the beginning stages of a raging fire.

"You say that like it's a perk."

For some reason, her tone made him grin. "If it is, it goes both ways."

Her chuckle was silky. "Spoken like a man comfortable with his skill set. I do generally find confidence attractive, but don't worry. You're not my type."

"Same." *Liar.* She was everyone's type and he was probably going to spend the next forever doing a terrible job of resisting her. But he had to—she was literally his prime suspect. "So, no kissing. Fine. But we have to make it believable. Plus, I have to have free rein without raising eyebrows. Solution?"

"You have to move in here. Obviously." She crossed her arms and stared him down. "After you pass a background check and I see official orders regarding my aunt's cause of death."

"Done." As long as she didn't have a problem with dogs, anyway. Not that she had a choice. Alfred came with the deal.

She had the grace to let her surprise show, as if she'd convinced herself he wouldn't cross the line she'd drawn. *Let that be the first lesson to you then, Ms. Wagner.*

There were no lines he wouldn't cross to get another shot at Ruiz.

Chapter 4

Samantha hovered in the doorway, staring at the imposing leather duffel that Dean had plunked down in the guest room—one of nine in the house, because apparently Aunt Greta had expected a small army to visit. She reminded herself that this was her idea, and he'd merely called her bluff. In all honesty, she'd expected more pushback on the whole fake dating scheme.

What did it say about her dating life that every man she'd invited to sleep over in the past decade had made excuses about early meetings, but the investigator who suspected her of murder didn't hesitate?

Nothing flattering, that was for sure.

Across the room, Dean methodically unpacked, stacking T-shirts with military precision. The scene was so domestic she had to suppress a hysterical bubble of laughter. How had her life come to this? Two weeks ago, she'd been a sales executive at EchoForge with a corner office and an assistant who remembered how she took her coffee. Now she was playing landlord to an annoyingly attractive investigator with shoulders like a linebacker and biceps that looked like they could bend rebar.

She had to get her head in the game.

"You know you're not actually moving in forever, right?" she quipped, nodding toward what appeared to be a professional-grade coffee setup emerging from his bag. "Are you always this prepared?"

Dean glanced up, a hint of amusement flickering across his usually stoic face. "I take coffee seriously."

"Clearly." She crossed her arms, leaning against the doorframe with studied nonchalance. "What's wrong with the perfectly functional coffeemaker downstairs? It has buttons and everything."

"It makes brown water, not coffee." He continued unpacking, pulling out a chrome French press and a manual grinder that looked like it belonged in a museum of coffee torture devices. "This room okay? It has the best sightlines to the front entrance and vineyard access roads."

Of course he'd selected this room for tactical advantage rather than the four-poster bed or the antique writing desk that she'd been oddly proud of when showing him the options. The man probably approached breakfast cereal with the same strategic assessment.

"It's fine," she said. "Though I didn't realize I was hosting a one-man security detail."

"You're not," he replied, shooting her a look. "You're hosting your boyfriend who happens to be reasonably cautious."

Boyfriend. The word hung in the air like a soap bubble, deceptively light, but ready to burst at the slightest touch.

A decidedly non-boyfriend-like growl came from near her feet as Alfred, Dean's blue heeler, appeared in the doorway, vibrating with the need to explore his new territory. Aka not a curve ball she'd been expecting, since he'd never mentioned a dog. On purpose, she was fairly certain.

Dean paused his unpacking, tipping his chin toward the dog. "Alfred, you can go check things out. Just don't chew anything that looks expensive."

The dog didn't need to be told twice. He shot past Samantha like a furry bullet, toenails clicking rapidly down the hallway.

"Don't worry," Dean said, noticing her expression. "He's well trained."

Was her distaste that transparent? "It's not that. I've never had a dog before."

"City girl through and through, huh?"

She lifted her chin. "I had a fish once. Named Gordon. I think we were together longer than most of my relationships."

Dean snorted, the sound startling and genuine. Score one for her.

Silence settled between them as he continued unpacking with efficient movements, but she couldn't figure out why it didn't feel uncomfortable. She should leave, should go check inventory or review quarterly projections or pick any of the million things on her to-do list, but something kept her rooted to the spot. Something beyond professional curiosity.

There was nothing professional about any of this, no matter how she tried to dress up being a murder suspect in her head.

Dean lifted his arms to place something on the top shelf of the closet, and his Toby Keith concert T-shirt rode up, revealing a jagged scar on his right side. It was puckered and angry, even though it was clearly not recent. The kind of scar that came with a story. The kind that changed a person.

Because he wasn't sexy enough already? *Come on.*

She looked away quickly, but it was too late. The thing unfurling in her belly had many names, but she'd stick with *inconvenient*. This was what she got for lurking in doorways—details she absolutely did not need to see.

"You can come in, you know," Dean said without turning around. "It's your house."

"Just making sure you have everything you need." She gestured vaguely. "Clean towels in the bathroom. Wi-Fi password is on the desk. Anything else?"

"I'm good." He finally turned to face her fully, and the force of his blue eyes nearly knocked her back a step. "But there's something we should talk about."

Her pulse skittered. Could the man read minds too? Had he known the whole time she'd been ogling him? "Oh?"

"Security." He closed the distance between them with purposeful strides, stopping short of invading her personal space. "Someone cut that ladder. Someone wanted to hurt you. Until we figure out who, we need to be careful."

The flutter in her belly turned into a tornado. Prior to this second, she'd have insisted that protective, overbearing men had not one attractive quality.

Obviously, that was a complete lie.

Everything inside her that had turned cold the moment he'd mentioned "murder" in her office heated in an instant.

This was *not* happening.

"I think I can manage not to climb any more booby-trapped ladders," she said frostily—or what passed for icy when her body felt like she'd parked in front of an open oven door.

"It's not just that." Dean ran a hand through his hair, a gesture that seemed at odds with his usual controlled demeanor. "We don't know what else might be waiting. I want to set up some basic security measures around the house and main facilities."

"Like what? Trip wires and bear traps?"

"Motion sensors. Extra locks. I'll do a perimeter check." His lips quirked up slightly. "No bear traps. Unless you have a bear problem I don't know about."

"Just the usual wine country hazards. Pushy tourists. Drunk bachelorette parties. The occasional snobby sommelier." Good. Crisis averted. She could still speak and keep her wits about her in the presence of so much masculinity.

His smile deepened, revealing the hint of a dimple. Oh, dang, that was way more adorable than it should be on a guy. What was she supposed to *do* with him? None of this was in the murder-suspect-investigator handbook.

A bark from downstairs broke the moment. Alfred had apparently found something interesting.

"I should go check on your dog before he decides to redecorate." She stepped back, suddenly aware of how close they were standing.

"Our dog," Dean corrected, his expression unreadable. "For all intents and purposes."

She rolled her eyes. "Right. Fake dating, fake dog co-parenting. Any other relationship milestones you want to fast-track while we're at it?"

"Let's start with breakfast in the morning. We should go over our backstory."

The unexpected invitation tripped something in her already questionable stomach regions.

"I'll have to check my extremely busy social calendar," she said dryly, backing toward the doorway. "All those wine tastings and harvest parties to attend."

"I'll take that as a yes," he replied, turning back to his unpacking.

Samantha retreated down the hallway at a furious clip before he caught her with this ridiculous grin on her face. What in the world had made her think this was a good idea?

Sure, having Dean here would keep employees from discussing murder suspicions. But now she had a new problem, a much, much bigger one—Dean. Dean with his coffee obsession and his unexpectedly deep blue eyes full of protectiveness on her behalf and his dog, who was currently sitting in her kitchen, head tilted expectantly as if they were already old friends.

"What are you looking at?" she asked Alfred, who thumped his tail against the tile floor. "This is a temporary arrangement. Don't get comfortable."

Alfred's tail thumped harder. *Ugh.* He was kind of cute.

"I mean it," she insisted, even as she opened the refrigerator to look for something dog-appropriate. "This is strictly business."

The dog's ears perked up at the sound of the refrigerator, and Samantha found herself slicing up leftover chicken for him before she could think better of it.

"Not a word of this to your owner," she murmured as Alfred delicately accepted the offering from her palm. "I have a reputation to maintain."

Alfred licked her fingers in what felt suspiciously like a pact of silence. Great, now she was conspiring with a dog. Next she'd be asking her cactus, Spike, for fashion advice. And admitting to Dean that she'd named her cactus.

Outside the kitchen window, the afternoon sun cast long shadows across the vineyard. In less than twenty-four hours, her carefully controlled attempt at a fresh start had transformed into a cohabitation with a suspicious sexy investigator and his dog, a murder investigation and the possibility that someone had tampered with a ladder in hopes she'd be killed. Or, at the very least, severely injured.

Samantha Wagner, Vineyard Slayer, was now also roommate to a man who thought *she'd* killed Aunt Greta.

This was not in any business school case study she'd ever read.

Allowing Dean to pick a guest room near hers might have been a logical arrangement on paper, but in practice, his proximity created its own unique form of tension. Especially when the rooms shared a connecting balcony.

The next morning, Samantha stood at the French doors leading to said balcony, coffee mug in hand, watching Dean through the glass. He'd set up his laptop on the wrought iron table outside her door, apparently unbothered by the early morning chill. Alfred lay at his feet, occasionally lifting his head to track the movements of birds in the nearby oak tree.

Dean was still in what appeared to be sleepwear—a faded Kenny Chesney T-shirt and joggers—but he was already fully immersed in whatever was on the screen of his slick laptop. The intense focus made her wonder what kind of investigative work happened before 7:00 a.m. Was he researching her? Compiling evidence? Planning the most effective interrogation strategy over his meticulously brewed coffee?

Figuring out how to get her to confess she'd dreamed about him?

She should have asked for more specific terms in their arrangement.

Steeling herself because she'd agreed to breakfast but not where to have it or that she'd actually eat, Samantha slid open the door and stepped onto the balcony.

"Morning," she said brightly, employing the same tone she'd used for early conference calls with Tokyo.

Dean glanced up, his eyes doing a quick assessment that made her suddenly aware she was wearing silk pajamas with tiny cacti printed on them. The corner of his mouth twitched. "Nice pajamas."

Her hand went to the cactus print before she could stop herself. "A gift from a friend. Apparently, I have a reputation for being prickly."

"No way," Dean deadpanned, looking up again with those startlingly blue eyes. "You're prickly with your friends?"

"Ouch," she commented mildly without affirming or denying that few people escaped her tendency to shoot first and ask questions next week. She settled into the chair opposite him, maintaining what felt like a professional distance. The table wasn't large, so their knees grazed each other.

Alfred chose that moment to abandon Dean and pad over to lay his head on Samantha's bare foot. The warm weight was oddly comforting.

"Traitor," Dean muttered to the dog, though there was affection in his voice.

"He has excellent taste," Samantha replied, reaching down to scratch behind Alfred's ears. The dog closed his eyes in bliss. "You never mentioned your dog was a social climber."

"Must be all that leftover chicken you fed him."

She froze, hand still on Alfred's head. Man, her stealth needed work, obviously. "You saw that?"

"He had chicken breath all night." Dean's expression softened into something almost like a smile. "It's fine. I appreciate you looking out for him."

"Well, don't get used to it." She sipped her coffee, which suddenly tasted bland compared to the rich aroma wafting from Dean's cup. "We need to talk about boundaries."

"Already setting relationship ground rules? Most couples wait until after the honeymoon phase."

"Very funny." She gestured between them. "This balcony situation. We need some guidelines."

Dean leaned back, crossing his arms over his chest in a way that made his biceps flex alarmingly. "Such as?"

"Morning hours. I'm out here from six to seven—Pilates and meditation. Then I have breakfast meetings with staff starting at eight most days. Your turn."

"I like being out here in the early morning and late evening. I can work around your balcony Pilates."

The way he said it made it sound vaguely scandalous, and Samantha felt heat creep up her neck. "And then there's the matter of personal space inside. The house is huge, but we're going to cross paths. If we're supposed to be dating, we should probably, you know, act like we like each other."

"You don't find me likeable?" His expression was neutral, but there was something in his eyes that looked suspiciously like teasing.

"I find you skeptical, irritating and inconvenient," she replied sweetly. "But that doesn't mean I can't pretend to be en-amored with your many charms."

"My *many* charms?" He leaned forward, resting his fore-arms on the table. "Name three."

Samantha narrowed her eyes. Two could play this game. "Fine. You're dedicated to your work. You obviously care about Alfred. And you have—" she waved vaguely at his upper body "—reasonable muscles."

Dean's eyebrows shot up. "Reasonable muscles?"

"Don't let it go to your head." She took another sip of her coffee, trying to maintain a straight face, because she'd let on how much she was enjoying this over her dead body. "What's attractive about me?"

"You're determined," he said without hesitation. "You don't back down easily. And you have good taste in dogs."

No hesitation. Almost as if he'd already figured out what he liked. On purpose. And not because he'd expected to be asked, but because he'd evaluated her as a woman.

The twisty tornado in her belly flared up again.

"Well," she said, slapping corporate composure all over her expression. "That should be sufficient for public consumption. No one expects us to be writing sonnets to each other."

"Speak for yourself. I've been working on one that rhymes 'determined' with 'German shepherd.'"

A startled laugh escaped her. "That's not even close to a rhyme."

"I never said I was good at sonnets."

Oh, dear Lord. The man had a wry, well-hidden sense of humor, which increased his attractiveness quotient.

And against everything smart and rational, she liked him.

With the morning sunlight warming their shoulders, Alfred's gentle snoring at their feet, this scene felt more domestic and comfortable than she could credit. If she weren't careful, she might forget why Dean was really here—to investigate a murder he thought she might have committed.

As if sensing her thoughts, Dean's expression shifted back to professional. "About today," he said, closing his laptop. "I need to start interviewing staff."

And the comfortable bubble burst. "We agreed—"

"We agreed I wouldn't tell them about the investigation," he cut in. "But I still need to talk to them. Get a feel for the place, for Greta's relationships, for potential enemies. Trust me, I can be subtle." Dean stood, stretching in a way that made his T-shirt ride up slightly. "I'll keep it casual."

What he should have said was *This was your idea*, but he didn't, and for that, she blessed him. She didn't have a choice about any of this, other than to make the best of it.

"Nothing about you is casual," she muttered, definitely not fixating on the strip of exposed skin.

He looked down at her, a hint of that almost smile playing around his mouth as he collected his laptop and coffee mug. "I'm going to shower and head out to check the perimeter. Want to join me?"

Her coffee went down the wrong way, sending her into a coughing fit. "Excuse me?"

"The perimeter check," he clarified, his face a mask of innocence that didn't quite reach his eyes. "What did you think I meant?"

The thing where they were both naked with water sluicing over them as he aimed those intense blue eyes in her direction before kissing her senseless.

"Nothing," she managed, still recovering. "I have work to do. Wine club proposals to review. Go…perimeter…whatever."

Dean disappeared into his room, leaving Samantha alone with Alfred, who gave her a look that seemed altogether too knowing for a dog.

Samantha sighed, leaning back in her chair to stare at the

vineyard stretching out below. Sunlight had started to creep across the valleys and rows of grapevines, giving the landscape an otherworldly quality. It was beautiful in a way she was still getting used to—so different from Houston's urban skyline.

And now she had to navigate it with Dean Carter as her shadow. Dean, with his reasonable muscles and his perimeter checks and his French press coffee that smelled a million times better than hers.

From inside Dean's room came the sound of the shower running. Samantha resolutely ignored the mental image that tried to form of what might be going on behind closed doors as Dean—okay that was enough of *that*.

Lots of other stuff to think about. Staff to manage. Vineyard to slay. Fake relationship to maintain.

And somewhere out there, someone who might want her dead.

Chapter 5

Dean's tactical assessment of Wagner Wines took approximately thirty-seven minutes.

His assessment of its new owner was proving considerably more complicated.

He tracked across the property line, noting each entry point, camera placement opportunity and security vulnerability with the efficiency that had once made him a top Ranger. The vineyard sat on gently rolling hills with excellent visibility in most directions—a defensive advantage. The processing facility was another story, with its multiple access points and blind spots that any halfway decent criminal could exploit seven ways to Sunday.

But it was the main house that concerned him most—specifically, the eight thousand square feet he now shared with a woman who smelled like expensive perfume and wore cactus pajamas.

Never in his life would he have said cactus pajamas were sexy. Apparently, it depended on the woman in them. Because she'd pulled it off.

And then even worse, Alfred had immediately cozied up to her. The dog had a keen sense of judgment about people—one of the things Dean had readily noted at the shelter and contributed to his reasons for picking Alfred—but it was disconcerting to see his four-legged partner switch allegiances for leftover chicken and ear scratches.

It meant something. What, he hadn't examined too closely. But he'd have to soon.

Dean circled back toward the main residence, noting a broken section of ornamental fence that would need repair. He'd spent the better part of his life looking for weaknesses—in perimeters, in testimonies, in himself. The vineyard had plenty, but Samantha Wagner remained a question mark.

Could she have killed her aunt for the inheritance? The timing was certainly suspicious. But if she had, what was the situation with the tampered ladder? Red herring or something more sinister?

His instincts, which he trusted more than people most days, were leaning in a direction he didn't like given his assignment at the vineyard. Which posed its own problem: Samantha could be in serious danger. *And* guilty.

His protective streak literally had no idea what to do with that.

After completing his perimeter check, Dean returned to the house, his shirt clinging to his back from exertion. Alfred padded alongside him, the dog's tongue lolling out in the late-morning heat.

"You need water, buddy," Dean told him, heading for the kitchen. They both did.

Inside, the house was blissfully cool, a stark contrast to the Texas summer outside. Dean filled Alfred's portable water bowl and set it down on the kitchen floor, watching as the dog eagerly lapped at the water.

"Getting soft already," he muttered, though there was no real admonishment in his tone. Alfred deserved the comfortable digs after months of living in a cage at the shelter. Maybe Dean did too, though he couldn't claim to be free of his bars.

Dean grabbed a bottle of water from the refrigerator for himself, downing half in one long swallow. The pristine kitchen reminded him he was a long way from his family's ranch in Blanco. Not in distance, but definitely in every other way. Everything here was high-end, gleaming, untouched. Like the rest of the sprawling house, it had a museum quality—beautiful but unlived in.

Samantha was the same way, he decided. Glossy and perfect on the outside, but what lay beneath that polished surface remained to be seen.

Time to find out.

He followed the sound of rapid typing to what appeared to be a home office off the main hallway. Samantha sat behind a large desk, surrounded by stacks of papers and two different jars of pens, furiously typing on her laptop. Her hair was pulled back in a sleek ponytail, and she'd swapped the cactus pajamas for a silk blouse and tailored pants that probably cost more than most people's monthly rent. Fancy. And untouchable.

But still very, very striking.

She hadn't noticed him yet, and Dean took the opportunity to observe her undetected. Her brow was furrowed in concentration, her posture impeccable despite the intensity of her focus. Occasionally, she'd pause to reference a document, make a note or tuck a stray strand of hair behind her ear.

It was the last gesture that caught him off guard—something so unconsciously human amid her otherwise perfect corporate facade. For a split second, he forgot she was a possible suspect and saw only a woman completely absorbed in her work.

"Productive morning?" he asked, breaking the silence.

She glanced up, her expression composed as if she didn't startle easily. "Very. I'm developing a wine club concept to boost direct-to-consumer sales. The current model is outdated, and we're missing key demographic opportunities."

Dean's mouth quirked up. "Is that English or MBA?"

"Both," she replied, though a hint of amusement flickered

across her face. "Some of us communicate with more than grunts and tactical jargon."

"Sounds exhausting."

"What sounds exhausting is whatever you've been doing." Her eyes swept over him, taking in his sweat-stained shirt and dirt-smudged hands. "Did you dig a moat around the property?"

"Security assessment," Dean replied, choosing not to elaborate on the broken fence he'd discovered. Better to fix it quietly than alert her to yet another vulnerability. "Your place isn't exactly Fort Knox."

Her expression remained perfectly confident. "I'm sure it's sufficient. We have an excellent security system."

Dean had to admire her composure. Not even a flicker of concern showed on her face, despite the fact that someone had literally tried to harm her yesterday. Either she was remarkably resilient or remarkably good at projecting strength. Both possibly.

He stepped farther into the office, noting the meticulous organization of her desk despite the volume of paperwork. Everything in its place. Even the pens were sorted by color. This was a woman who liked control and order.

They'd probably get along all right. In certain circumstances. Possibly these.

"Tell me about this wine club idea," he said, curious to see how her brain worked.

"It's a subscription model with tiered memberships. Quarterly shipments, exclusive access to limited releases, special events." Her eyes lit up as she warmed to her subject, missing not one beat despite having zero warning he was about to spring a test on her. "Most wineries have something similar, but I'm developing a more personalized approach with algorithm-based recommendations based on a user profile, purchase history—"

"Like Netflix for wine," Dean interjected, surprised at how

easily he'd understood her explanation. The strategy wasn't half bad either, though he'd never tell her that.

"Exactly!" Samantha leaned forward, enthusiasm apparent. "But with a premium experience element. VIP tastings, harvest participation opportunities, behind-the-scenes tours."

Dean studied her as she continued outlining her plan. She was impressive, there was no denying it. Her corporate approach might not sit well with the local vineyard crowd, but he couldn't fault her business sense.

While he didn't have sexy cactus pajamas on his list before today, confident, capable women had always done it for him. So he was in trouble, obviously.

"Sounds like a solid business approach," he said noncommittally, while wondering if he could will himself out of his attraction to her.

"The vineyard has excellent products. They just need proper positioning in the market." She gestured to her laptop. "I've been studying the competition. Most local vineyards are behind the curve on digital marketing and customer analytics."

"You're treating it like a corporate client."

"Because that's what it is." She fixed him with a look of absolute certainty. "A business is a business, whether it's producing software or wine."

This woman could sell chainsaws to a forest. No doubt.

Or she had a significant bit of skill covering her deficiencies. Either way, he needed to snap out of whatever spell she'd put him under and get his head on straight. Because a woman like that could very easily commit murder and pull off a snow job on the investigator charged with proving it.

And none of that would lead to his shot at Ruiz.

"Would you like to continue this conversation over dinner tonight?" Dean asked.

She smiled, something he couldn't read flashing through her gaze. "Trying to maintain our cover?"

"Among other things." Like keeping her close. Dosing himself with as much of Samantha as he could in hopes of diluting her effect on him. It was his only hope of maintaining his sanity.

"How dedicated of you." She turned back to her laptop. "Seven o'clock?"

"Works for me."

"I'll meet you downstairs."

The dismissal was clear. Dean retreated to his room, Alfred following along with happy steps because it didn't matter to him either way if Samantha was guilty.

She wasn't what he'd expected. Strickland had briefed him on her corporate sales background, her rapid rise at EchoForge, her reputation for ruthless efficiency. But he hadn't mentioned her determination, her resilience, her unwavering confidence.

She reminded him, uncomfortably, of himself. The mask of certainty, the refusal to admit weakness, the drive. They were practically twins.

The thought was unsettling.

Dean stripped off his shirt and headed for the shower. He caught sight of his reflection in the mirror, the bullet scar on his side a stark reminder of what happened when you let your guard down. When you trusted the system to work.

When you believed in people rather than evidence.

He turned away from the mirror and stepped into the shower, cranking the water as cold as it would go. He needed to cool off in more ways than one. And spend some time examining his priorities.

Dean arrived in the dining room at precisely seven o'clock, freshly showered and dressed in the closest thing to formal wear he owned—a button-down shirt that wasn't faded and a pair of dark slacks that he'd last worn to his father's funeral.

The massive dining table could have seated twenty, but Samantha had set up dinner at one end, with two place settings catty-corner to each other rather than directly across. More intimate that way. The woman didn't miss a detail.

She appeared a moment later, having changed into a simple dress that somehow managed to look both casual and elegant. Yet another thing about her he found sexy—though maybe he just liked the full package and he should stop being shocked when she got his motor humming.

"Right on time," she commented.

"Always." Dean took in the professionally arranged table. "Did you cook?"

Her laugh was genuine. "Ha ha. I had Calla order dinner from a place in Fredericksburg. Hope you like Italian."

"I eat anything that isn't moving," he replied honestly.

"Such refined tastes." She gestured for him to sit. "Wine?"

"Please."

She poured them each a glass of red, her movements practiced and graceful. If Dean hadn't known better, he might have believed she'd been entertaining at the house her whole life. Had she dreamed of one day owning this place? Dinner was the perfect place to find out more about this woman. Helped that he had a keen interest anyway, but anything he discovered could and would be used in the case against her, if it came to it.

"So," she said once they were seated, "given that we're supposed to be a couple, shouldn't we know more about each other? Basic information, at least."

"What did you have in mind?"

"Ever been on a speed date?" she asked, taking a sip of her wine. "Lay everything out in rapid fashion. Drink from the fire hose, so to speak. Couples know things about each other."

"Speed dating," he repeated, amused despite himself. "All right. Hit me."

"Where did you grow up?"

"Blanco. Family ranch. You?"

"Houston, but spent summers in Dallas with my father." She leaned forward slightly. "How did we meet?"

Someone had strategically placed candles around the table and the soft lighting caught gold shimmers in her eyes. He blinked and forced himself to stop staring. "Coffee shop in San Antonio. You spilled your latte on my shirt."

"How cliché," she said with a smile that transformed her entire face. "I think we met at a charity gala. You were there providing security, and I outbid you for a silent auction item you really wanted."

"Which was?"

"A vintage motorcycle restoration experience."

Dean raised an eyebrow, impressed by the specificity. More than that, he was struck by how she'd somehow guessed his interest in classic motorcycles. "How did you know I'd want that?"

"You have that look." Her eyes traveled over him appraisingly, lingering long enough to send an unexpected gush through his gut. "Capable hands. The kind that would enjoy rebuilding something from scratch."

The observation was surprisingly perceptive. "You'd be right."

"I usually am," she replied, the confidence in her voice softened by the playful curve of her lips.

"How long have we been dating?" he asked, surprised by how easily the question came.

"Eight months," she replied without hesitation. "Long enough that I can finish your sentences, but not so long that I've started rearranging your closet."

"You'd organize my shirts by color, wouldn't you?" Like the pens in her office.

"Within a week," she admitted with a laugh that seemed to fill the cavernous dining room.

Dean leaned closer, drawn by the sound. "First kiss?"

The question slipped out silkily and she reacted by leaning

in herself, closing the distance between them as if she couldn't help herself either. That was nice. The spark between them glowed, a hairbreadth from bursting into flame.

"Third date," she replied, her voice dropping slightly. "You walked me to my door after dinner. Very traditional."

"Sounds like me," he agreed. The door-walking part. Not the kissing part. He'd never wait that long to kiss a woman who intrigued him.

"Your turn," she said, tilting her head. "What's my morning routine like?"

"Hmm." Dean studied her, allowing himself to study her because he wanted to and he could. "Up before dawn. Obviously Pilates before anything. Emails before coffee."

Her eyebrows lifted. "Not bad. Though you forgot the part where I curse the alarm clock."

"I stand corrected."

"What's my biggest pet peeve?"

"People who show up late," he answered immediately. "And incomplete spreadsheets."

She laughed again, the sound rich and genuine. "How did you guess that?"

Because he'd become a student of her the moment he walked onto this property. "You've got your napkin folded at a perfect ninety-degree angle, and you lined up your silverware twice during dinner."

"Observant."

"It's part of the job." And the longer he could convince the both of them that was all it was, the better.

"And what else have you observed, Mr. Carter?" The question hung between them, layered with meaning. She wanted something personal. He wanted to give it to her.

Dean met her gaze. "That you're not what I expected."

She smiled, a genuine one that reached her eyes. "My work here is done."

"Worst date ever?" he asked, curious to see how she'd respond.

"Guy took me to an Astros game, then spent the entire time explaining baseball to me, despite the fact that I told him my father played minor league. Your worst?"

Every single one he'd ever been on. Except this one. But he didn't think it would be a smart move to admit that. "Corporate dinner where my date spent the entire evening networking with everyone but me."

"That's—" she winced dramatically "—painful."

"She was very strategic."

"And clearly not very smart," she murmured, her gaze lingering on his mouth. "I can't imagine my attention would stray from you for a moment."

That made two of them.

Exactly how far from the original intent of this speed date were they going to veer? No one on the vineyard staff was going to ask him about his worst date. He should guide them both back to basics, before he did something supremely stupid, like start doing the math on how long he was going keep thinking about kissing her.

She was his *suspect*. Full stop. Why was it so hard to remember that?

"What would you normally be doing on a Friday night?" she asked, her voice softer. "If you weren't here playing my fake boyfriend?"

The question backed him up a step. "Honestly? Probably sitting on my porch with Alfred, drinking a beer, watching the sunset over the hills."

Something flickered in her eyes, an unexpected softness. "That sounds peaceful."

"It is." And somewhat surprising that she'd agree. "What about you? Big-city nightlife? Corporate happy hours?"

"Working, most likely," she admitted. "Or at the gym."

"Sounds thrilling."

"Says the man whose social life revolves around his dog."

"Alfred is an excellent conversationalist."

She laughed again, and Dean couldn't stop his return smile. Didn't want to. This unexpected connection shouldn't exist, but he enjoyed so little about life lately that this felt like a reward. He hadn't died when Ruiz shot him, but neither had he figured out how to live.

"If we were really dating, what would you want to know about me?" she asked, her voice still on the low end of the register, as if they were a couple having dinner and a conversation because they liked each other.

And maybe they were. The space between them seemed to shrink, the massive dining room contracting until it felt like they were the only two people for miles.

Dean considered the question carefully, all too aware of how the air between them seemed to have thickened. "What scares you?"

Her expression flickered with surprise. "That's unexpectedly deep for speed dating."

"You asked."

She twirled her wineglass slowly, considering. "Failure, probably. Not measuring up." A small vulnerable smile touched her lips. "Your turn. What scares Dean Carter?"

Their eyes locked, and for a moment, he considered giving her the practiced answer. But something about the moment demanded honesty.

"Being wrong about people," he said quietly. "Trusting the wrong person at the wrong time."

Instead of pulling back, she leaned closer. "And how do you know who to trust?"

"I don't," he admitted. "Not anymore."

The confession hung between them, heavy with implication. She was close enough now that he could detect the faint scent of her perfume, something floral and subtle. Her eyes searched his, and for a brief, disorienting moment, Dean forgot why he was here, forgot everything except the woman sitting across from him.

He *never* got caught up like this. It was thrilling to know it was possible.

He leaned forward, drawn into the heat bubbling between them. His muscles strained to reach for her, to lay his palm along her jawline and lift it—

Her phone chimed with an incoming text message, shattering the moment. Samantha blinked and glanced at the screen, her professional composure sliding back into place like armor.

She stood, gathering her wineglass with a hand that wasn't quite steady, clearly affected by his nearness in kind. "I need to make a call. Would you mind clearing the dishes? I gave the maid the night off."

"Sure." He kept his tone neutral, though his gut screamed at him to do anything to get her to stay.

Would she? If he asked? What would she say if he told her he wanted to renegotiate their fake relationship parameters and kissing was back on the table?

"Thank you for dinner," she said, her voice carefully controlled. "It was…educational."

She disappeared down the hallway before Dean could respond, leaving him alone with half-finished plates and the lingering sense that something significant had happened—and been interrupted.

He cleared the table methodically, his mind turning over every aspect of their conversation. She'd been surprisingly open, genuinely engaged in a way that seemed inconsistent with someone hiding murder.

But everyone had secrets.

Dean settled on the porch, Alfred lazing at his feet as they both watched darkness fall over the vineyard. The silhouettes of grapevines stretched into the distance, shadows lengthening in the fading light. It was peaceful, eerily so. Hard to imagine that somewhere on this property, a murder might have taken place.

His phone vibrated. Samantha's name flashed on the screen along with a text message.

Sorry for the abrupt exit. Need to deal with staff issue. Don't wait up. Separate beds, right?

The message landed like a bucket of ice water, dousing the warmth that had been building between them all evening. Dean stared at the screen, reading between the lines. She was rattled by whatever had happened between them, retreating behind her professional walls.

And asking him to do the same. Which he should have been the one to suggest. But in reality, he hadn't looked for the escape route once during dinner.

He texted her back: Of course.

Professional. Appropriate. The right call.

So, why did it feel like he'd lost something he hadn't even known he wanted?

Dean headed back inside to find his focus. He had a murder to solve and a job to win. Everything else—including the unsettling pull he felt toward Samantha—was a distraction he couldn't afford.

No matter how many times his thoughts drifted to the way her eyes had dropped to his mouth, or how close they'd come to crossing a line that couldn't be uncrossed.

Professional distance. He still had it.

Mostly.

Chapter 6

The sun beat down on Dean's neck as he lugged the picnic basket through the vineyard rows. Perfect day for a fake date with a woman he'd almost kissed last night. Then again, Dean had always excelled at making things harder than they needed to be. His specialty, really.

"The Cellar Door Vineyard does guided tours with air-conditioning," Samantha informed him, striding along the dirt path in what had to be four-inch heels that would probably lead to a broken ankle before too long. "Just throwing that out there."

"Hard to have a heart-to-heart surrounded by tourists with cameras," Dean replied, adjusting his grip on the basket. The weight wasn't a problem—he'd spent summers hauling hay bales across his family's ranch—but watching Samantha navigate the uneven terrain in those shoes was giving him visions of having to carry her, which he didn't need. "Besides, your staff needs to see us together. Can't sell the boyfriend story if we're hiding."

"You sound like you're enjoying this a little too much." She shot him a sideways glance, the sun making honey out of the highlights in her hair.

"What's not to enjoy?" He gestured at the landscape with his free hand. "Beautiful woman, perfect weather, five-star dining."

"It's sandwiches and wine."

"Like I said. Five stars."

The smile that tugged at her lips put his blood on simmer. After last night's dinner and their near-kiss moment, Dean had promised himself he'd keep things strictly professional today. Five minutes in, and that plan had already been crushed.

But really, he did have a good excuse. They were leaning into this idea of fake dating. The sooner he established their cover, the sooner he could get on with questioning the staff and poking around—his real purpose here, which he did have at the forefront in his mind. Just not 100 percent of the time.

"If I trip in these shoes, you better catch me again," she warned, neatly sidestepping a puddle that would have ruined her white linen pants.

"Is that why you wore them? Looking for an excuse to fall into my arms?" *Oof.* He could have reeled that one back.

"In your dreams, cowboy." She bumped his shoulder lightly with hers, and he enjoyed that so much, he promptly trashed the idea of reeling back much of anything.

They were supposed to be bonding and flirting and dating, and he wasn't going to apologize for liking it.

Dean paused at a fork in the path. "North field, right? Your vineyard manager said that's where she'd be working today."

Samantha nodded, her expression shifting to something more guarded. "Jules and her team. Though I'm not sure parading around with my new boyfriend is going to improve her opinion of me."

"That's exactly why we're doing it." Dean resumed walking, keeping his pace measured to match hers in those ridiculously sexy shoes. "People reveal more when they're annoyed. Plus, it explains why I'm hanging around asking questions."

"So, I'm your cover story?"

"And I'm yours." He caught her eye, holding her gaze a moment longer than necessary. "Mutually beneficial arrangement, remember?"

She didn't look convinced but followed him anyway. The

Texas Hill Country spread out in every direction, vibrant green splashed with wildflower colors under a brilliant blue sky. Despite his general irritation with the assignment, Dean had to admit it was beautiful here. Peaceful in a way his life hadn't been for a long time.

Until he looked in the other direction. Toward Samantha. That way lay utter chaos.

They crested a small hill that offered a better view of the operation. Farther down, Dean spotted Jules, her weathered hat making her instantly recognizable from the profile Strickland had given him, even at a distance.

"This looks like a good spot," he said, setting down the basket under the shade of a large live oak tree. "Visible but not in the way."

Samantha surveyed the location with the critical eye of someone used to evaluating prime real estate. "Acceptable. Though I would have brought a blanket if I'd known we'd be sitting on grass while I'm wearing white pants."

"Way ahead of you." Dean pulled a checkered blanket from the basket with a flourish.

Her eyebrows lifted slightly. "Impressive. What else do you have in that magical basket, Houdini?"

"Lunch. Wine. Actual glasses, because I figured you'd draw the line at drinking from the bottle." He arranged the items on the blanket with more care than he'd typically bother with. "Habit from growing up on a ranch. Always be prepared, or you'll wind up hiking a mile back to the house."

"Apparently applicable to vineyards as well."

"I wouldn't steer you wrong." He handed her a glass of chilled wine—her own chardonnay, which seemed fitting—then sat down beside her, close enough that their shoulders nearly touched.

The proximity was deliberate. People watching needed to believe they were a couple after all. At least that was what he told himself as the scent of her perfume—something expensive and floral that hit him in the gut sideways—drifted over him.

"So," Samantha said, turning toward him slightly, "am I finally going to learn who you're really working for? Or do fake boyfriends not share that kind of information?"

The question chilled the action going on beneath his skin. "What makes you think I'm not a private investigator?"

"Please." She rolled her eyes. "No PI I've ever met carries himself like you do. Military or law enforcement, definitely. And that gun you try to hide in your boot isn't exactly standard private sector issue."

Dean masked his surprise with a sip of wine. She was observant—dangerously so. Especially if she could identify his biometric weapon as a level up from normal guns. "You've been checking me out."

"A hard requirement for anyone sleeping twenty feet away." She didn't miss a beat. "So, who are you, really? And if you say Batman, I'm walking away right now."

He considered his options. Complete honesty was out of the question. But a partial truth might satisfy her curiosity enough to build trust.

"Former Texas Ranger," he admitted. "Now I work…consultations."

"Consultations," she repeated skeptically. "For whom?"

"People who need answers."

"That's conveniently vague."

"It's all you get for now." He unwrapped a sandwich, offering her half. "Turkey and avocado. Alfred helped me make them."

"Your dog is a chef now?"

"He supervised. He's shockingly judgmental about my avocado slicing technique." The joke was worth it for the laugh it got out of her.

He really, really needed to stop making her laugh if he wanted to have a prayer of focusing.

"You're dodging my question," she said, accepting the sandwich half. "Fine. Keep your secrets, Mr. Former Ranger. But don't expect me to believe you're a concerned citizen investigating a natural death out of the goodness of your heart."

"Never claimed to be good-hearted."

"No," she agreed, her eyes meeting his. "But you're not as hard as you pretend to be either."

The crude joke died in his mouth as he registered that she'd made up her own story about him, and apparently, she'd cast him in the role of Onion Boy—with layers she wanted to peel back. She could keep dreaming. There were no layers here. His insides were as crusty and hard as the shell.

"What about you?" he asked, strictly to change the subject. "Sales executive turned vineyard owner overnight. That's quite a career pivot."

"Nothing about this was planned, believe me."

"Try me."

She took a bite of her sandwich, chewing thoughtfully before responding. "What do you want to know?"

"Everything," he said simply. And meant it. For the investigation, of course, no other reason.

Samantha studied him for a moment, as if deciding how much to reveal. "I was in sales at EchoForge. I'm good at it. Very good. But there was a merger, restructuring, and my former best friend Caitlyn decided my strategies would look better with her name on them."

"Ouch."

"Yeah. Not my favorite memory." Her fingers tightened around the wineglass. "I'd been effectively demoted when the lawyers showed up at my office."

"Lawyers?"

"From Finch and Associates. They informed me that my Great-Aunt Greta Wagner had passed away and named me her sole beneficiary." She shook her head slightly, still seeming bewildered by it. "The vineyard, the house, the business, everything."

Dean fought to maintain a neutral expression, but dang, if this was an act, she was *good*. "I'm sorry for your loss. You two must have been close."

"That's the thing," Samantha said, meeting his eyes. "I never even met her."

What? The admission hung in the air as he processed this new bombshell.

Obviously, Dean had done research. Background checks. Strickland and his team had done a lot themselves before he'd come on board. Someone in the governor's office had somehow developed suspicions that had led him here.

But no one had ever even *hinted* at this huge black fly in the ointment of a murder charge.

If Samantha had never met Greta, it potentially changed everything. Tying a motive to murder, for example. The possibility of Samantha knowing she was the beneficiary of her aunt's trust became that much harder to prove.

Unless she was lying.

"Never?" he repeated, watching her face carefully.

"Never. Not once." She took another sip of wine. "My family was estranged from her before I was born. Some falling out no one ever explained to me. No Christmas cards, no birthday calls, nothing. I knew she existed, but that was it."

This got weirder and weirder. "Yet she left you everything."

"According to the lawyers, she'd been following my career for years. Collected articles about EchoForge's press releases, kept tabs on my promotions." Samantha's expression was a mix of bewilderment and something else—pride maybe. "Apparently, she saw something of herself in me."

"That didn't strike you as strange?" he asked, genuinely curious now. "A relative you'd never met leaving you millions?"

"Of course it did. But what was I supposed to do?" Her laugh was sharp, almost brittle. "Say no to a fresh start when my career was imploding? I'm ambitious, not stupid."

"So the timing was convenient."

"Suspiciously so. Is that what you're getting at?" She fixed him with a look that could have frozen the sun. "I didn't even know she was sick, let alone dying. How exactly would I have engineered that?"

Dean held up his hands in a pacifying gesture. "Just establishing facts. You have to admit, inheriting a fortune from a stranger right when you need an escape route sounds like something from a movie plot."

"My life is not a movie," she said firmly. "And if it were, I'd demand better writing."

The comment startled a genuine laugh out of him. "Fair enough."

Samantha's expression softened slightly. "I get it. You're doing your job. But I didn't kill my aunt, Dean."

That was the straw. He shouldn't like the way her gaze got all melty when she said his name, but he did. He shouldn't like the sheer backbone on this woman, but he did. He shouldn't believe her, but God help him, he did.

This was years of investigative training and experience talking. A gut feeling he couldn't ignore and still say he was doing his job.

"Then someone else killed her," he said quietly. "And they might be after you next."

She didn't flinch at his bluntness, which surprised him. Most people would have balked at the suggestion they were in danger. But Samantha nodded, accepting the reality with remarkable composure.

"Hence the ladder incident."

"Hence my being here at all." Dean shifted closer, lowering his voice though no one was within earshot. "Have you noticed anything else suspicious? Anyone paying too much attention to you, asking odd questions, behaving strangely?"

"You mean besides the totally hot former Ranger pretending to be my boyfriend?" The teasing smile she shot him put them on even more perilous ground, because if she wasn't the killer, it changed everything.

"Besides me," he agreed, his internal grin so much bigger than it should be right now, but she'd called him *hot*. She couldn't unsay it.

"The entire staff treats me like I'm carrying the plague, but I think that's because I'm an outsider who caused their beloved manager, Ben, to quit." She picked at the edge of the blanket absently. "Mike gives me the creeps sometimes, but that might just be his personality."

"Mike," Dean repeated. "Worked here long?"

"According to his file, about fifteen years. Started as seasonal help during harvest, eventually became full-time maintenance." She tilted her head. "Why? You think he had something to do with Aunt Greta's death?"

"I think everyone's a potential suspect," Dean replied, feeling way too giddy about the complete 180-degree turn the conversation had taken. "Including the guy who sent you up a sabotaged ladder."

Samantha considered this, her expression thoughtful. "So, what's your professional assessment? What exactly happened to Greta?"

"Honestly? I don't know yet. The official cause of death was heart failure—natural causes. But my…employer has reasons to believe it wasn't natural at all."

"What reasons?"

"That's classified."

She rolled her eyes. "Of course it is."

"The important thing," Dean continued, "is figuring out

why anyone would want Greta dead. And why they might be targeting you now."

"I've been wondering the same thing." Samantha leaned back on her hands, her shoulder brushing against his. Not on accident either. "It doesn't make sense. If someone wanted the vineyard, killing Greta just means I inherit it. How does that help them?"

"Unless they didn't know you'd inherit," Dean suggested. "Or they thought they would."

"But then why come after me?"

"To scare you off, maybe. Make you sell."

She snorted. "Clearly, they don't know me very well."

"No," Dean agreed, studying her profile. "I don't think they do."

The sun had shifted, casting dappled light through the live oak leaves above them. It heightened the shadows on Samantha's face, and he couldn't look away, couldn't stop contemplating the determination in her eyes, the curve of her mouth.

Dangerous territory. Especially if she was somehow actually guilty. Even worse if she was innocent.

"Tell me more about your staff," he said, shaking off the what-ifs. "You've been here a week. First impressions?"

"Jules knows the vineyard inside and out, but resents my existence. Carlos—the winemaker—is brilliant, but keeps to himself. Lyn, the marketing director, thinks all my ideas are garbage. Calla's friendly enough, but cautious." She ticked them off on her fingers. "And Mike, well, you know about him already."

"Anyone particularly close to Greta?"

Samantha considered. "Jules, probably. She's been here the longest, and from what I've gathered, Greta trusted her judgment about the vines. Though that's based on staff comments. Again, never met the woman myself."

Dean nodded, filing away the information. He'd already run preliminary background checks on all the key personnel, a standard step in any investigation. Nothing had immediately raised red flags, but that didn't mean the answers weren't there, buried beneath the surface.

And the things Samantha had perhaps unwittingly revealed…she'd given him a lot to unpack. If the staff didn't like her, there might be more to the reasons than she'd assumed.

"You've got that look," Samantha observed.

"What look?"

"Like you're mentally cataloging everything I say and cross-referencing it with whatever other information you've gathered." She smirked. "It's your investigator face."

"I don't have an investigator face." Just the normal one.

"You absolutely do. Your eyes narrow slightly, and there's this little crease right here." She reached out, her finger brushing lightly between his eyebrows.

The unexpected touch lit him up. Her finger was cool from holding the wineglass, a stark contrast to the warmth spreading through him with dangerous speed. She started to pull away and he caught her wrist. *Not so fast.*

"Is that so?" he murmured, watching her pupils dilate slightly.

"Mmm-hmm." Her voice had dropped to match his. "Dead giveaway."

"I'll have to work on that."

"Don't." She still hadn't pulled her hand away. "I like being able to read you."

Yet another thing he shouldn't like. But he did.

The moment stretched between them, electric and dangerous. Dean was acutely aware of how easy it would be to lean forward, to close the distance between them. After being interrupted at dinner last night, the temptation to stop her from getting away a second time was almost overwhelming.

It would be so easy to pretend it was for show, just maintaining their cover in case anyone was watching. But he knew better. There was nothing fake about the way she scattered his pulse, and nothing professional about the thoughts crowding into his mind.

Their fingers intertwined almost of their own accord. Dean's thumb traced a small circle on her wrist, feeling her shiver beneath his touch.

"We should probably try harder to be a convincing couple," he said, his voice like sandpaper. "For anyone watching."

"Absolutely," she agreed, shifting closer. "Thoroughness is important in any operation."

He found himself drowning in her eyes, in the faint smile playing around her lips, in the scent of her perfume mingling with the vineyard air.

The sound of approaching footsteps jerked them both out of the bubble. Dean released Samantha's hand, though not without reluctance, as Mike, the handyman, made his way toward them with purposeful strides. There was something about that guy. His body language set off all kinds of bells and whistles in Dean's gut, none of them good.

"Heads up," he murmured, nodding toward the approaching figure. "Mr. Ladder himself."

Samantha tensed slightly beside him. "Perfect."

"Ms. Wagner," Mike called as he neared them. "Sorry to interrupt your…picnic."

The way he said "picnic" made it sound like a euphemism for something illicit. Dean instinctively shifted closer to Samantha, his arm brushing against hers in a gesture that could be interpreted as protective and territorial. Because it was both.

"It's fine," Samantha replied, her voice cool but professional. "What can I help you with?"

"There's a delivery at the main building. Need your signature." Mike's eyes flicked to Dean, assessing. "You must be the boyfriend everyone's talking about."

Dean extended his hand, deliberately rising to his full height. "Dean Carter."

Mike shook it with a grip that was slightly too firm to be friendly. "Mike Thompson. I keep this place running."

"Maintenance?" Dean asked, though he already knew the answer.

"Among other things." Mike turned back to Samantha. "The delivery guy says he can't wait. Something about a temperature-controlled shipment."

Samantha sighed. "I'll be right there." As Mike nodded and turned to leave, she called after him. "Mike? Next time, please feel free to text me rather than hiking all the way out here."

The handyman's shoulders stiffened slightly before he continued walking away.

"Not a fan of proper communication channels?" Dean asked once Mike was out of earshot.

"He's old-school. Prefers face-to-face." Samantha gathered her wineglass. "But he most likely wanted to get a look at you."

"At us, you mean. See if we look like a real couple."

"And? What's the verdict?" Something playful danced in her eyes. "Do we need to practice some more? Mike did interrupt a very important assessment."

Dean considered the question as he folded the blanket. They'd been sitting close together, sharing food and wine, talking intimately. He'd held her hand, touched her, looked at her in ways that had nothing to do with their cover story.

Well, it did as far as she knew. He'd take his own reactions to the grave.

"I think we're selling it," he said, his voice catching in his throat. "Though we might need to work on our nonverbal cues."

Samantha's eyebrow arched. "What did you have in mind?"

Before he could overthink it, Dean stepped closer, tucking a strand of hair behind her ear. Her breath stuttered at the contact, her eyes widening slightly.

"Little things," he murmured. "The way you touch someone when you're comfortable with them. Familiar. Automatic."

His fingers lingered near her jaw, and he could reel her in right now. Selling it, he told himself, but that was a lie.

He wanted her in every way a man could want a woman.

His phone rang, shattering the moment *again*. Dean recognized the ringtone—Strickland. Of all the timing. He could *not* catch a break.

"I should take this," he said, reluctantly stepping back. "My boss."

Samantha nodded, disappointment flashing across her face, but to her credit, she didn't push for more details. "I need to deal with that delivery anyway."

Dean watched her gather the last of their picnic items, then answered the call as she started back toward the main complex.

"Carter," he said, keeping his voice neutral.

"How's the investigation going?" Strickland's voice held a warmth that put Dean on edge for some reason.

Most likely because he wasn't doing his job and Strickland had no idea.

"Gathering information. Building rapport." Dean turned away from the vineyard, lowering his voice. "New intel has made this investigation somewhat complicated. I'm still working on untangling it all."

"Sounds like I sent the right man for the job."

Strickland's confidence came through loud and clear, but all that did was remind Dean this was still an audition. A place on the team would only be available to someone who delivered results—a murder conviction.

And then he'd have a shot at Ruiz.

The reminder hit Dean like a bucket of ice water. *Ruiz.* The reason he'd agreed to this assignment in the first place. The man who'd put a bullet in him and walked free. The justice he'd been denied.

"You did send the right man," Dean replied, his voice hardening. "I'll get you results."

"See that you do." Strickland paused. "And, Carter? Watch yourself. There's a lot of money at stake. People can and will do anything to protect themselves if something they want is being threatened."

People. As in Samantha Wagner. A woman he barely knew and had spent a handful of hours with thus far. A woman who had the biggest motive for killing her great-aunt. A woman he'd cavalierly decided could be innocent for possibly—probably— reasons that weren't entirely professional.

The call ended, leaving Dean standing alone under the live oak. Reality doused the warm glow his picnic with Samantha had created. This wasn't a real relationship. Dating was a cover story. This was work. And he had a job to finish if he wanted his shot at Ruiz.

He watched Samantha disappear into the main building, her confident stride still doing a number on him despite the harsh reminder that he couldn't afford to trust her. But everything he'd learned about her today pointed to a woman who was am- bitious, resilient and direct—not someone who would poison her aunt for an inheritance she didn't know was coming. The timeline didn't make sense. The motive was tenuous at best.

The thing was, he wanted her to be innocent. His profes- sional judgment was becoming clouded by something he had no idea how to control.

Dean picked up the picnic basket. Strickland wouldn't like this development at all. This was precisely the kind of emotional entanglement that had no place in an investigation.

Yet as he made his way back toward the house, he couldn't deny the truth that was becoming increasingly difficult to ignore.

He was teetering toward being convinced she wasn't a mur- derer.

And that made things ten times more difficult than if she were guilty.

Chapter 7

Dean Carter drove like he did everything else—efficiently. And with so much competence that it became insanely sexy. Which was also like everything else. So Samantha was aware 24/7 that her fake boyfriend might be the hottest man on the planet.

And *painfully* aware that he hadn't kissed her yet.

Not for lack of opportunity. There'd been plenty of those, and she'd been around interested men enough times to know when one was. Dean fit the category. They were supposed to be dating. It made zero sense that he hadn't made a move yet—totally under the guise of their fake relationship, of course—and she had a feeling she knew why.

He was trying to drive her batty. Spoiler alert: it was working.

This was what she got for telling him their arrangement did not include kissing. Of course she'd get the one Boy Scout in the world who stuck to the strict letter of the law. Now she'd have to be the one to make the first move, which normally she'd be all over. But she did have that one tiny little insignificant detail to contend with.

He'd told her she wasn't his type. So now she had a complex about it.

See: *batty.* The man was going to drive her straight out of her gourd.

Time for a distraction. Samantha surveyed the quaint main street of Strassburg as Dean parked his truck near the town square. Compared to touristy Fredericksburg with its manicured German-inspired storefronts, Strassburg was unapologetically authentic—weathered buildings, practical exteriors, and a quiet main street that probably hadn't changed much in the last fifty years.

Unwelcome pre-meeting nerves sparked in her stomach. This was just another business interaction. Except she wasn't walking into a boardroom with a PowerPoint presentation and a fabulous sales pitch. She was heading into a small town where everyone had known Greta, and they'd all be measuring Samantha against whatever yardstick small-town winery people used.

Dean climbed out of the truck, then came around to her side and opened the door like a bona fide *gentleman*. Then he iced that cake by holding out his hand to help her down, which she was not turning down, no way, no how. The moment his fingers found hers again, she had the ridiculous impression that her skin knew his touch and had *missed* it. That this clasp of hands completed something previously separated.

She needed serious professional help.

The morning market buzzed with activity. Vendors called out greetings to customers they clearly knew by name. Children darted between stalls while parents shopped for produce and homemade goods. The scent of fresh bread and roasted nuts wafted through the air, mingling with the earthy smell of just-harvested vegetables.

It was picturesque, charming and completely intimidating.

Samantha squared her shoulders. This was not that different from a tricky sales meeting. She could do this in her sleep.

"Let's start with produce," she suggested, nodding toward a stall piled high with vibrant vegetables. "Nothing says, 'I'm a normal human,' like buying zucchini."

Dean chuckled, his thumb tight against hers as they walked

hand in hand. "Strategic zucchini purchase. Your business degree is really paying off."

"Mock all you want, but relationship-building starts with shared experiences." She slipped naturally into her pitch-meeting mode. "We need to establish common ground with the locals, demonstrate that we value their products and expertise, and—"

"Or we could just talk to people," Dean suggested mildly. "Like humans."

She rolled her eyes. "That's what I meant."

"Sure it was." The warmth in his eyes threatened to make her forget her own name, so she forced her gaze forward.

They approached the vegetable stand where a weathered man in his sixties was arranging tomatoes with meticulous care. He looked up as they neared, his smile friendly until his gaze landed on Samantha. The transformation was immediate and unmistakable—his expression closed, eyes narrowing with suspicion.

He'd recognized her. And that was a bad thing.

"Morning," Dean offered easily.

The man's eyes flicked between them, recognition dawning as he realized they were together. His face shuttered completely. "We're closed."

"You look open to me. Is there a problem here?" she asked, striving to keep her voice level.

"You're the problem, Ms. Wagner." The man practically spat her name, clearly recognizing her. "Everyone here knows what your aunt did. And you're cut from the same cloth."

Wait. What? He thought her aunt had done something bad? And by extension, Samantha was bad, too?

If she'd been wearing her power heels, Samantha might have been able to brush this off more gracefully. As it was, the accusation hit her like a slap. This wasn't just rudeness; this was personal, targeted animosity directed at her solely based on her last name.

"I'm not my aunt," Samantha said, fighting to maintain composure. She felt like she'd shown up to give a presentation only to find everyone speaking a different language.

"You're a Wagner. Same thing," an older woman chimed in from the next stall. "You can't walk her name around here and expect a welcome."

The unfairness of it stung. They knew nothing about her, yet had already decided who she was? Based on what—her aunt's personality? Which Samantha could now guess might not be all that sweet and loving given the animosity.

Dean's arm settled around her waist, a subtle gesture of support that grounded her against the unexpected hostility.

"Seems to me," he drawled, his voice carrying enough to reach every eavesdropper, "that judging someone before you know them says more about you than it does about them."

The observation landed in pin-drop quiet. Some onlookers shifted uncomfortably, the murmurs suggesting Dean's words had struck a chord.

"You're not from around here," the farmer said firmly. "You wouldn't understand. We don't do business with Wagners. Never again."

He turned his back on them, making it clear the conversation was over.

Samantha bit her lip, the dismissal stinging more than she'd expected.

As they moved away from the hostile vendor, Dean's hand found hers again, giving it a reassuring squeeze.

"Welcome to small-town politics," Dean murmured, guiding her toward a quieter corner of the market. "Want to head back to the vineyard?"

"Absolutely not." The idea of retreating after one confrontation was unthinkable. "I need to understand what we're dealing with here. Knowledge is leverage, and right now, we're operating with an incomplete data set."

A smile ghosted across his face. "There's my corporate warrior."

It took her a full second to pick her jaw up off the floor. The fact that she was his anything came from clear out of left field. Wait. Did he mean it as a compliment? It felt like a compliment.

And now her brain had completed its evolution into spaghetti with Dean's name on it.

"Old habits," she admitted, proud that her voice sounded level. "But seriously, what is going on around here? I need to know what Greta did that made these people hate her so much. It could be relevant to your investigation, right?"

"Very relevant. Let's try there. Different approach this time." He nodded toward a honey vendor whose stall was momentarily customer-free. He guided her with a gentle pressure at the small of her back that branded her skin as effectively as a cattle prod. "Sometimes it's what people don't say that matters most."

The honey vendor, a woman in her fifties with laugh lines around her eyes, greeted them with cautious neutrality. She'd clearly witnessed the earlier confrontation but seemed willing to reserve judgment.

"Morning," Dean said with that easy charm he could apparently summon at will. "Is this local honey?"

"Sure is. From my hives outside town." She gestured to the jars of amber liquid displayed in neat rows. "Wildflower, clover and mesquite. The wildflower's my personal favorite, but the mesquite has a deeper flavor."

"I'll take one of each," Dean decided. "My girlfriend here has a sweet tooth."

He pulled Samantha closer, his arm settling comfortably around her waist like it belonged there. Felt like it belonged there too.

The vendor's eyes flicked to Samantha, still unreadable. "You're the Wagner girl, aren't you?"

"Samantha Wagner," she confirmed, bracing for another onslaught.

But the woman simply nodded. "Heard you inherited the vineyard. Big responsibility."

"It is," Samantha agreed, surprised by the neutral tone. "I'm still learning the ropes."

"We were curious," Dean interjected smoothly, "did Wagner Wines source locally? We're considering expanding some of our vendor relationships."

The honey seller's expression tightened slightly. "Not exactly. Greta preferred to work with larger suppliers from outside the area. Said it was more efficient."

"Efficient isn't always better," Samantha commented, desperately hoping she'd read the room right. "Sometimes quality comes from more personal connections."

It seemed to thaw the vendor slightly, thank goodness. "That's what I always thought. But Greta had her ways."

"What kind of ways?" Dean asked, his tone casual as he examined a jar of honey.

Good grief, he was slick. She'd seen some smooth talkers in her day, but this one took the cake and a pot of honey or two.

The woman glanced around before lowering her voice. "She wasn't one to play fair, if you understand my meaning. Used her money and connections to get what she wanted, regardless of who got hurt in the process." She looked directly at Samantha. "No offense."

"None taken," Samantha assured her. "I'd rather hear the truth."

The vendor seemed to make a decision. "Truth is, Greta made a lot of enemies in this town. People who crossed her tended to regret it."

"Sounds like a tough businesswoman," Dean commented.

"Tough isn't the word most folks would use," the vendor replied. "There were rumors she was getting threatening messages in the months before she died. Can't say many people were surprised."

Samantha exchanged a quick glance with Dean. *Threatening messages—do tell.*

"What kind of threats?" Dean asked as if he did this every day.

The vendor shrugged. "Just talk. But if you're taking over, you might want to consider a different approach than your aunt. This town has a long memory."

"I appreciate the advice," Samantha said sincerely, more grateful than she could fully articulate for it. "And the honey looks delicious."

As they continued through the market, Dean used his natural charisma to engage various vendors while subtly extracting information. The pattern became clear: Greta Wagner had been ruthlessly efficient in business, leveraging her wealth and influence to gain advantages for the vineyard at the expense of local farmers and smaller businesses.

What disturbed Samantha most wasn't solely what Greta had done, but how familiar some of the tactics sounded. The strategic elimination of competitors. The leveraging of resources for maximum advantage. The single-minded focus on success at any cost.

That's how you got ahead in the corporate world. Samantha had done all of that and more during her own rise at EchoForge.

She pushed the uncomfortable thought away. Business was business. Sometimes tough decisions had to be made. That didn't make her anything like Greta. She'd sold software, not crushed family farms. Totally different.

By the time they'd circled the market, Samantha was emotionally exhausted. She'd been glared at, snubbed, reluctantly served and outright refused business by at least half a dozen vendors. Without Dean beside her, she suspected it would have been even worse.

"Time for a breather?" he suggested, noticing her flagging energy.

"Please," she agreed, letting him lead her to a bench in the shade of an ancient oak tree.

Once seated, she closed her eyes briefly, gathering herself. "Well, that was overwhelming."

"Productive," Dean corrected. "We learned a lot about Greta. And potentially why someone might have wanted her dead."

"The list of suspects seems to be the entire population of Strassburg," she muttered. "Fantastic. Just what I need—to own the business equivalent of the Death Star."

Dean's shoulder pressed against hers, solid and reassuring. "Not everyone hated her. The honey lady seemed neutral."

"She was the only one. I can't believe this is the legacy I've inherited. A business built on bullying and strong-arm tactics." She shook her head and side-eyed him. "How am I supposed to overcome that perception?"

"By being different," he said simply.

The answer was so Dean-like that she just shook her head. "You make it sound easy."

"Not easy. Straightforward." His blue eyes latched onto hers. "You're not Greta. You didn't build the business her way. You have a chance to run it your way."

She could. This was her chance, her fresh start staring her in the face. It might be a steeper climb than she'd anticipated, but so what? No one got to the summit by moping around base camp after a few people threw some nastiness in her direction.

"Okay, now I'm ready to go home," she said and let Dean lead the way back to the truck.

Once Dean helped her up into the cab and then climbed behind the wheel, Samantha leaned her head back against the seat, the full weight of the day's emotional roller coaster reeling through her body. "I feel like I just pitched to the world's toughest client panel, except instead of pointed questions, they were armed with tomatoes and personal grudges. At least in sales, people try to hide their contempt until after you leave the room."

Dean's mouth quirked. "For what it's worth, I think you handled that better than most people would have."

"You sound surprised," she replied, trying to keep her tone light despite the elephant sitting on her chest.

"Not surprised." At a red light, he contemplated her with those blue eyes that drilled right through her. "Impressed."

That was a compliment. No question. It crawled inside her and took root, simple but potent. She wasn't used to men noticing anything about her except her looks. *Off-kilter* didn't begin to describe what was happening inside right now.

"I still lost," she pointed out. "No one's inviting me to the town picnic anytime soon."

"Some battles aren't about winning." His gaze shifted back to the road. "They're about showing up and standing your ground."

The drive back to the vineyard passed in silence as she contemplated her next move. By the time they arrived, the sun was high overhead, casting short shadows across the rows of grapevines.

"Coffee?" Dean suggested once they were inside. "I'll make you a cup strong enough to revive the dead. Exactly what the doctor ordered for sloughing off mean people's opinions."

After the morning they'd had, it sounded perfect. "Trying to convert me from lattes?"

"One cup at a time," he confirmed, the corner of his mouth lifting in that half smile that did dangerous things to her pulse.

Samantha watched as Dean moved around her kitchen with surprising grace for such a big guy, grinding beans and preparing his fancy French press with the focus of someone performing a sacred ritual. Alfred appeared from wherever he'd been napping and settled at her feet, his warm weight oddly comforting.

"The people in town," she said finally, breaking the comfortable silence. "They really hated her. And now they hate me by extension."

"They don't know you yet," he pointed out. "First impressions can change."

"Is that what happened with us?"

Dean's hands paused on the grinder for a beat. "Maybe," he admitted, glancing up with an expression she couldn't quite read. "First impressions aren't always accurate."

It might be the closest he'd come yet to admitting he might be changing his opinion about her guilt in the matter of her aunt's death.

"No," she agreed softly. "They're not."

And the closest she'd come to telling him he definitely wasn't her type, but that had ceased to be a problem.

He finished preparing the coffee and poured it into two mugs, sliding one across the counter to her. "Try this. Guaranteed to make everything look better."

She took a cautious sip and was surprised by the rich, complex flavor. Strong but not bitter, with subtle notes that danced across her palate. "Okay, you're a genius of the highest order. This is actually good. Like 'make you reconsider your entire relationship with caffeine' good."

"High praise from the latte connoisseur," he teased.

"Do you think what we learned changes things?" she asked in all seriousness. "About Greta's death?"

Dean leaned against the counter, considering her over the rim of his mug. "It gives us more potential suspects. And it confirms that someone might have been threatening her."

"Which means whoever was threatening her might be after me now."

"We've established that as a possibility since the ladder incident," he reminded her.

"It's different now," she insisted. "Today made it real in a way it wasn't before. These people really despised her. Enough to—"

"To kill her?" he finished. "Maybe. That's what we need to find out."

The "we" didn't escape her notice. Somewhere along the line, this had become a joint investigation rather than Dean working alone. It meant something to her that he might be willing to treat this as a full partnership, instead of just a fake relationship cover.

"So what's our next move?" she asked.

"Our next move," Dean echoed, his mouth quirking upward, "is for you to finish that coffee. Then we regroup and plan."

The way he'd emphasized "our" made it clear he'd noticed the shift too. But instead of correcting her, he'd embraced it. The realization warmed her more than the coffee ever could.

Samantha found herself smiling despite the crappy day. She might have inherited a vineyard with a heap of trouble attached, but she'd also gained an ally she hadn't expected.

And that felt dangerously close to something worth celebrating.

Chapter 8

Dean stared at his phone with the kind of side-eye usually reserved for telemarketers and unregistered firearms. Strickland's message glowed on the screen, worse than either.

Video briefing. 30 minutes. Full team.

Full team. He'd conveniently forgotten that a "team" existed.

What he hadn't forgotten was that he didn't need anyone's help. Teams came with complications, expectations, disappointments. Like your partner deciding a woman was more important than years of having each other's backs.

He'd been operating solo since arriving at the vineyard, partly because that was how he dealt with the world now, and partly because this whole undercover boyfriend situation would not benefit from extra guys running around the place.

Lone Wolf might as well be his code name, assuming he actually earned one. It covered all the bases.

Somehow, he didn't think Strickland would accept a no from what didn't present as an invitation to the meeting in the first place. It was a command. Dean would be there, period.

So that meant he had to be prepared to speak to the case, though his big fat nothing solid would go over like an anvil balancing on spaghetti noodles. As had become his habit, he'd parked on one of the loungers on the balcony outside his room and scrolled through his notes on the case.

The facts weren't adding up the way they should. Especially not after yesterday's town visit, where half of Strassburg seemed ready to nominate Greta Wagner for Villain of the Year. If anything, the suspect pool had widened to include basically anyone who'd ever done business with the woman.

Except Samantha, potentially. Which complicated matters in ways he wasn't prepared to unpack before caffeine.

"That's your 'someone moved my favorite gun' face."

Dean glanced up to find Samantha leaning against her doorframe, coffee in hand, wearing a sleek workout outfit that looked like a million dollars on her. Not an accident. He strongly suspected she'd gone shopping since he'd moved in with the express goal of driving him off his rocker.

Not that he was complaining about the view. At all. She'd taken to joining him on the balcony in the morning, a cute couple's habit for the benefit of the staff that he got to enjoy. Win-win.

"Work stuff," he said, holding up his phone and leaving it at that.

"Ah, your mysterious business." She took a sip of her coffee, eyeing him over the rim. "While you're playing cowboy spy, I need to head to the tank rooms. Refrigeration system's throwing a tantrum, and Carlos is having an existential crisis about our Tempranillo."

"Say that five times fast." His joke made her eyes dance with amusement.

"I can barely say it once," she admitted with a laugh. "My tongue trips over itself just thinking about it."

Dean's brain conjured up a few thoughts about her tongue that were decidedly unprofessional. He cleared his throat. "I should get busy."

"Right." She stepped forward and dropped a casual kiss on

his cheek, lingering a beat. "Jules walked by," she whispered near his ear, then vanished as if that little bit of contact hadn't floored her the way it had him.

As she disappeared down the stairs, Dean did his best to jump-start his heart, which had stopped long about the time she leaned in. His skin burned where her lips had touched his skin, and he wanted more. Other places.

And not for the cover story. Not because their relationship was fake. There had been nothing fake about how that had felt.

If they'd reached the casual-morning-affection stage of this charade, he was here for it. Now that he knew the rules, he could stage his own version tomorrow morning.

Alfred, the traitor, chose that moment to abandon him in favor of trotting after Samantha.

Enough with the distractions. He had bigger problems than sorting out whatever was happening between him and Samantha Wagner. Like this impending team call that was going to force him to admit he hadn't made much progress on his own.

Dean headed to his room and opened the way too fancy laptop Strickland had issued him on the desk. Dang, he should have practiced how to sound like he wanted to be on this video call instead of doing anything else, like getting a root canal.

He'd spent the last year doing everything alone. The bullet scar on his side twinged, a reminder of what happened when you trusted the wrong people.

Thirty seconds later, two faces appeared on his screen. Tanner Callahan, with his perma-grin and eyes that crinkled at the corners, and Beckett Granger, whose expression made concrete look emotional.

"Carter!" Tanner said with enthusiasm that bordered on offensive for this hour of the morning. "How's life at the vineyard? Wining and dining the pretty suspect?"

"It's an investigation, not a vacation," Dean reminded him. "And she isn't officially a suspect."

Beckett's eyebrow lifted a millimeter, the equivalent of a shocked gasp from anyone else. "How much more official does it need to be?"

Dean ignored the jab. "Based on what I've learned from the locals, half of Strassburg wanted Greta dead. Samantha never even met the woman before inheriting the vineyard."

"First-name basis," Tanner noted with a smirk. "Things must be going well."

"I'm undercover as her boyfriend," he reminded them with an exaggerated eye roll meant to come through as loud and clear as his tone did. "What am I supposed to call her? Ms. Wagner?"

"Fair point," Tanner conceded. "Though you seem pretty committed to the role. What I saw of your little picnic yesterday was practically romance-novel-cover material."

Dean's blood turned to ice as he internalized that this operation had layers no one had clued him in to. "You were watching us?"

"Providing backup," Tanner corrected, enjoying this way too much. "Strickland's orders. Got some interesting intel from the locals while you were busy with your boyfriend routine."

The idea that Tanner had been surveilling him without his knowledge wasn't just irritating; it was embarrassing. Dean had been in law enforcement long enough to know when he was being watched. Or he used to be, anyway, before wine country and silk blouses and afternoon picnics started making scrambled eggs out of his professional instincts.

"You could have told me," Dean said, reeling back the hundreds of other things he wanted to say.

"Would you have agreed to it?" Beckett asked with infuriating logic.

No, he wouldn't have. But that wasn't the point. If they were a team, he should be informed about what was happening.

But that would require *him* to act like this was a team too.

Time for a new strategy. "So, what's this intel you supposedly gathered while stalking me?"

"Not stalking. Multitasking," Tanner said cheerfully. "And it's good. The town gossip circuit is buzzing about Wagner Wines. Greta had enemies. Lots of them. Business rivals, jilted partners, vendors she squeezed too hard."

"That tracks with what I've been hearing," Dean acknowledged coolly. "But it doesn't tell us who might have escalated from angry to lethal."

"That's why we're here," Beckett interjected. "To help you narrow it down. I've been analyzing the vineyard staff backgrounds. There are irregularities."

Dean's eyebrows rose. "What kind of irregularities?"

"Employment gaps. Financial discrepancies. Previous workplaces with suspicious patterns." Beckett's fingers clacked across his keyboard. "I need more time to be thorough."

It grated on Dean to admit it, but he needed this. He did not like spinning his wheels while trying to juggle an investigation, a protective detail and a fake relationship that was starting to feel uncomfortably real.

"I could use the help," he found himself saying, words that would have been unthinkable a week ago.

The admission hung in the air for a moment, both men on screen looking at him like he'd suddenly started speaking in tongues.

"Say that again?" Tanner asked, cupping his ear. "I think my audio glitched."

"Don't push it," Dean growled. "This is bigger than it seems on the surface. Too many angles, not enough eyes."

"That's what we're here for," Beckett said, with what might have been the ghost of a smile. "I'll focus on financial records and staff backgrounds. Particularly interested in this handyman, Mike Thompson. His employment history has red flags all over it."

That tracked. And made Dean's senses tingle, even as he kicked himself for not checking up on Mike personally. These guys were filling gaps that shouldn't have needed filling, but while they were at it, at least they were doing well.

"I'll work the local angle," Tanner added. "Hit the bars, charm the townspeople. Find out who had genuine beef with Greta beyond the usual small-town grudges."

They were good at this, Dean realized with something like reluctant admiration. Splitting responsibilities, targeting different aspects of the case, complementing each other's skills. Almost like they'd worked as a team before.

"I'll keep working the vineyard angle," Dean said after a moment. "Staff interviews, personal effects, physical evidence."

"A three-pronged approach," Tanner noted with approval. "Much more efficient than whatever Lone Ranger routine you've been working over there thus far."

"Lone Ranger had a partner," Dean pointed out. Maybe that would be a good code name if he got any kind of choice in the matter.

"So do you," Beckett replied simply. "Two of them."

Well, that walloped him where the sun didn't shine, and it took him a minute to recalibrate.

Looked like this was a thing then. A thing he didn't think would be wise to reject. They weren't Jake. They weren't the Rangers. This was something different. Something new. He'd do everyone a favor if he kept an open mind instead of galloping off in the other direction.

Yeah, teams fell apart. Partners let you down. Going solo meant controlling all the variables.

But it also meant limiting what you could accomplish. And right now, with a murder to solve and Samantha's safety at stake, being smart suddenly seemed like the priority.

Strickland's face suddenly appeared on screen, his silver

hair and shrewd eyes filling a fourth window. "Gentlemen. Progress report?"

Dean let Beckett summarize their plan, watching as Strickland nodded along, clearly pleased with what he was hearing.

"Good. You're thinking like a unit," Strickland noted. "That's what this team is about, Carter. Seeing how it feels to be part of something bigger than yourself again."

"I thought it was about finding out who killed Greta Wagner."

"It's about both," Strickland replied mildly. "I need leaders. I need you to remember how to be one. That's what I'm counting on."

A leader? "That's not me, Strickland. I'm barely a team player."

His former mentor's gaze drilled through the screen, as vibrant as if the man stood right in front of him in the flesh. "We disagree on both counts. Group check-in Friday, same time. And Carter? I didn't make a mistake putting you on this team. Don't treat it like one."

The call ended, leaving Dean staring at a dead, black screen. Might as well be looking at his own heart. What was left of it.

Bottom line, this audition wasn't earning him any glowing reviews. And his shot at Ruiz depended on two things—how well he conformed to the team he'd joined and results.

Looked like it was going to be a long few days until the Friday check-in.

Dean worked through lunch, sorting Greta's files in the relative safety of his bedroom with the door closed. He told himself he was keeping the staff out, but it served as a great barrier against Samantha too.

No distractions.

He kept up that mantra until he picked up an invoice from a company with an address in El Paso.

Cadiz Street. Like it was yesterday, he transported back to that frigid February outside a warehouse near the border. One of the worst operations in the history of time.

Six hostages. Three gunmen. No clear leadership. Local law enforcement was overwhelmed, the feds were stuck in jurisdictional red tape, and DPS's tactical team was en route but too far out. Someone had to take control before the whole thing imploded.

So Dean had stepped up.

He'd worked with the sheriff's office and state troopers to establish a perimeter, coordinated with DPS's Special Operations Group as they deployed tactical units, and made the call to stall negotiations long enough for the breaching team to get into position. He hadn't been the one kicking down doors, but he'd been the one making sure it all happened in sync. A wrong move, a delay of even a few seconds, and innocent people would have died.

When the situation escalated, he adapted. A hostage tried to run, a gunman panicked, the strategy had to shift—fast. Dean had thrown the whole plan in the trash and instantly redirected the teams to keep the chaos from spiraling into bloodshed.

In the end, all six hostages walked out alive. The gunmen went to prison. DPS still used that case as a training example. Not for the tactics, but for the leadership that had turned a near disaster into a textbook resolution.

Yeah, okay. He'd been a leader once, and Strickland had witnessed it from the front row.

Then Jake had met Aubrey. Ruiz had kidnapped her to get to her senator father. Another warehouse, another opportunity to dominate, and instead, Jake's priorities had shifted to *her*. Away from Dean. Ruiz had put a bullet in Dean's side and then walked free.

And suddenly, being any part of a team seemed like a liability rather than an asset.

Dean rubbed absently at the scar beneath his shirt. The wound had healed, but the lesson remained embedded like a bullet fragment: don't rely on anyone and *don't* risk the mission for a woman.

A lesson he was willfully ignoring every time Samantha Wagner walked into the room.

By midafternoon, Dean had a stack of files spread across the table—records he'd managed to retrieve from Greta's office with Samantha's permission. Employee files, property records, business contracts. Nothing that screamed, "I was murdered!" but enough to paint a picture of a woman who'd clawed her way to success, leaving scratches on anyone who got too close.

His phone buzzed. A message from Beckett to their group text.

Found something on Mike Thompson. Sending file now.

Dean's phone buzzed again. Tanner this time.

Local gossip gold mine. Will call later.

Two solid leads he hadn't had to turn over a single stone to get. It was unsettling. Helpful but unsettling. Like finding out the math homework you'd been sweating over already had the answers written in invisible ink.

Except it wasn't like that at all. This was what a team could accomplish—distribute the workload. Cover more ground. Play to individual strengths.

"What's next, trust falls and friendship bracelets?" he muttered to himself.

The door from the balcony opened and Samantha swept in. Her hair was slightly disheveled, a smudge of something dark on her otherwise immaculate blouse. She looked…amazing. Like a woman who wouldn't mind a man tussling her up some.

A sharp ache in his gut spelled a different kind of trouble, because this was a woman he wasn't just marginally attracted to. This was a woman who could destroy kingdoms.

Who knew he'd prefer this earthy version of Samantha to the uber-polished one?

So much for keeping her out. It hadn't occurred to him that she'd sneak into his room via the balcony. And now this whole interlude felt vaguely illicit, and he did not need any help on that front.

"If you're planning to become a permanent fixture in this room, I'm going to start charging you rent," she said, dropping into the chair across from him with an exhausted sigh that made him want to spread his hands across her shoulders and indulge them both in a relaxing massage. "Though I suppose sharing the dog makes us even."

"Alfred has made his preferences clear," Dean replied, nodding toward the dog who'd settled at Samantha's feet the moment she sat down. "Traitor goes to the highest bidder."

"Or the one with access to the good cheese," she admitted with a guilty smile. "Are those Greta's files?"

"Some of them." Dean discretely closed his laptop lid before she spied Beckett's newly arrived file on Mike. "Getting a feel for how she operated."

"Finding anything useful?"

"Some," he admitted. "My associates are helping with the background work."

Samantha's eyebrows shot up. "Associates? As in plural? I thought you worked alone."

"I never said that."

"Didn't you?" She ticked off points on her fingers. "You've never once mentioned colleagues or partners. You handle everything yourself—from security checks to interviews to research. Plus, you have that whole sexy loner cowboy vibe going on."

He blinked. She thought he was sexy?

"Even investigators need specialized perspectives sometimes," he mumbled.

"So, who are these mysterious associates?" Samantha asked, pulling one of the files toward her. "Other investigators? Analysts? Computer hackers?"

"Something like that," Dean hedged. Strickland's operation was classified, and the less she knew, the safer she'd be. "Let's just say they each bring different expertise to the table."

"Different expertise," she repeated with a smirk. "Very diplomatic. You're not going to tell me anything concrete, are you?"

"Classified," he replied with a half smile that did nothing to soften the wall he'd erected. It was necessary. He'd sucked at doing it so far.

"Fine, keep your secrets," she said, waving a hand dismissively. "I'm calling you the Shadow in my head. Always in the background, rarely revealing anything, surprisingly substantial when needed."

"Please don't," Dean said, though the corner of his mouth twitched upward.

"Too late. It's decided." She grinned, returning to the file she'd pulled. "It's interesting though. I didn't peg you for a team player."

Sometimes she showed up in totally unexpected ways and he shouldn't like that she saw as much as she did.

"Even lone wolves need a pack sometimes." The words landed weird, but he didn't hate the way they felt in his mouth. He did mourn the loss of that as his potential code name though. "Especially when the territory gets complicated."

Her expression softened. "Like when half a town decides to hate you on sight?"

"You handled that well yesterday."

"Because you had my back." She met his gaze with warmth that had a lot of *my hero* in it. "Made me feel less like I was facing a firing squad alone."

Something dangerous uncurled in his chest. "Team effort."

"See? You're better at this collaboration thing than you think." Her smile did nothing to help this situation.

Not Samantha too. First Strickland with his leadership speech and now this. What was with the universe conspiring against him like this?

Before everything had gone sideways in his career, he'd had a totally different opinion of his skill set. Now it was easier to be alone. Depending on no one meant no one could let you down.

"Maybe," was all he said, though something shifted in his chest, like a key turning in a lock long rusted shut.

Samantha seemed to sense she'd pushed far enough. She shoved her chair back and stood. "I should go check on the Tempranillo situation. Carlos is probably hugging the tank and singing lullabies to the grapes by now."

"The life of a vineyard owner is never dull," Dean remarked.

"You have no idea." She paused at the doorway, her expression thoughtful. "You know what's funny? I spent my entire career proving I could succeed on my own. That I didn't need anyone's help to climb the corporate ladder. And now here I am, running a vineyard I know nothing about, still trying to do it solo. And I'd be lying if I said I was doing it well."

The parallel wasn't subtle, but he got the point. Dean watched her walk away. She was right, of course. They were facing similar challenges from opposite directions—they were both being forced to rely on others after bulldozing through challenges with the armor of self-sufficiency.

After she left, Dean stared at the stack of files without really seeing them. His phone buzzed again with more information from Beckett about Mike Thompson's suspicious employment history, followed by a message from Tanner confirming he'd dug up some interesting local gossip about Greta's final days.

Working with these guys was producing results faster than

he could have achieved alone. It was a fact, plain and simple. And Dean Carter had always prided himself on dealing in facts.

Alfred trotted back into the room, immediately making a beeline for Dean this time. The dog dropped his head in Dean's lap and looked up at him with those soulful eyes that always seemed to see right through him.

"Don't give me that look," Dean muttered. "I'm getting there. Maybe having backup isn't the worst idea in the world. As long as it's the right backup."

As he opened the file on Mike Thompson and saw the red flags Granger had mentioned, he cursed. Somehow, without his permission, he'd accepted that this was happening. He was part of this team, like it or not. A team with purpose. A team with specific skills. A team with Tanner's charisma, Beckett's analytical precision and his own...what? His own ability to see how they fit together.

To lead, whether he wanted to admit it or not.

And somewhere deep inside, in a place he'd locked away with everything else, Dean knew that accepting this part of himself was the first step toward being whole again. Toward moving past the betrayal and the bullet and the bitterness.

Toward becoming the kind of man who might actually deserve a place on this team.

Maybe even toward whatever was growing between him and Samantha Wagner.

Chapter 9

Nothing in the corporate world could possibly prepare you for what to do when you'd accidentally ruined five thousand dollars' worth of wine because you grabbed the wrong container off the shelf.

Samantha stared at a steel vat of what should have been the vineyard's award-winning Syrah, now bubbling with angry, chemical-scented foam that oozed from the pressure release valve at the top like something from a B-grade horror film.

"I'm so fired," she muttered, before remembering she was, technically, the boss. "Correction—I'm so screwed."

She'd handled hostile boardrooms with less panic than she felt watching this wine die before her eyes.

At least she'd been alone when the disaster happened, having insisted on performing this simple task herself.

Simple. That was the kicker. Carlos had offered—no, practically begged her to leave it to the professionals. But she'd been so determined to prove she wasn't just some city girl playing vineyard dress-up that she'd assured him she could manage.

Carlos had looked like he wanted to handcuff himself to the vat to prevent her from touching it, but had reluctantly backed down when she'd pulled the owner card.

Now she understood his panic. Winemaking wasn't a Power-Point presentation where you could simply edit out a mistake. It was irreversible chemistry. And she'd irreversibly chemistried this batch into oblivion.

"Perfectly executed self-sabotage," she announced to the empty tank room. "Ten out of ten. Would recommend if your goal is abject humiliation."

She couldn't blame sleep deprivation or multitasking. No, this had been pure, unfiltered determination to prove herself worthy of the Wagner name. To show the staff, who still looked at her like she was a corporate raider in stilettos, that she belonged here.

And, okay, maybe to show Dean she wasn't as hopeless as she'd come across at the market the other day. She could earn people's respect. This fish could adapt to dry land, yes, sir.

The thought of Dean finding out about this disaster sent a fresh wave of nausea through her that had nothing to do with the chemical fumes. So this plan had worked out great.

The steel door to the tank room swung open with a metallic groan to admit another fun addition to her nightmare. Jules Foster stood in the doorway, her weathered face transitioning from neutral to thunderstruck as her gaze locked onto the frothy disaster.

"What. Did. You. Do?" Each word dropped like a stone into a very deep, very quiet well.

Samantha straightened her spine, channeling the poise she'd maintained through boardroom slaughters much worse than this. Allegedly worse. Currently, this felt like the business equivalent of showing up to a presentation with the wrong client's numbers.

"There appears to have been a slight miscalculation with the additives," she said. Understatement. Jules would likely realize that instantly.

"A slight miscalculation," she repeated flatly as she tracked the foam dripping down the sides from the pressure valve.

"You've destroyed an entire batch of our Syrah. Do you have any idea what that's worth?"

"Approximately five thousand dollars," Samantha answered promptly, because of course she knew. She'd memorized the production costs of every varietal within forty-eight hours of inheriting the vineyard.

Jules stared at her, clearly thrown by the precise response. "And you're just…what? Standing here watching it disintegrate?"

"I was contemplating my options," Samantha replied, though her options mainly consisted of variations on finding a hole to crawl into.

"Your options?" Jules barked out a laugh that contained zero humor. "There are no options. It's ruined. Carlos spent months nurturing this particular batch. It was going to be submitted to the Hill Country Wine Competition next month."

Oh. That particular detail hadn't been in any of the spreadsheets Samantha had reviewed. The knot in her stomach tightened to bowling-ball density.

"I'll take full responsibility," she said, which seemed inadequate given she was already technically responsible as both the perpetrator and the owner.

"You bet you will," Jules confirmed unnecessarily. "This is exactly why Ben quit, you know. He said Greta's replacement would be the death of this vineyard. I didn't believe him at first, but now…" She gestured at the foaming vat with a sweep of her arm.

The words hit with precision, targeting every insecurity Samantha had been battling since arriving at Wagner Wines. Because honestly? Jules wasn't wrong. Samantha was in over her head, drowning in grape terminology and production processes while pretending she had a clue what she was doing.

The familiar sensation of not measuring up crashed over her like a wave. It was the same feeling she'd had as a kid, coming home clutching a math test with a 98 percent score scrawled across the top in red ink.

Her parents always wanted to know what had happened to the other 2 percent.

If on the next test, she'd scored 100 percent, her parents nodded with approval but not surprise. It was expected, not exceptional.

Two decades later, and she was still chasing that elusive sense of "good enough." Still trying to avoid disappointment when she didn't achieve perfection. Except now the disappointment came from a staff that had never wanted her here in the first place.

Samantha's throat tightened. She would not cry. Not in front of Jules. Not over ruined wine, no matter how expensive or competition-worthy. She'd navigated sexist investors and corporate backstabbing without shedding a tear; she could handle this.

"I'll speak with Carlos about making this right," she said stiffly.

"There's no making this right," Jules replied, her voice hard. "This was our showcase wine. Wagner Wines hasn't won the regional competition in three years, and Carlos thought this batch had a real shot." She shook her head. "I knew letting you near production was a mistake."

With that parting shot, Jules turned and stalked out of the tank room, leaving Samantha alone with the evidence of her failure.

The moment the door closed, Samantha allowed her shoulders to slump.

"Stellar performance," she muttered. "Samantha the Vineyard Slayer strikes again. Only this time, it's actual slaying. Of actual wine."

A soft whine from the doorway caught her attention. Alfred stood there, head tilted, regarding her with what looked suspiciously like concern.

"Don't look at me like that," she told the dog. "I don't need your pity."

Alfred padded over anyway, nudging her hand with his nose. Despite her best efforts to maintain some dignity, she found herself crouching down to smooth the fur behind his ears.

"At least you don't care if I'm competent or not," she murmured, the stroking motion managing to soothe her a tiny bit. "You'd probably still like me if I burned the whole vineyard to the ground."

"I wouldn't go testing that theory if I were you," a deep voice drawled from the doorway.

Dean.

Samantha's head snapped up to find him leaning against the doorframe, arms crossed, his expression maddeningly indecipherable. He looked tired, the lines around his eyes slightly deeper, as if he'd been up half the night.

Looking for evidence to convict her? Or exonerate her? That would be better.

"How did it go with your team?" she asked quickly, desperate to direct attention away from the bubbling disaster behind her.

His eyebrows lifted slightly, clearly not expecting that question. "Productive. Unexpected. Humbling." He moved into the room, surveying ground zero with slightly widened eyes. "Looks like your morning's been eventful too."

Samantha straightened, mortification heating her cheeks. "If by 'eventful' you mean 'catastrophically incompetent,' then yes."

"What happened?" he asked, eyeing the bubbling mixture visible through the sight glass.

She gestured at the chaos. "Chemistry did its thing. Wine died a dramatic bubbly death."

"Why were you doing this yourself?"

The question was identical to one she'd asked herself moments ago, but coming from him, it carried a different weight. She felt a flicker of defensiveness.

"Because I'm the owner? Because I should know how this works?" She crossed her arms. "Because I'm tired of looking incompetent in front of my staff."

"So you decided to risk a batch of wine rather than risk looking incompetent," Dean said, his tone matter-of-fact but not unkind.

Put that way, it sounded ridiculous. But wasn't that exactly what she'd done?

"I thought I could handle it," she admitted after a moment. "Carlos offered to help, but I…wanted to prove I could do it myself."

Dean's mouth quirked in what might have been recognition. "Funny how that works, isn't it?"

It took her a second to make the connection between her parting words to him and this eerily similar situation. "This isn't the same thing."

"Isn't it? I spent the morning getting schooled by my teammates after spending a week trying to solve everything alone." His expression softened. "Sometimes the hardest thing isn't the task itself, it's asking for help with it."

The unexpected parallel hit her crossways. Dean Carter, the man who earlier this week had insisted he worked better alone, was standing here drawing connections between his resistance to teamwork and her need to prove herself.

"It would be easier if you sounded less reasonable," she said, fighting a reluctant smile. "It's hard to feel properly sorry for myself when you're making sense."

"I have my moments," he replied, the corner of his mouth lifting. "Usually around eight thirty-seven on alternate Tuesdays."

The joke was so Dean that she couldn't help but laugh. His sense of humor hooked her in unexpected places sometimes, so much so that she had to take a moment to appreciate it, even in the midst of failure. Especially in *this* moment.

"You're running yourself into the ground," he continued,

his voice gentle but firm. "Trying to master every aspect of a business you inherited two weeks ago."

"That's my job," she countered, though with less conviction than before.

"Your job is to run the vineyard, not personally handle every aspect of it." His eyes held hers, steady and certain. "That's why you have specialists. Carlos knows wine production better than you ever will."

Her pride stung at the blunt assessment. "So, I should be a figurehead? Pay bills and stay out of the way?"

"No. You should be a leader." Dean gestured at the ruined batch. "This happened because you're trying to prove something instead of focusing on what actually needs doing."

It was such a practical solution, and yet it challenged everything she'd been forcing herself to do since arriving.

"I hate when you make excellent points I should have already realized," she muttered. "It ruins the image in my head of you being this infuriating cowboy."

The corner of Dean's mouth ticked up in that half smile that never failed to make whipped cream out of her bones.

"You're burning the candle at both ends," he said. "And in the middle. And probably from a few extra wicks you've added for good measure."

"I wanted to show them I belonged here," she said quietly, the admission sliding free into the space he'd created for truth. "That Greta didn't make a mistake choosing me."

Dean's expression shifted into something so gentle her throat hurt. "You don't have to earn your place here by being perfect at everything. You just have to show up and keep showing up, even on the days when it's hard."

The simplicity of it struck her. So different from the messaging she'd absorbed her entire life, that her worth was tied to achievement, that anything less than excellence was failure.

"I've been working myself to death trying to be the perfect

vineyard owner," she admitted. "But maybe what this place needs isn't perfection. Maybe it needs someone who cares enough to keep trying, even after destroying a vat of award-worthy Syrah."

Dean's eyes crinkled slightly at the corners as he treated her to the half smile she'd started craving. "That sounds about right."

Alfred, who had been watching their exchange with apparent interest, chose that moment to lean against her leg, his warm weight a steady pressure against her calf. The gesture seemed like canine affirmation.

"Your dog seems to agree," she said, reaching down to stroke his head. The simple, uncomplicated affection from the animal was unexpectedly comforting.

"He's got good instincts about people." Dean watched them for a moment, then added, "Though he's also partial to anyone who feeds him leftover chicken, so take that with a grain of salt."

She laughed, and it cleansed something inside. It felt good to momentarily set down the crushing weight of her own expectations. To let him do that for her.

"So, what now?" Dean asked, nodding toward the still bubbling vat.

"Now I go find Carlos, admit what I did, and ask him to show me how this should have been done." The prospect wasn't pleasant, but it felt like the right next step. "Not so I can do it myself next time, but so I understand the process better."

"Sounds like a plan," Dean agreed. "Knowledge without needing to master every skill personally."

"A novel concept," she admitted wryly. "I guess leadership doesn't mean you have to do everything yourself."

Something flickered in Dean's eyes at that—recognition, perhaps, or his own private realization. "I'm learning that too," he said quietly.

The moment stretched between them, this unexpected connection binding them together. Here they were, both struggling with similar issues from opposite directions—her desperate need to prove herself through personal achievement, his stubborn insistence on handling everything alone. Both of them learning, albeit reluctantly, that there might be better ways.

Together. Not because of the fake relationship. But because this was who Dean was at his core—someone who cared. She liked being included in those who got to see this side of him.

"Thank you," she said finally. "For not laughing. Or telling me everything will be fine when we both know I blew several thousand dollars of product."

"You're showing up," Dean said simply, the words carrying more weight than their simplicity suggested. "Every day, trying to figure this out, stepping up to challenges most people would run from. That counts for something."

The words settled around her like a warm blanket. *You're showing up.* Not "you're succeeding" or "you're failing," but simply acknowledging the effort. The persistence. The willingness to keep going even when things got hard.

It was a completely different metric than she'd ever applied to herself. In her world, effort without results was just failure by another name. But the way Dean said it—like showing up was its own kind of success—rearranged a few pieces inside.

And that meant more than she was ready to admit.

"I should go find Carlos," she said, reluctant to end this moment but aware of her responsibilities. "Confess my sins and see if there's any chance of salvaging even a drop of this batch."

Dean nodded. "Probably wise."

She started toward the door, then paused, turning back. "How did you know? That I needed—that this happened?"

"Alfred," Dean replied, a hint of amusement warming his voice. "He came and told me. He has a thing for you, by the way."

"My very own canine emotional support alarm." It was supposed to be a joke, but if anything, she felt oddly touched that the dog had sensed her distress and sought help. It was more than most humans in her life had ever done.

Dean shrugged. "You could do worse."

As if understanding he was being discussed, Alfred trotted over to her, looking up with expectant eyes. Impulsively, she crouched again to scratch his ears, murmuring, "Thanks for the rescue, buddy."

When she straightened, she found Dean watching them with an expression she couldn't quite translate, made up of warmth and surprise and something else that made her skin feel like it was on wrong side out. For a moment, they stood there, close enough that she could feel the heat of him, could catch that woodsy scent that was becoming dangerously familiar.

"I'll see you back at the house," she said, suddenly self-conscious of how aware she was of…everything. His height, his breadth, the way his eyes seemed to darken when they held hers a beat too long.

He nodded. "I'll be there."

Three simple words, but they carried a weight of reassurance that stayed with her as she left the tank room, shoulders straightened, mentally rehearsing her conversation with Carlos.

Alfred trotted alongside her, a surprisingly comforting presence.

As disasters went, this one had taken an unexpected turn toward something else entirely.

Samantha the Vineyard Slayer might have decimated a batch of award-worthy Syrah, but for the first time since arriving at Wagner Wines, she wasn't facing these challenges entirely alone. Dean was here. Somehow the universe had dropped a good one in her lap.

And that was worth more than any ruined wine.

Chapter 10

Dread settled in Samantha's stomach as she stared at the row of bottling equipment now spitting and hissing like an angry cat. Which was *not* her fault! This time. She'd been having a perfectly decent morning until ten minutes ago, when Jules had stormed into her office, face flushed with fury.

"The equipment's malfunctioning again," Jules had announced, her tone implying this was absolutely Samantha's fault. "Carlos needs you. Now!"

Of course he did. Because when you screwed up royally with a five-thousand-dollar batch of wine, you naturally got called in to handle the next crisis. Perfect sense.

Now, standing in the processing facility surrounded by stainless steel machines that looked more suited to a sci-fi movie than a vineyard, Samantha fought the urge to turn around and flee back to Houston. At least corporate backstabbing came with familiar equipment and jargon she understood.

Every dawn at Wagner Wines brought home the point that she had no idea what she was doing.

"I swear it was working perfectly an hour ago," Carlos insisted, his normally calm demeanor frayed at the edges. He fiddled with control panels while eyeing her suspiciously. "I've run diagnostics three times."

"And?" She braced herself for the verdict.

"Something's been tampered with." Carlos wiped sweat

from his brow. "This isn't a malfunction. Someone deliberately messed with the calibration settings."

The knot in Samantha's stomach tightened. "Could it be a mechanical issue? Maybe vibrations from—"

"No." Carlos cut her off firmly. "These settings require manual override codes. Someone intentionally recalibrated the pressure gauges, which would have ruptured the main line if we hadn't caught it in time."

Jules, who'd been hovering nearby with arms crossed and judgment radiating from every pore, let out a pointed sigh. "First the wine batch, now this."

The implication hung in the air like a bad smell. Samantha's cheeks heated.

"You think I sabotaged my own equipment?" The words spit out with razors attached. "That makes absolutely zero sense, Jules."

"I didn't say that." Jules's eyes, however, said plenty.

"You didn't have to." Samantha smoothed her expression into what she privately called her Boardroom Blank—the carefully neutral mask she'd perfected during particularly vicious quarterly reviews. "Carlos, can you fix it?"

"Already working on it." He turned back to the control panel. "But we can't bottle today. We'll lose a full production day."

Great. Another financial hit she couldn't afford. Add it to the growing list of disasters that had occurred on her watch. The wine batch failure had been her fault, but this? This was something else entirely.

"I want to take a closer look at that control panel," she said.

Reluctantly, he stepped aside. Samantha leaned in, studying the digital display with its blinking warning lights and error messages. She might not know much about winemaking, but she understood technology. And security protocols.

"Carlos, who has access to these override codes?"

The winemaker ran a hand through his already disheveled

hair. "Me. Jules. Ben had them, obviously, before he quit. And your aunt kept a master list."

A master list that was now presumably in Samantha's possession somewhere. She made a mental note to search Ben's former office—her office—more thoroughly.

"Anyone else?"

"Mike does maintenance on the equipment," Jules volunteered, her tone slightly less accusatory. "He'd need access for troubleshooting."

Mike. That guy's name kept showing up in places where trouble happened. Coincidence, maybe. But she didn't think so.

This wasn't just about a ladder or malfunctioning equipment. Someone was doing this on purpose.

She wanted to know who. And why.

Samantha excused herself and headed outside, needing air that didn't taste like tension and suspicion. The late-morning sun beat down on her shoulders as she stalked back to the house, her brain whirling with the overload of information.

These weren't random accidents. Someone wanted to send a message, harm her, maybe drive her off—or at the very least make her look grossly incompetent. Given the staff's already low opinion of her, it wasn't exactly a challenging mission.

As she hit the steps, the only person she had any interest in seeing came through the door.

Dean. Looking far too delicious for a guy whose style trended toward "lazy Sunday afternoon." She nearly flung herself into his arms, but that would be weird. Plus, she didn't need him or his quiet strength or his crinkly eyes. Not really. She was fine. It was fine.

She'd take a joke though. She did like the way he made her laugh.

And he came with a dog. Alfred sat at his feet, tail thumping against the ground as he spotted her.

"Rough morning?" Dean asked, his shrewd gaze sweeping over her.

"You could say that." How did he *do* that? One look and he knew something was up. "Someone sabotaged the bottling equipment."

Dean straightened, Ranger mode activated. "Tell me everything."

"Carlos is resetting the system now." She fell into step beside him as he started walking toward the processing facility. "Someone messed with the calibration settings. Could have caused a major pressure breach if they hadn't caught it in time."

"Anyone get hurt?" His hand hovered near her waist, not quite touching but present enough that she could feel heat through her silk blouse.

"No, thankfully. Carlos noticed something was off before they started the full bottling run." She glanced at him. "This is the second incident, Dean. Someone tampered with that ladder, and now this."

"Third, if we count your aunt's death." His gaze scanned the landscape as they walked, taking in details other people didn't, her included.

That was why she trusted him. He didn't miss things, and he wouldn't in this situation either.

"Everyone thinks it's me," she admitted quietly. "After the wine fiasco, the timing doesn't exactly work in my favor."

Dean stopped walking, turning to face her. "But you didn't do it."

The certainty in his voice licked through her, soothing edges that had frayed more than she'd realized. Her eyes drifted shut for a beat, and she grabbed onto the lovely floaty feeling before it faded.

And then it did, leaving her with a somewhat cold reality.

"How can you be so sure?" she murmured, needing to know, dreading the answer.

The question hung between them, bigger than the simple vowels and consonants that made up the words. She was asking him whether he thought she was capable of doing terrible things, right here, right now.

"Because you didn't," he said simply, in no way missing the point. "You're ambitious, determined and occasionally terrifying, but you're not stupid. And ruining your own vineyard would be stupid."

She quirked a brow at him even as a laugh bubbled up, which she'd absolutely wanted more than she wanted her next breath. "Occasionally terrifying?"

"When you're in full corporate warrior mode." His eyes finally crinkled at the corners, and everything inside her settled. "It's actually impressive. Frightening but impressive."

"I'll take that as a compliment." She started walking again, absurdly pleased. "Though I seem to be failing spectacularly at being impressive here."

"You're learning." Dean didn't even have to hurry to catch up, his long legs matching her stride easily. "Learning isn't failure."

"Tell that to Jules. And Carlos. And literally everyone else who looks at me like I'm a walking disaster in designer shoes."

"I like your shoes."

She glanced down at her stilettos with the silk ankle ties and then back at him with an eye roll. "Of course you do. They're Louboutins. You'd have to be blind not to like them."

"I should have said I like them on you." He treated her to a slow smile, and there was nothing halfway about it. "They're the sexiest pair you own, and I thought so last Thursday too, the first time you wore them."

Her extremities lost all feeling.

He'd noticed her shoes. Noticed them like that. Her skin flashed hot as electricity shot across it. She covered her reaction with a cough. Probably. "Smooth, cowboy. How many times did you practice that?"

He shrugged, seemingly unbothered. "Zero. It came out that way. We have an audience, by the way."

We have a...what?

Sure enough, she spotted Calla watching them from the tasting room window, her expression openly curious. Oh. Oh! Duh. This was all an act for the fake relationship.

Oddly disappointed, Samantha forced a relaxed smile, leaning slightly closer to Dean as if sharing a private joke. Because this was her life now, he slipped his arm around her waist, the weight of it shockingly familiar even as she registered that he'd never touched her quite like this.

"See? Working like a charm," he murmured, close enough that she could feel his breath against her ear. And then he iced that cake by lifting the back of his hand to her cheek, sweeping away a lock of hair as if he'd done exactly that so many times it came second nature.

"What is?" she squawked, fighting the urge to lean into him.

"Our cover story." His fingers traced a small maddening circle against her hip. "Nobody watching us right now is thinking about sabotaged equipment. They're thinking about how nauseatingly into each other we are."

She arched an eyebrow. "Spoken like a true romantic."

"You know what I mean." His gaze never left hers, this conversation riveting, obviously. "Convincingly. Believably."

"Right." She nodded, as if the distinction mattered. As if she wasn't hyperaware of every point of contact between them.

As if she didn't think about leaning into the space between them and seeing what kinds of things this cowboy might be good at doing with his mouth.

A sudden commotion from the equipment shed interrupted their performance. Shouting voices and the sound of something heavy crashing to the ground had them both instantly alert.

"Stay here," Dean ordered, already moving toward the disturbance.

"Fat chance," she muttered, following him.

They raced across the lawn toward the growing commotion. Well, he raced, she stumbled after him as best she could in her heels. As they neared the shed, Samantha saw what had happened. A heavy metal shelf had collapsed, bringing down barrels of chemicals and supplies. Smoke rose from some sort of reaction between spilled substances, creating an acrid cloud that made her eyes water.

Jules and Carlos were already there, attempting to contain the mess.

"Everyone alright?" Dean called as they approached.

"No injuries," Jules reported, her face smudged with soot. "But we've lost most of our maintenance supplies."

The chemicals couldn't have been cheap either. Another costly loss. They were starting to stack up.

"How did this happen?" Samantha asked, though she already suspected the answer.

Jules gestured to the metal brackets that had once supported the heavy shelving. "Looks like the bolts gave way. But they were inspected recently. They should have been secure."

"When?" Dean asked, crouching to examine one of the fallen brackets. "When were they last inspected?"

"Last week," Carlos supplied. "Mike checked all the storage areas during routine maintenance."

Mike again. Not a coincidence, and his probable involvement was becoming impossible to ignore.

"Where is Mike now?" Dean's voice had taken on an edge that made several staff members glance at him nervously.

Jules frowned. "I haven't seen him since early this morning."

Dean and Samantha exchanged a look loaded with meaning. Without a word, he straightened and moved closer to her, his hand coming to rest against the small of her back in a gesture that might have looked casual to observers but felt distinctly protective. And inclusionary. He made them look like a team effortlessly.

She liked that idea more than she should.

"Jules, can you handle the cleanup?" Samantha asked. "I'll send some additional help, but I need to get back to the house."

Dean followed her from the shed. Once they were out of earshot, she let out a shaky breath. "That wasn't an accident."

"No," Dean agreed grimly. "It wasn't."

"This is getting out of hand." She raked a hand through her disaster hair that had been carefully styled at some point. "First the ladder, then the bottling equipment, now this? What's next? The main house going up in flames while I'm sleeping?"

She'd meant it as a joke, but Dean's expression darkened.

"That's not going to happen," he said, his voice dropping to a register that sent a shiver down her spine. "I won't let it."

The fierce declaration should have raised her feminist hackles. Instead, it sent a completely different kind of heat spiraling through her. When was the last time someone had been so firmly in her corner? None of this made any sense. She'd met Dean Carter five minutes ago, and he already felt like her strongest ally.

"We need to find Mike," she said, refocusing on the problem at hand instead of the fireworks going off inside.

"My team has already checked into his background and found a few red flags," Dean said, scanning the property. "Let's see if he's in the maintenance shed."

She nodded, falling into step beside him. "You have people looking into him?"

"Just my teaxm, yeah," he admitted. "They're good at finding things most people miss."

Samantha tried to picture what kind of team Dean worked with, but her imagination supplied only vague outlines of equally attractive men with guns and serious expressions. With them on the job, no women anywhere would get any work done ever again, obviously.

They searched all over the property, eventually spotting Mike near the tank rooms, toolbox in hand as he exited the building. Thank goodness. Samantha was about to pull off her shoes and go barefoot.

"Mike," Dean called out, his voice casual but carrying an undercurrent of authority that made the handyman freeze momentarily. "Got a minute?"

Mike turned slowly, his weathered face revealing nothing. "What can I do for you?"

"We had another incident," Dean said, closing the distance between them with Samantha at his side. "Heavy shelving collapsed in the equipment shed. The one you inspected last week."

Mike's expression remained neutral. "Accidents happen."

"Do they?" Samantha couldn't keep the edge from her voice. "Because we've had quite a run of them lately."

"Coincidence," Mike replied, but his eyes narrowed slightly.

"Mind if we take a look at your maintenance logs?" Dean asked, though it didn't sound like a request. "Just routine follow-up."

Mike's jaw tightened. "They're in my office. This way."

He led them to a small room off the main equipment building, little more than a closet with a desk crammed inside. As he bent to retrieve a binder from a drawer, Samantha noticed the slight tension in his shoulders, the careful way he kept his face turned away from them.

Because he didn't like her. Or was there a more sinister reason?

"Here," he said, handing the binder to Dean. "Everything's documented."

Dean flipped through the pages, his expression giving nothing away. "Looks like you inspected those brackets last Thursday."

"Like I said, they were secure then." Mike crossed his arms, leaning against the desk. "Sometimes equipment fails."

"Three different types of equipment in two weeks?" Samantha asked. "That's an unusual failure rate for a place that's supposedly well maintained."

Mike's eyes met hers, something cold flashing in their depths. "Maybe the vineyard is trying to tell you something."

"What does that mean?" she pressed, stepping closer despite knowing in her gut he was somehow responsible for all of this mayhem.

"Some people don't belong here." His voice had dropped, the words carrying a weight that felt distinctly threatening. "Some people are not supposed to own vineyards."

Dean closed the binder with a deliberate snap. "Sounds like you have concerns about Ms. Wagner's management."

"Just stating facts," Mike replied, his gaze never leaving Samantha. "City people come out here thinking they can run a vineyard because they've had a few wine tastings. It doesn't work that way."

"And what way does it work?" she asked, refusing to back down from his challenge.

His mouth curved in a humorless smile. "Not like whatever you're doing, that's for sure. You think you can waltz in here because your name's on the deed? You don't know the first thing about what Greta built."

"Or what happened to her?" Dean's question landed like a stone in still water, sending ripples through the room.

Mike's composure slipped momentarily. "What do you mean, what happened to her?"

"Just curious about your thoughts," Dean said, his tone deceptively casual. "Since you worked closely with her for so long."

"Heart attack," Mike replied shortly. "Doctors confirmed it."

"Convenient timing," Samantha observed, watching his reaction closely. What might he give away if they pressed him even further?

"For who?" Mike's eyes flashed dangerously. "For you? The niece who's never been here before, who never visited but inherited everything without lifting a finger?"

"I was thinking more about people who might have wanted the vineyard for themselves," she replied evenly. "People who've been here a long time, who might have thought they deserved it."

Mike took a step toward her, his bulk suddenly seeming more threatening. "You don't know what you're talking about."

Dean moved between them, crossing his arms across his impressive torso in a show of dominance that Mike didn't miss. "Where were you when the shelves collapsed today, Mike?"

"Irrigation system," he replied too quickly. "North field."

"Funny," Dean said, "Jules said she hasn't seen you all morning."

Mike's face hardened. "What's with all these questions? I don't answer to you."

"No," Samantha agreed, "you answer to me. And I want a full accounting of your movements today, along with a complete report on all equipment you've inspected in the past month."

For a tense moment, she thought he might refuse. Then he nodded slowly, his eyes never leaving hers. "Whatever you say, Ms. Wagner. You're the boss." The words carried a subtle mockery that raised the fine hairs on her neck.

"That's right," she said firmly. "I am."

As they left the cramped office, Dean's arm slipped around her waist, guiding her away from Mike with a gentle pressure she leaned into automatically. Because she was just that weak and his fingers felt good.

But she'd say it was for balance if he asked. Dang stilettos.

When they hit the steps of the house, she grimaced. "He's definitely hiding something."

"More than something," Dean agreed grimly. "According to my team, Mike's employment history has some suspicious gaps, and he was fired from his last job under unusual circumstances."

"What kind of circumstances?"

"The kind that get buried with the right incentives." Dean's expression was dark. "We need to dig deeper."

"He's dangerous, isn't he?" She hated the slight tremor in her voice.

"I wouldn't trust him with a dandelion." Dean met her eyes, his gaze bleeding with concern and assurance and something else she didn't know how to name. "But he won't get near you again."

She should have bristled at his caveman routine. Should have reminded him that she was perfectly capable of handling difficult men. Instead, she nodded as relief rushed in so hard, she saw stars.

"Fine, but only because he gives me the creeps," she informed him loftily. "Not because I need protecting."

The corner of Dean's mouth lifted in that half smile that did ridiculous things to her equilibrium. "Of course not. You're terrifying, remember?"

"Occasionally terrifying," she corrected with a reluctant smile.

"More often than not." His expression grew serious again. "We need to figure out why Mike—or anyone else—would be sabotaging equipment."

"The timing can't be coincidental," she mused, thinking out loud. "These incidents started right after I inherited the vineyard."

"And after Greta died," Dean said carefully. "It could be related."

The implications settled like bad Chinese food in her stomach. "You think these events might be connected to what happened to her?"

"I think someone doesn't want you here. And they're willing to go to extreme lengths to make that happen." The words hung in the air between them, stark and unarguable. "But they'll have to go through me if they want to hurt you."

Dean did that thing again where he lifted a hand to her face, sweeping back her hair, but this time, they didn't have an audience.

And she let him.

For a moment, Samantha allowed herself to believe him. To trust that this sexy cowboy investigator with the shadowy connections and capable vibe would indeed keep her safe.

It was a strange feeling for someone who'd spent her adult life relying solely on herself. But not entirely unwelcome.

"So, what do we do now?" she asked.

Dean's gaze was steady. "Now, we find proof. And we make sure whoever's behind this doesn't get a chance to try again."

We. As in the two of them. Together.

Dean wasn't the type to misspeak. He meant it, and the concept carried weight she hadn't expected. She'd preferred to handle challenges on her own terms, at her own pace. By herself.

But standing there with Dean, facing threats she couldn't have anticipated, Samantha was grateful not to be alone. Dean's steady presence felt right in a way few things had since her arrival at Wagner Wines.

"We will," she agreed, and it carried weight coming from her too.

After all, she'd never been one to back down from a challenge. And this one threatened her business, her livelihood.

But somehow, the sabotage seemed to have shifted things between her and Dean. He didn't think she'd done these things. His belief in her meant something. Especially if it was the catalyst to convince him she hadn't killed her aunt.

Had someone else though? The same someone who had continued their reign of terror at the vineyard? It felt probable. Which meant Samantha was in even more danger than she'd originally thought.

Chapter 11

Dean's body burned the midnight oil without his permission. Had since the hospital.

Restlessness drove him toward the perimeter path that circled the vineyard's main house, a route he'd worn into a rut over the past week. The Texas night stretched around him, inky black with pinpricks of starlight overhead, the moon hanging low like a scythe blade without a handle. His bullet scar throbbed against his ribs, a relentless pulse that matched his stride.

Midnight walks had become his ritual. Not that walking helped the scar itself—that pain was a souvenir he'd carry forever. What the dark solitude actually eased was the insomnia, the nightmares where he relived that moment over and over— the gun, the impact, the cold concrete against his face and the certainty he was going to die right there.

Those dreams still jerked him awake, his heart hammering against his ribs and sweat cooling on his skin. Tonight had been one of those nights. So he walked.

The rhythm of his footfalls helped untangle the knots in his head. And there were plenty to work through.

Like the sabotage incidents that kept piling up. The ladders. The bottling equipment. The collapsed shelves. Each pointed to someone methodically working to either drive Samantha away or hurt her in the process.

The thought of Samantha in danger did a number on his

stomach. Which had nothing to do with his job and everything to do with why he was currently screwing up this assignment. If he could just focus for a minute, he could find the killer and then see what was what with Samantha.

Mike Thompson sat at the top of that suspect list, with his suspicious gaps in employment history and his thinly veiled hostility. Dean's fingers curled into a fist. The handyman was careful, calculated. Dean had tangled with men like that before—wolves who waited for the right moment to show their teeth.

Swishing sounds behind him got 100 percent of his attention instantly.

Footsteps. Light ones. Deliberately placed. Someone was following him, trying to be quiet about it.

He pulled his biometric weapon from his boot seamlessly and palmed it, every muscle poised and ready to defend. Then he caught the faint scent of perfume on the light breeze. Floral with a hint of something deeper. Unmistakable.

Samantha.

His pulse tripled, and not from alarm. A hot woman roaming around in the dark gave him many ideas that he might not entertain at a reasonable hour, but this wasn't one and she also shouldn't be out here unprotected.

Dean pivoted and closed the distance between them in three swift strides. Her eyes widened as she spied him coming in the scant moonlight.

"Hey," she called and was strangled on it as he backed her up against the trunk of a massive oak.

Her gasp brushed against his cheek as he caged her between his arms, his body a shield from any watching eyes. A shield that no one had asked for. This was all for his own benefit. He'd been looking for an excuse to touch her, and this one checked all the boxes and then some.

She was wearing some kind of filmy top with shorts that

showed an enormous amount of leg. Did she *sleep* in this out-fit? Because he never would again now that the visual had been burned into his brain.

"Hey, yourself," he murmured. "You shouldn't be out here. It's not safe."

"Am I in danger from some unknown assailant?" Her brows lifted. "Or a cocky cowboy? Because you're the only one around, Carter."

Yeah, she was no dummy. She'd known they were blissfully alone—and that he'd have sensed any real threats long before she reached him. It was a neat compliment and a trap all in one.

Might as well call a spade a spade. "It's possible I slightly overreacted, given the actual threat level."

She laughed, making absolutely no move to break free of this…whatever it was. "You're forgiven. I should also clarify that I wasn't complaining."

"Well then." Good grief, she smelled like heaven and he leaned in even closer, weighing whether he could get away with burying his nose in her hair.

Her breath hitched, pushing her chest against his. "This is all faking it for the audience. Right?"

He nodded toward the tree line beyond her shoulder, where absolutely no one stood, using it as an excuse to dip his chin to graze her cheek. "Could be someone watching. Better safe than sorry."

"Always the professional," she murmured, her gaze drop-ping to his mouth before flicking back up. "Is that why you make rounds at midnight each night? Professional vigilance?"

The genuine curiosity in her voice caught him off guard. Most people wouldn't have noticed his nightly absences, let alone cared enough to follow him.

That was when he dropped his arms. And the pretense.

"Can't sleep sometimes," he admitted, cursing himself for

wanting to be honest. The half-truth felt too close to a lie, so he added, "Not since I was shot."

Understanding dawned in her eyes. "Your scar. It's a bullet wound."

She'd seen it. When? The fact that she hadn't asked him about it meant she'd opted to give him his privacy, and he couldn't figure out why that mattered so much.

Or why that fact alone made him want to tell her about it.

His jaw tightened reflexively. He never discussed that day, not with anyone. But standing in the darkness with Samantha, her face tilted up toward his, the words tumbled out almost as if he'd been gearing up to spill them.

"Sometimes I can still feel it. The impact. Like it just happened." His hand drifted to his side, fingers pressing against the ridge of scar tissue beneath his shirt. "Doctors say it's normal. Phantom pain or something."

She didn't offer platitudes or pity, just a quiet nod. "Is that why you left the Rangers?"

"Part of it." The muscles in his neck tensed, memory constricting his throat. "The system failed. Ruiz walked. And Jake…"

Her hand settled lightly on his forearm, an anchor as the words tangled in his throat. Her touch burned through the fabric of his shirt, a warmth that traveled up his arm and settled somewhere inside in a place that he didn't have a name for.

"Jake?" she repeated in a murmur.

"My partner. We'd been a team for years." The betrayal still tasted bitter, even now. "Our last case together, this kingpin, Ruiz, kidnapped a senator's daughter. Aubrey."

"I heard about that," she said. "That was you?"

Dean swallowed and nodded, the memory still raw. "Jake and Aubrey had been high school sweethearts. He'd ended things when he became a Ranger, thought the job was too dangerous to drag her into. But seeing her again…" His jaw tightened.

"He went off-book, put her first. I supported that. Saw what she meant to him. But then I got shot trying to rescue her while he was busy making up for lost time."

Jake hadn't been there for Dean.

"I'm sorry."

Her fingers tightened slightly on his arm, grounding him. Pulling him back to the here and now, which he'd sorely needed. Because she'd instinctively known, or did she just have that kind of effect on him?

Alfred materialized from the shadows, nosing at their legs before settling nearby, his alert ears swiveling to monitor their surroundings. Reminding Dean that he had a different life now with different loyalties.

"When did it happen?" Samantha's voice was gentle against the night in a way that made his chest ache.

"Eight months ago." The night air suddenly felt cold against his skin as memories rushed back. "When I woke up in the hospital, it was over. They'd captured Ruiz, locked him up."

"And that's when Jake chose her?" Samantha asked.

"He quit the Rangers. Married her." Dean's jaw clenched, the phantom pain flaring as if summoned by the memory. "Said his years on the force had been a mistake, that he should never have let her go in the first place. Everything we'd been through together…he just walked away from it."

"The woman over the job," she murmured.

"His personal feelings over justice," he corrected, though the distinction felt paper thin now. "There are lines you don't cross in this profession."

A small smile touched her lips. "Says the man pretending to be my boyfriend."

"That's different."

But was it? Her point nagged at him. Not because he'd crossed any lines pretending to be her boyfriend. But because he wasn't out here having a conversation with Samantha about his investigation into Greta's murder. This was personal in every way.

He stepped back from the tree. From her. Cool air filled the gap between them, the distance a void full of nothing, as if he'd wrenched away something essential.

He didn't like it.

"We should keep moving," he said, glancing around as if some threat might lurk in the shadows. "Standing in one place too long makes us an easy target."

Samantha didn't call him on it, though she should have. She fell into step beside him, their shoulders occasionally brushing as they continued along the path. Alfred trotted ahead, his nose working overtime as he patrolled their route.

"So that's why you work with your team now instead of the Rangers," she said after a long silence had stretched between them. "What you said earlier about trusting the right people, you're building that back up. Slowly."

Had his skin vanished and allowed her to peer around inside him, or was she really just that good at reading him? He'd mentioned the team during their earlier conversation, but for her to connect those dots so quickly... Samantha was a force to be reckoned with.

"Something like that," he admitted. "It's a work in progress."

"I can relate." Her voice carried far more weight than a platitude should. "Corporate backstabbing makes you paranoid."

"Your friend?" He remembered her naming someone during one of their get-to-know-you sessions.

"Caitlyn." Samantha's laugh held no humor. "My best friend at EchoForge. At least, I thought she was."

"What happened?"

"She used everything I told her against me. Every strategy, every plan I shared. She took it all to the sales team, presented it as her own work." The moonlight caught the hard edge of her profile. "I walked into a meeting to find my ideas on the screen with her name on them."

"Ouch."

"The worst part wasn't losing the promotion she stole from me. It was realizing that every late night, every working dinner, every confidence shared…" Her voice tightened. "She was mining me for information the whole time."

The pain in her voice plucked an unexpected chord in Dean's chest. Betrayal. By a close friend. Of all things to have in common, that had not made the list. His fingers flexed to reach for hers, to comfort, to be comforted in kind, to connect. All of the above.

He resisted. Barely.

"Hard to trust after something like that," he acknowledged, fighting to keep his tone neutral instead of spilling out the avalanche of feeling behind them.

"Impossible," she corrected. "Which is why I'm so bad at the whole team player thing. Delegation means vulnerability. Relying on others means risking betrayal."

"So you do everything yourself." Not a question.

She shot him a sideways glance. "Says the man all but wearing an 'I work alone' T-shirt when he first showed up."

"Touché."

Her smile tore through him like the first rain after a drought. Something cracked open between them—raw wounds exposed to identical scars. Different injuries, same patterns. She understood. Maybe too well.

The heat between them had nothing to do with the night's temperature and everything to do with recognition. Dangerous. Unplanned. Addictive.

Ahead, Alfred froze, nose twitching, tail brushing from side to side in the tall grass.

"Alfred is such an odd thing to call a dog," she murmured. "Family name?"

"Batman reference." His lips twitched. "He came with the name but it was pretty perfect. Alfred Pennyworth is Batman's right-hand man. Loyal. Reliable. Has everyone's back."

Unlike people.

She shot him a glance. "That's unexpectedly adorable."

"Tell anyone, and I'll deny it." He shoved his hands into his pocket where they couldn't accidentally stray into places they weren't supposed to be. "Strenuously."

"Your secret's safe." A pause, then hesitantly, "My cactus is named Spike."

"As in...?"

"*Buffy the Vampire Slayer*," she confessed, moonlight catching the blush creeping up her cheeks. "Ridiculous, I know."

"Prickly exterior, secretly fabulous." The assessment tumbled out unfiltered. She deserved to hear the truth after her brave confession.

She stared at him for a beat. "I don't think anyone has ever put that together quite like that."

This easiness between them was another thing he hadn't prepared for. Hadn't armored against.

The trail opened to a clearing with the valley sprawled below, a patchwork of shadows and silver. Dean scanned the perimeter. Habit. Always. Nothing moved in the darkness. Just leaves rustling, moonlight shifting, Samantha's quiet breathing beside him. Her scent teased his senses, floral notes and something uniquely her.

"It's beautiful here," she murmured.

"Peaceful," he agreed. "Sometimes."

She turned, moonlight catching the sudden seriousness in her eyes. "These sabotage incidents, they're connected to Greta's death, aren't they?"

The shift to business snapped him back to reality. Safe ground. "Too many coincidences otherwise."

"So, someone killed my aunt and now they're trying to— what? Scare me off? Hurt me? Kill me too?"

"Maybe all three." His jaw locked. "They'll have to go through me first."

The fierce declaration startled them both. Her eyes widened, searching his face in the darkness.

"You really don't think I did it." Not a question. A realization. "You don't think I killed my aunt anymore, do you?"

"No." The certainty washed over him. He'd been aware of his doubts for a while, but it was only in this instant that he was sure. "I don't."

Something flickered in her eyes. Relief layered with something deeper, harder to name. "Why? You barely know me."

The truth stacked up like evidence he couldn't ignore. Her shocked face at each sabotage. The way she faced down hostile vendors despite her shaking hands. The determination that drove her despite being thrown into the deep end.

The knot in his throat tightened as he registered how deep she'd infiltrated his defenses. Strickland would have a stroke when he found out how compromised Dean was.

But he still believed her.

"Investigator's instinct," he said, which was practically the same thing. That gut-level feeling had served him his entire career, and he didn't think it was failing him now.

"Is that what this is? Instinct?" Her probe carried weight his sleep-deprived brain wasn't equipped to lift. Not with her standing close enough that her scent wrapped around him like an embrace, asking questions he didn't want to answer.

"Among other things."

The silence thickened, heavy with a charge as if they might see lightning strikes in the distance. Darkness cloaked them, pulled them together. One step and he would be able to taste her. Find out if her lips were as soft as they looked. Surrender to whatever magnetic pull kept yanking him toward her.

His pulse hammered in his throat. Warning him. Reminding him. The job. The mission. Jake's choices with immeasurable cost.

Alfred's low whine sliced through the moment. The dog's ears pricked forward, attention locked on something in the darkness.

"We should head back." Half relief, half disappointment churned in his gut. "It's late."

Samantha nodded, something unreadable flicking across her face before she masked it. "Early mornings and all that."

They walked back in silence, their fingertips brushing. Each contact sent electricity jolting through his system. Sparks he couldn't afford. Awareness he couldn't shake.

The porch light caught her face as they approached the house, but it was a mask he couldn't read. He wished he could. At least to know if the midnight stroll in the dark had affected her like it had him.

Probably it was better not to know.

"Thanks for letting me tag along," she said as they reached the patio. "And for telling me about Jake."

Dean shifted his weight. Vulnerability chafed like an ill-fitting uniform. "It's good for you to know. For our cover story."

Something darkened her expression before she nodded. "Right. The cover story."

She turned to leave. Before he could think better of it, he caught her wrist. Her pulse fluttered beneath his fingertips—too fast. Matching his own thundering heartbeat.

"Samantha." Her name roughened his voice. "Be careful. These incidents are escalating. Don't take unnecessary risks."

The warning felt hollow against the vise tightening around his chest. She could be in grave danger, and he'd done nothing to fix that for her. The urge to protect, to fight, clawed at his rib cage.

"I'll be careful," she promised, her gaze holding his a beat too long. "Good night, Dean."

She slipped inside, footsteps fading down the hallway. The echo of her pulse still throbbed against his fingertips.

Alfred sank down beside him with a sigh that sounded too knowing for a dog.

The lines Dean had marked so carefully were smudging. He was fighting instincts that had nothing to do with duty and everything to do with the way his lungs seized when she looked at him with those eyes.

Jake had crossed a line for a woman and lost everything. Dean had sworn never to make the same mistake. Now here he stood, ground shifting beneath his boots, lines he'd already crossed invisible in the distance behind him. And his toes edged up to brand-new ones.

Chapter 12

Samantha's mental checklist of "Things That Are Going Spectacularly Well" contained exactly zero items as she rifled through yet another stack of Greta's paperwork.

After last night's moonlit confession session with Dean, she'd slept better than any night since she'd arrived in the Hill Country. Not because unburdening her soul to a man who no longer thought she'd murdered her aunt had been cathartic or anything.

Thinking like that was going to get her into trouble.

And if that midnight chat on the vineyard path had left her feeling lighter somehow—well, that was just the relief of finally having an ally. Nothing to do with the way Dean's voice had roughened when he'd spoken her name, or how hot it was to have a man back her up against a tree, or the way his fingers had felt against her skin.

Nothing at all.

"Focus, woman," she muttered, turning back to the stacks of folders on the massive desk. "No vineyard slaying happens while daydreaming about sexy cowboys."

Two days ago, she wouldn't have thought to dig through Greta's personal papers. But something had shifted during that midnight walk. Dean, who'd shown up convinced she was a cold-blooded killer, now believed her. Actually *believed* her. The sheer novelty of it still had her stomach doing flips.

If it also meant he might start seeing her as more than a murder suspect—or even a fake girlfriend—well, that was a dangerous train of thought leading to a station she wasn't ready to visit.

Besides, there were more pressing matters, like the fact that someone kept trying to sabotage her vineyard. And according to Dean, that someone might be connected to Greta's death. Solve the latter, stop the former. At least that was the operating theory.

"If I were threatening messages from a potential murderer, where would I hide?" she asked the empty office.

No response from the universe. Typical.

She'd already gone through the filing cabinets twice, finding nothing but vineyard records, tax documents and enough paperwork to give her accountant nightmares. The desk drawers had yielded little beyond expensive pens and forgotten paper clips.

If she were hiding incriminating evidence at EchoForge, she'd have used—

Samantha froze, then dropped to her knees, running her fingers along the underside of the massive oak desk. Her fingertips brushed against something cool and metallic—a small button. She pressed it, and a soft click rewarded her as a hidden compartment popped open on the right side of the desk.

"Jackpot."

She took a half second to do a little shimmy, hips *and* shoulders.

Inside lay a leather-bound book and a manila folder. She pulled them both out, setting them on the desk gingerly, as if the items might explode. Which, given what they might contain, wasn't far off.

The leather book was a journal, its pages filled with Greta's precise handwriting. Samantha flipped it open to a random entry dated two years earlier.

Watched Samantha's case study presentation at the technology summit online. Masterful takedown of competitors. She has the Wagner instinct for the jugular. Her method-

ology in how she'd closed that multi-million-dollar ac-count was particularly impressive. Ruthless efficiency without sentimentality. Perhaps there is something of me in her after all.

A chill ran down Samantha's spine. This wasn't the fond observation of a distant relative. This was something else—assessment, evaluation. Like Greta had been *scouting* her.

There were pages of these types of entries, all with her name in them.

Her fingers trembled slightly as she turned to the last entry, dated days before Greta's death.

I've made the necessary arrangements. Samantha will inherit everything. She has the Wagner steel to handle this place, to continue what I've built, regardless of who stands in her way. She's worthy. The others never were.

Worthy. The word she'd spent her entire life chasing, and here it was, bestowed by an aunt she'd never met. It should have felt like victory.

Instead, an uncomfortable hollowness spread through her chest.

Worthy of what, exactly? Of being the next Greta? The woman half of Strassburg apparently hated enough to celebrate her death?

With growing unease, Samantha set aside the journal and opened the manila folder. Inside were a dozen handwritten notes, their crude block letters a stark contrast to Greta's elegant script.

YOU CAN'T KEEP STEALING WATER FOREVER

PAYBACK'S COMING, WAGNER

BACK OFF OR SUFFER THE CONSEQUENCES

The last note made her blood run cold:

DEATH IS THE ONLY THING YOU DESERVE

Each note was dated with a different pen, likely her aunt's handwriting, the most recent three weeks before Greta died. Beneath the threats lay documents: water rights agreements, land surveys, and what looked like private investigator reports on local farmers and competing vineyards.

As Samantha read through them, her stomach grew a dozen Gordian knots. These weren't just business records. They were evidence of systematic manipulation: strong-arm tactics, exploitation of legal loopholes, and deliberate moves to undercut competitors.

The same tactics she'd used to snip clients from competing sales teams.

The same aggressive approaches that had earned her the nickname "The Diamond" in the EchoForge boardroom—cold, hard, brilliant, and capable of cutting glass.

The same cutthroat strategy that had made Greta deem her *worthy*.

"Find anything interesting?"

Samantha started, nearly dropping the stack of threatening notes. Dean stood in the doorway, shoulder propped against the frame, arms crossed over his chest. Normally, she sensed him or at least heard him coming with his heavy boot tread, but she'd been so engrossed, he'd snuck up on her.

Looking like *that*. She'd wasted precious seconds staring at papers when she could have been absorbing the male perfection lounging at her door.

"You could say that." She gestured to the spread of documents. "Greta wasn't exactly winning any popularity contests."

He strolled into the room and crossed to the desk, picking up one of the notes, a swath of Dean-scented air enveloping her with his citrusy goodness that made her want to dive right in.

His eyes narrowed as he read. "These are death threats."

"I noticed."

"Why didn't you call me the moment you found these?" There was an edge to his voice—concern, not accusation. The distinction made something flutter in her chest.

"I found them two minutes ago," she said, watching as he methodically examined each note. "Hidden compartment in the desk. Apparently, Greta had secrets."

"Everyone does." His fingers traced the edges of one note, his sharp gaze missing nothing. "This is exactly what we need. Concrete evidence someone was threatening her before she died."

Samantha hesitated, suddenly uncertain about having Dean dig deeper. These notes were about to unleash a storm she wasn't sure she was ready for.

"Maybe we should be careful with these," she said, reaching to gather the notes. "We don't know what kind of hornets' nest we're kicking."

Dean's eyebrows shot up. "Are you suggesting we ignore death threats against your aunt? When someone's also trying to harm you?"

"Of course not. I just—" She glanced toward the door. "The staff is already on edge. If we start a full-blown murder investigation while I'm trying to keep this place running—"

"These notes could lead us to whoever's behind the sabotage incidents." His voice was steady but firm. "Someone in this town wanted Greta dead. And they might want the same for you."

"I understand that." She gestured to the threatening notes with a flick of her wrist. "But stirring up all this while I'm still trying to manage a vineyard that's barely functioning because half the staff hates me? Maybe we need to be strategic about this."

Dean studied her, his expression unreadable. "This is about more than operational challenges."

"I found something else." She sighed and tapped the journal. "Greta's been following my career for years. She chose me as her heir because she admired my sales tactics. My 'ruthless efficiency,' as she put it. Saw herself in me. That's why she left me everything."

Dean picked up the journal, scanning the pages with unsettling intensity. "This is not insignificant. Someone else may have known about her interest in you. It establishes potential motive, gives us solid suspects. I need to talk to my team about this."

"Dean, wait." Samantha's tone stopped him halfway to the door. "I'm trying to build something here. This is my second chance, my only shot at having a new career. If we go full FBI on this place, I'm not sure where that leaves me."

"Alive. This isn't just about solving a murder anymore," he said firmly. "It's about keeping you from joining your aunt in the grave."

Like that was an option she would choose? Except Dean seemed to think that's exactly what she was doing. Maybe she could step it back a notch.

"Fine. But let's be careful how we handle this," she said. "At least let me talk to the staff first, feel out what they know about these threats."

Dean crossed his arms. "Not alone."

"I've handled difficult clients and cutthroat competitors. I think I can manage a handyman and a vineyard manager."

"This isn't a sales meeting, Samantha." His expression hardened. "Someone sent death threats to your aunt, and that same someone might be targeting you now. I'm not letting you question potential suspects alone."

What, like she couldn't handle herself? She let the mad poke at her for a second or two and then got over it. He cared. For whatever reason. It wasn't a terrible thing.

And okay, maybe she wasn't entirely opposed to having backup.

"Fine," she conceded. "But follow my lead. These people already think I'm an incompetent city girl who drove away their manager. Having my boyfriend interrogate them like they're criminals won't help."

"I can be subtle," Dean deadpanned.

"You? Subtle?" She raised a skeptical eyebrow. "You radiate 'law enforcement' so hard you might as well have 'cop' tattooed on your forehead."

"Yet somehow people buy that I'm your boyfriend." That half smile again, the one that did ridiculous things to her pulse.

"The jury's still out on that," she countered, gathering the threatening notes. "Come on, then. Let's see what the staff knows."

"Ms. Wagner." Mike's face betrayed nothing as they approached the equipment shed where he was inventorying what was left of the supplies. His gaze slid to Dean, a flicker of wariness crossing his features. "Something I can help you with?"

"Just some questions about my aunt," Samantha said, keeping her voice casual, channeling her best "this client is hesitating but I'll close the deal anyway" tone. "You worked with her for fifteen years."

Mike's movements slowed fractionally. "What do you want to know?"

"What was she like to work for?" Samantha kept her tone conversational.

He shrugged, not meeting her eyes. "Fair enough. Paid well. Didn't micromanage."

Dean wandered around the shed with calculated casualness, picking up tools and examining them as if he were merely a curious boyfriend, but Samantha noted how he positioned himself between her and Mike.

"That's not what I heard in town." She leaned against the doorframe. "In Strassburg, people talk about her like she was one step away from a comic book villain."

"People talk a lot." Mike's jaw tightened. "Doesn't make it true."

"So she didn't use what they called 'aggressive business tactics'?" Samantha pressed. "Didn't put pressure on local farmers? Didn't manipulate water rights?"

Mike set down the clipboard with deliberate care. "Ms. Wagner built a successful business. That doesn't happen by being nice all the time."

"I'm familiar with the concept." Samantha exchanged a quick glance with Dean. "Did you know she was receiving threats?"

A muscle jumped in Mike's jaw. "Everyone around here knew she had enemies."

"People who might have wanted her dead?" Dean's voice was deceptively casual as he picked up a wrench, turning it over in his hands.

Mike's gaze snapped to him. "I didn't say that."

"But you're not surprised." Dean set the wrench down with a deliberate click that seemed to echo in the small space.

"What are you two getting at?" Mike's eyes narrowed.

"I found threatening notes in her office," Samantha said bluntly. "Death threats. Along with documents showing she was deliberately diverting water from neighboring properties, undercutting local farmers, hiring private investigators to dig up dirt on competitors."

Mike's expression hardened. "Your aunt knew what she wanted and how to get it. Made enemies in the process. That's business."

"Was it just business when she threatened to expose the Martins' tax problems unless they sold her their south field?" Samantha pressed, referencing a document she'd found. "Or when she manipulated the water board to reclassify the creek boundaries so neighboring farms couldn't access irrigation during drought season?"

Mike's face flushed. "You digging all this up for a reason? What's done is done."

"We're trying to figure out if someone had enough motive to kill her," Dean said, his demeanor shifting subtly into investigator mode.

Mike's eyes darted between them. "You think someone killed her?"

"I think it's awfully convenient that she died after receiving death threats," Samantha said.

Mike took a step closer, his bulk suddenly seeming more threatening. Dean immediately moved forward, his posture casual but his eyes sharp.

"You want my advice?" Mike addressed Samantha, though his gaze kept flicking to Dean. "Let sleeping dogs lie. Some things around here are better left buried."

"Like what happened to my aunt?"

"Like anything that might stir up old grievances," he said, eyes cold. "People around here have long memories."

"Is that a threat, Mike?" Dean's voice carried a quiet warning.

Mike stepped back. "Just being helpful. For the new boss. And her boyfriend." Said with enough texture to make it sound like he didn't quite buy the lie at this point. He turned to his clipboard with deliberate focus. "Don't go digging where you don't belong."

As they walked away, Samantha felt Dean's hand slip into hers, a steadiness that both grounded and unsettled her.

"Well, he's not suspicious at all," she muttered once they were out of earshot.

"Definitely hiding something," Dean agreed. "Or covering for someone. Or both."

Jules was in the north field kneeling beside a vine, examining leaves with meticulous focus. She looked up as they approached, wariness immediately replacing concentration.

"If it's about the inventory reports—"

"It's about Greta," Samantha interrupted. "And the people who might have wanted her dead."

Jules's eyes flicked to Dean, who had hung back slightly and still managed to give off vibes like he might pull out the firearm in his boot at any second.

"That's awfully direct," she said. "Are you sure you want to have this conversation in front of your pretty boyfriend?"

Since he wasn't her boyfriend and he was far from pretty, she was more than okay with it. Intense and smoking hot, yes. Pretty, no. *Pretty* would imply he went to a lot of effort to get that way and he somehow just rolled out of bed like that—okay, way off subject here.

"It's fine," Samantha said with a fake smile. "He works in security consulting, so this is a normal day for him."

She caught the look on Dean's face and prayed he'd roll with it. They hadn't talked about any kind of shift in his role here, but honestly, it felt necessary at this point, especially after Mike's pointed reference to it. The staff might still wonder why he'd started taking such an active interest in all the suspicious things going on around the vineyard, but she and Dean could still sell the boyfriend angle at the same time, so hopefully it all worked out.

"I found death threats in her office," Samantha said, "along with records of how she built this business by destroying others."

"And you're surprised about her tactics?" The bluntness of the response caught Samantha off guard.

"You knew?" Dean asked, stepping forward.

Jules gave a humorless laugh. "Everyone knew. Your aunt didn't exactly hide her methods. She was proud of them."

"Proud of stealing water from neighboring farms? Of blackmailing competitors?" Samantha couldn't keep the disbelief from her voice.

"Proud of building a successful business by any means necessary." Jules shook her head in disgust. "She called it 'having the courage to do what others wouldn't.'"

Dean crouched down beside a vine, examining it with feigned interest. "You don't sound like you agreed with her approach."

Jules didn't answer immediately, her gaze drifting across the vineyard. "I stayed because I love these vines. Because the land itself deserves better than what she did with it."

"Tell me about the threats," Samantha pressed gently.

Jules's mouth tightened. "Started maybe eight months ago. After she diverted the creek during that drought, leaving the Hendersons' orchard to die. Then she bought their land at half its value."

The bitterness in Jules's voice was unmistakable.

"That wasn't the first time," Jules continued, anger seeping into her tone. "The Wilsons lost their vineyard five years back after she spread rumors about mold in their grapes. There's a reason half the county celebrated when she died."

Samantha felt sick. "And no one stopped her?"

"She had money. Connections. Got enough of those, problems disappear." Jules looked directly at Samantha, as if trying to convey something extra. "On the flip side, some of those connections are the kind that make sure a heart attack is never questioned."

Well, that wasn't subtle at all. Dean and Samantha exchanged a glance.

"Who sent the threats?" Dean asked, his tone casual but his attention razor-sharp.

"Could've been anyone. The Hendersons. The Wilsons. Mayor Brooks after Greta threatened to expose her husband's gambling debts." Jules shrugged. "Take your pick."

"And no one thought to mention all this when I inherited the place?" Bitterness crept into Samantha's voice. "Maybe a little 'Congratulations on your vineyard. By the way, half the town might want you dead by association'?"

Something like sympathy flickered across Jules's weathered face. "Would you have believed it? Or would you have thought it was just locals trying to scare off the city girl?"

Samantha had no answer for that. At least not one she liked.

By the time Samantha and Dean returned to the house, the sun was heading toward the horizon, painting the vineyard in warm golden light. Under different circumstances, she might have found it beautiful. Today, it only highlighted how much was at stake—this land, this business, these people's livelihoods.

And someone might be interested in eliminating her from the equation. Just as they might have eliminated Greta.

Dean vanished into his bedroom as soon as they hit the second floor, so she took some much-needed downtime to wash off vineyard dirt in the shower. Plus, it was where she did her best thinking, which she needed to do a lot of.

What, exactly, had questioning the staff gained her? Nothing, except the knowledge that something needed to change, fast.

When she got out of the shower, she threw on yoga pants and a top that left one shoulder bare, exposing her matching tank top. She found Dean on the back patio, laptop open, files spread across the table. Alfred sprawled at his feet, ears perking up as she approached.

"I hope your afternoon was more productive than mine," she said, sinking into the chair across from him.

"Very." His eyes held the intensity of a predator on a promising trail. "Those notes were exactly what we needed. I've sent the information to my team so they can work on identifying potential connections."

"Great. After talking to Mike and Jules, I'm convinced the entire county wanted Greta dead."

"Makes my job harder," Dean said, "but it confirms our theory. Someone had serious motive to want Greta gone."

"And might want the same for me, by extension." Samantha stared out at the vineyard, its neat rows stretching into the distance. "Especially if they think I'm planning to continue her approach."

"Are you?" The question was casual, but his gaze said he understood the gravity of the answer.

"Good grief, no." She shuddered. "You heard the things she did, Dean. She destroyed families. Businesses. Lives. All to build this place." Samantha gestured at the vineyard around them. "I can't continue that legacy."

"What are you thinking?"

"I need to make amends." The decision crystallized as she spoke. "Starting with the water rights—returning access to the creek for the neighboring properties. Reaching out to the families she drove out to offer compensation." She gave a small, humorless laugh. "Basically dismantling half of what made this place profitable."

"That's a big undertaking," Dean observed, his expression unreadable. "A lot to risk."

"Some things are worth the risk." She met his gaze steadily. "I've spent my entire career being exactly like Greta— aggressive, relentless, focused on results no matter the cost. I've poached clients, undercut competitors, pushed every advantage to close deals."

She thought of Greta's journal. *She has the Wagner instinct for the jugular.* Really, Caitlyn had learned how to do all of that from her. Samantha had a lot of nerve being upset that her friend had done the same.

"I never thought I'd be questioning my entire approach to success," she continued. "My whole life, I've believed that achievement was everything, that being the best, no matter the cost, was the only way to prove myself."

"And now?"

"Now I'm sitting in a vineyard that someone may have killed for, being targeted by the same person, wondering if everything I thought made me valuable is actually the thing making me a target." She gave a weak laugh. "Not exactly the fresh start I envisioned."

"Sometimes we don't get the fresh start we want," Dean said, his gaze holding hers. "We get the one we need."

Jeez. He really knew how to dig in and hit all the spots she didn't know were so tender. A ripple passed between them, something she'd likely have never noticed if she hadn't been paying such close attention.

It felt like connection. Because they weren't pulling punches any longer. Dean didn't judge, didn't seem bothered by anything other than whether she put herself at unnecessary risk. It was…nice.

"What Jules told me today, what I found in Greta's papers. It changed something." She twisted her watch around her wrist, a nervous habit from childhood. "I always thought success meant winning at all costs. Now I'm wondering if the cost matters more than I realized."

"The line you won't cross," Dean said quietly. "The one that defines who you are."

"Exactly." She looked up, meeting his gaze. "I think I need to redraw some lines."

Something like approval warmed his expression and it was

icing on the cake to have gained that from him. "Sounds like a good place to start."

"It won't be easy." She grimaced. "This whole place was built on Greta's approach. Changing that means risking everything she built."

"Not for you. It's only a risk if you don't succeed, and you will," Dean said quietly.

The weight of his gaze made her heart stumble. He believed in her. Without hesitation. Dean never said anything he didn't mean. It was his best quality, a rare one.

For the first time in her life, someone had her back, someone who had nothing to gain by telling her these things. He saw *her*. Not her achievements or whatever he hoped she'd accomplish in the future.

The realization terrified her.

"I should—" She stood abruptly. "I need to think about all this."

Dean nodded, watching her with those too-perceptive eyes. "I'll be here."

Three simple words that shouldn't have felt like a promise. But somehow, they did, every time he said them.

As Samantha walked away, she felt lighter than she had in days, despite the weight of the discoveries. Somewhere between finding Greta's journal and this conversation, something fundamental had shifted.

She'd come to Wagner Wines determined to prove herself worthy of the inheritance. Now she found herself questioning whether Greta's approval was something she wanted at all.

Perhaps it was time to establish her own definition of success—one that didn't require ruthlessness to achieve it. It felt like the first step on a path she actually wanted to follow.

Chapter 13

After two weeks of cohabitation in bedrooms connected by a balcony, Samantha would have thought she'd know everything about Dean Carter. But as she watched him stride across the vineyard toward her, Stetson tilted against the morning sun, she realized how little she actually knew. The man was an enigma wrapped in denim and quiet competence, and she still hadn't figured out how to crack his code.

"Morning," he called, voice like espresso: dark, smooth and guaranteed to kick her heart rate up several notches. "Ready for our field trip?"

"Field trip implies fun and educational value," she replied, raising an eyebrow. "Is that what we're doing?"

"Something like that." His half smile did that thing to her insides. Not the tornado this time, more like whipped cream being folded into hot chocolate. Warm, sweet and so very bad for her. "Figured if we're investigating water theft, you should understand how the land works first."

Because he knew stuff like that. Apparently. Since discovering Greta's threatening notes and sketchy water rights documents yesterday, Samantha had been itching for action. Dean's methodical approach sometimes made her want to scream, but she couldn't argue with results. If a vineyard tour conducted by her fake boyfriend would help connect more dots, she'd pull on her boots and smile the whole time.

Even if alligator Lucchese boots and a silk blouse ended up being a questionable fashion choice.

"Lead the way, Professor Carter," she said with a theatrical sweep of her arm. "I'm eager to see what counts as an educational date in your world."

His eyes brightened at the teasing tone, the blue in them deepening like the sky after a summer storm. "Don't get your hopes up for anything fancy. This is strictly business."

"With a side of maintaining our cover," she reminded him. "Fake dating field trips count as boyfriend duties."

"What a hardship."

His voice dipped lower, vibrating somewhere in her chest cavity, and he reached out to tuck a strand of hair behind her ear. The gesture was so natural, so unexpectedly tender, that her breath stumbled as he leaned closer.

"Jules is watching from the equipment shed," he murmured in her ear, his fingers lingering longer than strictly necessary.

The explanation shouldn't have disappointed her. It *shouldn't* have.

"Of course she is," Samantha managed, pressing her palm against the ghost of his touch once he'd turned away. "Come on, we'll start at the south property line."

The vineyard sprawled out before them, rows of grapevines stretching toward the horizon like meticulously planned highways. June heat pressed down, wrapping everything in a haze that made the landscape shimmer and blur at the edges. This wasn't her world—not yet—but something about it called to her anyway.

Dean set a steady pace, somehow knowing exactly which paths let her navigate without sacrificing her expensive boots that may not have been too much more of a practical choice than stilettos. Alfred trotted ahead of them, tongue lolling happily as he periodically circled back to make sure they were following.

"The original property was about forty acres," Dean explained, gesturing toward a distant tree line. "My team's research shows that Greta tripled it over fifteen years through acquisitions."

"Acquisitions is a nice corporate way to put it," Samantha noted dryly.

"I thought you'd like that," he replied, offering his hand to help her down a steeper section of the path, which she took for purely practical reasons, even as his callused palm sent warmth cascading up her arm. "Most of those acquisitions happened during drought years when neighbors couldn't afford to keep their land irrigated."

He didn't release her hand immediately after they navigated the tricky terrain. Instead, his fingers remained loosely intertwined with hers as they walked as if they did this all the time, a casual intimacy that felt anything but casual to her heart rate.

They crested a small rise that gave them a panoramic view of the rolling hills with their patchwork of vineyards, orchards and pastures. Dean stopped, raising his free hand to shield his eyes from the sun as he took in the landscape with a tactician's focus.

"See that?" He pointed to a line of darker green vegetation cutting across the property line, reluctantly letting go of her hand. "That's not natural."

Samantha squinted, seeing only sun-dappled greenery. "What am I looking at?"

"Plant indicators." He started walking again, this time off the path and down toward a shallow ravine. "Certain types of vegetation only grow with consistent water access. In drought years, they should die back. These haven't."

"And that's unusual because…"

"Because the creek that feeds this area was supposedly dry during last year's drought." His voice carried an undercurrent of certainty that hadn't been there before. "That's what your neighbors were told when they wanted to tap into it."

She paused, studying his profile as sunlight gilded the edge of his jaw. "How do you know so much about water systems?"

Something shifted in his expression. "Grew up on a ranch in Blanco, remember? Water rights are the lifeblood of any agricultural operation in the Hill Country. You pick things up when your family's survival depends on it."

Duh. She kept forgetting that he came from this area. She shouldn't have. He blended with the land, seemed a part of it in a way that she hadn't fully internalized. In reality, he belonged here far more than she did, his relationship with this environment part of his DNA bred into him through generations.

How many people on earth knew him like this? How many of them felt like they'd won the lottery when he revealed these pieces?

"What was it like?" she asked. "Growing up on a ranch?"

Dean was quiet for a moment, considering her question with the same careful attention he gave everything. "Hard work. Early mornings. Late nights during calving season." A ghost of a smile touched his lips. "But there's something about being connected to a place, knowing its rhythms, understanding what the land needs."

"Must have been different from growing up in Houston," she said, stepping carefully over a fallen branch. "No concrete in sight out here."

"Different worlds," he agreed, reaching out to steady her when her boot slipped on loose gravel. His hand lingered at her waist, warm and solid. "But you adapt quicker than most city people."

The compliment felt like a gift, and she tucked it away carefully.

"Don't tell anyone, but I'm starting to appreciate the quiet. The sky. All this is breathtaking." She gestured at the rolling landscape with its impossible expanse of blue overhead.

He led her down to where the ravine deepened, revealing a

small creek bed that should have been dry but instead held a trickle of water. Crouching down, he gestured for her to join him. After a moment of considering how many crawly things might be down there, she knelt beside him, close enough that their shoulders touched. Which of course meant he was close enough to wrangle anything that slithered.

"See how the soil's darker here?" he asked, fingers brushing against the earth with reverence that caught her by surprise. "There's been consistent moisture, even during drought months."

Even the man's hands—capable sun-worn hands that knew how to read the earth in ways spreadsheets and sales projections never could—were sexy.

She was having trouble focusing on the thing they were supposed to be looking at, but she gave it a shot to show she had been listening. "You're saying water's being diverted here when it shouldn't be?"

"I'm saying someone's rerouting the natural flow." He rose, moving upstream with the easy grace of a man who'd spent his life reading the land. "Let's see if my hunch is right."

He disappeared around a bend in the creek. Samantha followed, stepping carefully on rocks to keep her Luccheses moderately salvageable. She rounded the corner to find Dean crouched again, this time inspecting what looked like a metal pipe partially hidden by overgrowth.

"And we have our answer." His voice held a grim satisfaction. "This pipe shouldn't be here. It's tapping into the aquifer flow upstream of where the creek enters neighboring properties. Technically legal if you file the right paperwork, which I'm betting Greta did." His fingers traced the pipe's path. "But ethically? It's stealing water from every property downstream. Precisely where the Henderson orchard was located before they had to sell."

"The orchard Jules mentioned yesterday." The connections

clicked into place. "Greta diverted their water, forced them to sell when their trees died, then bought the land at a discount."

"And I'll bet this was installed right before those threatening notes started showing up." Dean straightened, dusting off his hands. "Nothing drives desperate actions faster than watching your livelihood die while your neighbor's land stays green."

The realization settled like lead in Samantha's stomach. Another piece of Greta's legacy, another ethical nightmare she'd inherited. It seemed the deeper they dug, the more rot they found.

"Did all of her business practices involve destroying other people's livelihoods?" Samantha checked her ire, grateful that Dean hadn't told her to look in the mirror. "I mean, I know I come from the corporate world, where it's mighty rich to throw stones. But still. This feels a lot more vicious."

He nodded graciously. "Different worlds, different rules. But even in the business I came from, there were lines most people wouldn't cross."

"Lines," she echoed, the word taking on new significance.

Everyone had them. Dean had drawn his lines with a giant Sharpie, living his black-and-white ethics without apology.

Where were hers?

Dean started walking again, following the pipe's path through underbrush and across rocky terrain. Samantha scrambled to keep pace with his ridiculously long legs, thoughts churning. Putting hands on physical evidence felt different from reading documents in Greta's office. This wasn't abstract business strategy. It had become real.

He took her hand again, leading her to a clearing where the evidence couldn't be mistaken. His fingers felt nice against hers, and she found herself reluctant to let go when they reached the clearing.

"I wouldn't have seen any of this," she admitted, casting her gaze across the landscape with new appreciation. "I'd have walked right past every clue."

"Different expertise." He shrugged, but his expression softened. "You'd spot financial irregularities I'd miss completely."

"Fair point." She smiled, appreciating the acknowledgment. "So, you're saying we make a decent team?"

His gaze met hers, something flickering in their depths. "We do."

The simple confirmation shouldn't have made her heart skip, but here she was, pulse jumping like she'd just closed a million-dollar deal. This was about water theft, not the way sunlight caught Dean's hair or how his voice settled inside her every time he talked.

They followed the pipe to where it connected to a larger system that fed directly into the vineyard's irrigation network. Dean traced the connections with practiced efficiency, taking photos with his phone and making notes in a small notebook he produced from his back pocket.

"Old habits," he explained when he caught her watching. "Some things stick, even without a badge."

"Do you miss it?" she asked, genuinely curious. "Being a Ranger?"

A shadow with a hundred shades passed across his face. "Parts of it. The purpose. Knowing where I stood." He tucked the notebook in a pocket. "But systems fail. People let you down. Sometimes you have to find a different path."

"I know a little something about that," she said with a laugh and held out her hand like a game show hostess to frame the vineyard.

As their gazes locked, the ripple passed between them again, the one full of shared experiences that acted like glue to bind them together. Astounding that she could claim such with a man like him, one she'd never have connected with under regular circumstances. No danger of the charity ball meet-cute actually happening in real life.

But she had met him in this stage of her life, and it meant

something she wasn't willing to ignore. What she was willing to do about it remained to be seen.

As they made their way back toward the main property, Dean pulled a water bottle from his back pocket and offered it to her first. The simple courtesy—putting her needs before his—wasn't lost on her.

"Thanks." She took a sip, then handed it back, hyperaware of his fingers brushing hers in the exchange and how not accidental it felt.

"What are you thinking?" he asked, his voice richer, less like an investigator and more like…something else.

She met his gaze, finding unexpected comfort in its steadiness. "How much it's going to suck to take the time and energy to fix this. Reroute the water back to its natural flow, reach out to affected neighbors, offer compensation. I'm going to do it though. I have to be different than my aunt."

Admiration flickered across his face, so genuine it made her chest ache.

"My father always said land has memory," Dean murmured, his voice hushed as if sharing a secret. "I like that you want to give it something new to remember."

"That's beautiful. Thank you for that."

This earnest, raw side of Dean was startling, and that was saying something when he constantly surprised her. She was in way over her head with this one, but she'd never backed down from a challenge yet.

They walked in companionable silence back toward the house, the afternoon sun casting long shadows across the land. Alfred dashed off to chase some creature through the underbrush a dozen times but always circled back to check their progress.

Samantha studied Dean with a serious side-eye so he wouldn't catch on. He was so easy to look at, the confidence of his movements, the conviction in everything he did and said.

It felt like an anchor in shifting sand.

"Thank you," she said when they reached the patio. "For showing me all this."

His eyes crinkled. "Just doing my job."

"No." She shook her head, her fingers seeking out his forearm, feeling the warmth of sun-soaked skin beneath her fingertips. "Your job is investigating Greta's death. Teaching me about the land? That was something else."

He held her gaze for a moment, something indecipherable flickering in his eyes. "You deserve to understand what you've inherited. Good and bad."

And something about the way he said it, about the quiet intensity in his expression, made Samantha realize she'd underestimated Dean Carter from the beginning. He wasn't just a former badge with a grudge against humanity. He carried wisdom and emotional intelligence that was hard to come by.

And he was far too good for her.

As Dean excused himself to call his team about their findings, a strange, unfamiliar ache settled beneath her ribs. From moment one, she'd acknowledged that any breathing woman would appreciate his broad shoulders and impossibly blue eyes.

This was different. Deeper. Dangerous.

She *liked* him, liked his principles. The way he saw the world in terms of what was right rather than what was easy. The clarity with which he drew his lines and refused to cross them.

And as she stood there, surrounded by a vineyard built on other peoples' suffering, Samantha realized she wasn't just changing her opinion about what made a successful business. She was changing her definition of what made a man worth falling for.

The list had Dean Carter on it and no one else.

The thought should have sent her running in the opposite direction. She'd built her entire life around precision and control, around knowing exactly what came next and how to leverage it.

Dean Carter was neither precise nor controllable, and the way her heart stuttered when he looked at her with those too-blue eyes was definitely not in her carefully crafted do-over plan.

None of this was.

But standing here, with the afternoon sun warming her shoulders and the vineyard stretching out before her, Samantha couldn't bring herself to care. Something had shifted between them today, something quiet but fundamental, like water changing course to find its natural path.

She didn't know how to be worthy of what was happening between them. After all, she was still a work in progress, one who hadn't earned her right to stand among these Hill Country people, especially not Dean.

But she could get there.

Chapter 14

The bullet scar on Dean's side throbbed, a residual reminder he could never shed. Midnight had become his time in the vineyard, quiet except for the whispering breeze through the grapevines. For a week now, these walks had been his ritual, circling the property, checking for weaknesses in the perimeter while he grappled with insomnia and his ethics.

And for five nights running, Samantha had joined him.

He wouldn't say he looked forward to it. You looked forward to going to a party or watching a baseball game.

This time with Samantha had become *necessary*.

He always started out the same way. Walking and bargaining with himself to not be disappointed if she didn't show. But he honestly didn't know if he took a solid, full breath some nights until he heard the soft crunch of gravel behind him, precisely seven minutes into his patrol—just like clockwork.

Tonight, she'd made it in six minutes. Something spread through his chest that had nothing to do with the mild June night. Relief and a lot of other stuff he had zero intention of examining.

"Right on time," he said without turning.

"Are you suggesting I'm predictable?" Samantha's voice carried a smile he could hear without seeing, and it lit him up so hard that his scar actually stopped hurting.

Or maybe tonight he had a lot more going on inside that he preferred to focus on.

That was when he turned. She stood a few feet away, silhouetted by moonlight, wearing loose cotton pants and a thin sweater that slipped off one creamy shoulder.

Sexy. But then she didn't have a look that wasn't.

Alfred trotted up, circling Samantha once before pressing against her leg in greeting, where he'd likely stay for the duration. His dog had switched teams again, apparently.

"Alfred and I had a bet going on whether you'd show up tonight," Dean said, falling back into their dynamic that had developed over these midnight walks. Jokes and lightness until it became something else.

"Who won?"

"He did."

She laughed, the sound skimming across his skin like a physical touch. "Smart dog."

"Don't tell him that. It'll go to his head."

It was ridiculous how easily they'd slipped into this routine. How natural it felt to walk these midnight paths together, their shadows stretching side by side in the moonlight.

That first night, she'd been curious enough about his nocturnal activities to follow him and they'd talked. Fine. He didn't mind the distraction from his demons. He hadn't expected to see her again, but the next night, she showed up again, seemingly content to walk with him as if they'd planned to meet. On the third night, they didn't even talk much, just sort of hung out.

On the fourth night, he'd waited for her without admitting it to himself, straining to catch the faint scent of her perfume on the breeze.

This was becoming a habit, though neither of them named it or claimed it. Just like no one brought up how the professional distance between them eroded more and more with each passing night.

They walked in comfortable silence for a while, tracing the familiar path along the southern perimeter. The ridge overlooking the creek had become their unofficial rest stop—a flat boulder beneath a sprawling oak where they'd pause every night. Five nights of companionship that grew deeper, more personal with each passing midnight.

Five nights of Dean's resolve weakening.

"How's the scar tonight?" she asked as they crested the ridge.

"Pulling no punches this evening, I see," he commented mildly, debating whether to be honest when she already saw too much. Understood too much. It was dangerous in ways that had nothing to do with his mission.

"Which means it hurts like the devil, but you're too stubborn to admit it."

He almost smiled. "Something like that."

They reached the oak where they always stopped, close enough that their shoulders nearly touched. The night spread before them, a canvas of silver moonlight and inky shadows. The vineyard stretched into the distance, rows of carefully tended vines creating a patchwork across the hillside.

"You're thinking so loud I can hear you," Samantha said after a moment, shooting him a sassy grin.

If she could, she'd already know none of his thoughts were appropriate. How the moonlight played with her hair. How her scent lingered in the air between them. How easy it would be to close the distance to her mouth, to discover if her lips would demand as much as he hoped.

"Just tactical assessment," he lied. "Thinking about case angles."

She turned toward him, moonlight illuminating the teasing glint in her gaze. "Liar."

She was getting better at reading him. Too good. "What am I thinking about then, smarty pants?"

"How long it's been since your last oil change, probably," she said with a chuckle.

It was such a goofy thing to say that she got a full-blown

laugh out of him, and he took a minute to enjoy it, because it had been a long time since he'd felt this...not terrible. "Well, now that you mention it, I'm way overdue."

All at once, he wanted to be behind closed doors with her. Not out here in the open under the guise of playacting for the audience that didn't exist.

What would it feel like to laugh with her for real because they were a couple and no one but the two of them cared if they were together? What if she could be the one lying on the next pillow, telling him jokes until closing his eyes didn't feel like a life sentence? He could watch her drift off to sleep, content and happy because *insomnia* was just a word in the dictionary.

All at once, she cocked her head and studied him with a serious expression. "Can I ask you something?"

"Sure," he murmured, though shifting vibes was last on his list of things he wanted to do.

"How can you possibly trust me?" She wrapped her arms around her waist as if holding herself in. "I've been wondering about it since you told me you changed your mind. I was suspect numero uno, and then all of a sudden, you went from seeing me as a killer to...whatever I am now."

It was a fair question. One he'd been asking himself with increasing frequency. What had changed? When had the scale tipped away from "suspicious character" and toward "intriguing woman"? From professional distance to this dangerous proximity?

He didn't know. And it was a problem regardless of whether he could pinpoint it.

"Should I not trust you?" he asked.

"I didn't kill my aunt." Her voice was quiet. "But not many people would believe me without some kind of proof, let alone the guy in charge of the investigation. I mean, I'm still the person who stood to gain the most. Still the convenient heir who showed up right after she died. All the evidence that made me your prime suspect still exists."

"Not all evidence carries equal weight."

"Meaning?"

Dean blew out a breath. This wasn't a conversation he'd prepared for, but their midnight walks had become something powerful that bound them together, and he wanted to honor that. More so than he would have expected.

And that meant laying some things on the line that he might not normally.

"Meaning I've been doing this job a long time. I know genuine reactions when I see them." He glanced her way. "Your shock when we found the sabotaged equipment. Your determination to fix what Greta broke. The way you fight for this place even though it's drowning you."

He studied her face in the moonlight. "People can fake a lot of things, but not the pattern of who they are when they think no one's watching. Not the small choices that add up to character."

"And my character says 'not a murderer'?"

Aw, dang. She was really asking, as if she couldn't quite credit what he was telling her. The vulnerability in the slant of her shoulders undid something inside him.

"Your character says you face problems head-on, not from behind," he told her, his voice dropping a notch spontaneously. "You're straightforward to a fault. Stubborn. Determined. If you'd wanted Greta dead, you'd have confronted her directly. Not plotted from a distance."

Samantha's face took on this glow. "That's shockingly accurate."

"You asked what changed. It wasn't one moment." His gaze held hers. "It was a hundred small things. The way you talk to Alfred when you think I can't hear. How you say good morning to Jules despite how badly she treats you. Your refusal to let the vineyard staff see how much their coldness affects you."

He hadn't meant to notice these things for any reason other than to gather impressions about his suspect list. It was only because of who Samantha Wagner was at her core that they'd become evidence of her character. And each layer had systematically dismantled his suspicion until nothing remained.

Well, nothing of his suspicion remained. But it had certainly been replaced with a whole lot of something else. Something far more hazardous to let off the leash.

But he'd been straining against it every minute of every day for an eternity.

"You've been paying a massive amount of attention to me when I wasn't looking," she murmured.

"That's the job." This was the part where she should definitely brand him a liar again.

"Is it?" Her gaze searched his face, drifting to his lips as if compelled. As if she could read him like a sales pitch.

"I am a professional," he reminded her, desperately trying to redraw some lines that they'd been erasing for days, the boundary dissolving faster than he knew what to do with.

"Right." A small but slightly wicked smile curved her lips. "The consummate professional who happens to be strolling in the moonlight at midnight with his girlfriend."

Something in her tone made his pulse kick up. "Fake girlfriend. Maintaining our cover story."

"Mmm-hmm." She shifted slightly, her shoulder bumping into his. Lingering, nuzzling even. "That's what we're doing. Keeping up appearances."

The contact cascaded electricity through his system. The scent of her, floral with an undercurrent of pure Samantha, made his head swim.

"In case someone is watching," he supplied automatically, because that was what they did. Repeated these lines because this was all fake, and he at least needed to keep the reminders front and center.

"You never know." She tapped her chin and glanced at him slyly. "That probably means we should practice kissing."

The suggestion unfolded in the thick atmosphere, and he couldn't look away from whatever was happening here. Didn't want to.

"In case someone is watching?" he repeated like an idiot, because of course that was the excuse they were sticking to.

She'd frazzled his brain.

Dean had built his life around clear lines—right and wrong, justice and injustice, professional and personal. Black and white. No gray areas.

Samantha Wagner was nothing but gray areas.

"I overheard Jules talking to one of the crew," she said. "They're totally convinced we're a couple. It would be a shame if we ruined the cover story because we weren't prepared for a kissing situation."

"A...*kissing* situation?" his mouth repeated without his permission before he could tell it to shut up and say, *Yes, ma'am. We need to be practicing kissing.*

She shifted closer, until her shoulder pressed against his. The contact sent very real, very not fake heat surging through his veins. That was the problem with practice kissing. He didn't want it to be practice. The first time he kissed Samantha Wagner should be about need and want and anticipation and *necessity*.

"Sure, like if someone catches us mid-investigation and we don't want them to know what we're doing." She placed a hand dead center on his torso and leaned in. "You could sweep me into a kiss. As a distraction."

"I could," he growled, mentally crossing his fingers for that exact scenario because, boy, could he visualize it perfectly.

He pressed her palm flat against his thundering heart before she got any ideas about moving it. Or herself.

"Don't you think we should be prepared ahead of time?" she

murmured, eyeing his lips again as if she would devour him with the scantest encouragement.

"I think it would be a shame to waste this moonlight," he corrected as his brain melted, scattering all of his wits at her feet. "We can let that other kissing situation take care of itself since we have a completely different kissing situation going on here."

"What situation is that?"

"The one where I want to kiss you, but I need to be sure it's what you want too," he told her bluntly as his ethics kicked in with a vengeance. "I'm not much for fake kissing."

They were doing this right or not at all. *That* was what had been holding him back, and only a single word from her would erase all of his problems.

"Dean." His name on her lips was barely a whisper.

Everything in him stilled, waiting. Wanting. "Say it, Samantha, or this is not happening."

"I want you to kiss me."

And then his mouth crashed down on hers, the last barrier between them crumbling like sand castles in the wake of a tidal wave.

The kiss was nothing like he'd imagined in the moments of weakness when he'd let himself indulge. It was better. Deeper. More real than anything he'd experienced since waking up in that hospital bed with the world irrevocably changed.

Her lips were shockingly soft beneath his, yielding yet demanding as her arms wound around his neck. He pulled her closer, one hand at her waist, the other tangling in her hair. She made a small sound deep in her throat that sent heat spiraling through him.

She tasted like mint and possibility and happiness.

The night cloaked them as the kiss deepened, evolved from urgent exploration to something more profound. Her body fit against his perfectly, soft curves meeting hard angles in a way that made his blood sing. His hand slid to her waist, pressing her closer as if he could push this feeling inside him to keep forever.

The kiss didn't end. Apparently, she didn't mind that he had a few dozen fantasies to enact and a strong urge to explore the skin near her ear, her throat, her jaw, and back to her mouth again.

When they finally broke apart, reality crashed back with brutal force, the weight of what he'd done settling in his chest like stone.

"Just so we're clear, that wasn't fake," she murmured, her breath warm against his lips.

"No," he agreed, voice ragged. "It wasn't."

He pulled back slightly, needing distance to clear his head. The moonlight highlighted her lips, still swollen from his kiss. She looked both vulnerable and powerful, a contradiction that mirrored the war within his own chest.

Jake's face flashed through his mind. Dean had sworn he'd never make the same mistake. Never let personal feelings compromise a mission. Never cross that line.

Yet here he stood, that line not just crossed but obliterated, with no idea how to go back. Or if he even wanted to. Kissing her went against everything he believed in.

That was what made it so significant.

He'd spent his life being certain, being righteous. Following rules, enforcing boundaries. The bullet in his side had shattered that certainty, leaving him adrift in a world where justice could be bought and partnerships betrayed.

But this pull toward Samantha—it wasn't about uncertainty. It was about recognizing something in her that called to him. They were the same somehow, underneath. They had a similar wounded understanding of betrayal. A shared strength that didn't need to be explained or justified.

He'd labeled Jake's decisions as mistakes. A betrayal. And

as he stared at Samantha's kiss-roughened lips, he couldn't help but wonder if he'd been the one in the wrong.

The admission cost him something, a certainty he'd clung to, a righteous anger that had fueled him for months. But in its place, something else was growing. Something unexpected.

Something that might be compromising his investigation. Something that had left him vulnerable with no clear exit path. The inability to see how to untangle himself might be the biggest red flag.

And he couldn't get his brain jump-started long enough to tell what was what.

"Dean?" Uncertainty threaded through her voice as she studied his face.

He took a step back, his body rebelling against the distance even as his mind grasped for control. "We should get back. It's late."

The flicker in her eyes condemned him. Hurt, confusion, resignation, it was all there. She nodded, wrapping her arms around herself as if suddenly cold despite the warm night air. "Right. Of course."

He'd hurt her with his retreat. That knowledge twisted in his gut. But what was the alternative? To pretend this wasn't a catastrophic breach of everything he believed in? To ignore that he'd compromised an active investigation for a kiss?

To admit that, for the first time since watching Ruiz walk free, something—someone—had become more important than vengeance?

He needed to process. Without her in the vicinity.

She turned to go, then paused, looking back at him. "For what it's worth, I don't regret it."

The words hung in the air between them, honest and unadorned. Before he could find a response, she was walking away, moonlight silvering her silhouette as she moved down the path toward the house. Alfred hesitated, glancing between them before trotting after her, of course.

Dean remained rooted to the spot, watching until she disappeared from view. His fingertips rose to his lips, still warm from her kiss. What had he done?

Become exactly what he'd judged Jake for being—a man who put a woman above the mission. Letting his guard down. Allowing someone to matter. Creating a vulnerability that could get him or, worse, someone else hurt or killed.

This was a disaster. Not because she wasn't trustworthy, but because she was. Because she made him want things beyond vengeance. Made him question certainties he'd lived by for months.

The stars offered no answers as he stood alone on the ridge, caught between the man he'd sworn to be and the man he was becoming. One who wanted to spend all his time with her instead of investigating the murder he'd been assigned to solve.

Because if he truly was walking the same path Jake had chosen, what would he sacrifice along the way?

Chapter 15

Afternoon sun poured through the windows of Samantha's office in the main house, but she barely noticed it. She'd been holed up for hours, creating spreadsheets for her new wine club concept, when the shout jerked her from her data-entry trance.

"Fire! Northeast field!"

What?

She launched herself from the desk chair, all thoughts of wine club membership tiers evaporating as she sprinted toward the commotion.

Outside, chaos reigned. Smoke billowed from one of the vineyard fields, thick plumes visible even from the main house. She stood there, unable to get her brain wrapped around the scene.

The vineyard was on fire. *Her* vineyard. On *fire*. The vines were burning to ash right in front of her eyes.

"Samantha!" Dean's voice, urgent and clear, snapped her from her trance. "Stay here."

He was already moving, heading straight for the utility shed where equipment was stored.

She'd spent all day avoiding him after last night's kiss, aka the kiss to end all kisses, the one that had shifted tectonic plates under the earth's crust. The kiss he'd abruptly backed away from, leaving her standing in the moonlight with her heart in her hands and a million unanswered questions.

Now, watching him sprint toward danger without hesitation,

something primal unfurled inside her. This man who couldn't figure out what he wanted to happen between them was somehow the first to run toward fire threatening *her* property.

It meant something and she wanted to know what.

Ignoring his directive, Samantha kicked off her heels and ran, feet finding purchase on the parched summer ground. Her Armani blouse and pencil skirt were hardly appropriate firefighting attire, but she didn't have time to figure out the dress code for a fire.

As she crested the small hill that separated the main buildings from the northeast field, the full scope of the disaster unfolded in real time. *Disaster* being the operative word. Gray-white smoke billowed upward in thick columns, partially obscuring rows of young vines being devoured by fast-moving flames. The fire snaked through the field like a living thing, advancing with terrifying speed across the dry vegetation.

Wind whipped the smoke into her face, acrid and choking. Her eyes instantly watered, vision blurring as the caustic cloud enveloped her. The crackling sound of vegetation burning filled the air, punctuated by shouts of workers trying to organize a response.

This wasn't just property damage. These were her vines. Her future. Her redemption.

"You shouldn't be here." Jules appeared beside her, face streaked with dirt, eyes reflecting the distant flames. "Fire Department's on the way."

"What do you need me to do?" Samantha countered, rolling up her sleeves.

Jules studied her for a heartbeat, surprise flickering across her weathered features. Then she thrust a shovel into Samantha's hands. "Dig. We need a firebreak before it jumps to the main field."

The shovel's wooden handle did not look like it belonged in the hand of someone with a French manicure, but she refused to stand idly by while everyone else helped. She'd built a reputation at EchoForge by diving headfirst into crises, by refusing

to be sidelined when stakes were high. This might be unfamiliar terrain, but the principle was the same—show up, step up.

That was what Dean had said she excelled at. She wasn't letting anyone down today.

She plunged the shovel into the earth, mimicking the actions
of workers around her. Pilates had not prepared her for anything
close to this sort of effort, and her muscles screamed at her to
stop. Which she did not. Each breath pulled more smoke into
her lungs, causing her to cough and wheeze. Ash and embers
floated through the air like snow.

Any filmmaker who needed a post-apocalyptic scene in their
movie should be lining up with cameras right about now.

Sweat trickled down her spine and across her forehead, mix-
ing with the ash to form a gritty paste that stung her eyes. Her
silk blouse clung to her skin, ruined beyond salvation. But it
didn't matter. What mattered was the strange belonging that
settled into her bones as she turned over shovelful after shovelful of her own dirt.

This is mine. This is mine. And she was going to protect it.

"Faster! It's picking up!" Carlos shouted from somewhere
to her right.

The wind had shifted. What had been distant flames moments before were suddenly much closer, feasting on dry summer vegetation with audible hunger. The heat pressed against
her exposed skin like an unwelcome touch, intensifying with
each passing second.

Through the haze, she glimpsed Dean directing a group of
workers with calm authority, organizing their efforts with tactical precision. Despite everything, her heart stumbled at the
sight of him. Good grief, why had no one told her how sexy a
capable man could be?

He wasn't in retreat mode now. Crisis had stripped away
everything but the essential core of who he was. This was the
real Dean Carter. And she was here for it.

They needed to talk. Later.

Sirens wailed in the distance, drawing closer. Oh, thank goodness. The cavalry was here.

"Fall back!" Jules ordered as the flames leaped ahead of their firebreak attempt, consuming vines with voracious hunger. "Safety first! Move!"

Samantha stumbled backward, the heat pulsing against her face even from this distance. The smoke had transformed into a wall, making it difficult to see more than a few feet ahead. Her lungs burned with each breath, and she stumbled.

Someone grabbed her elbow, steadying her.

Dean.

His face was grim, smudged with soot, but his eyes—those impossibly blue eyes that she'd seen in her dreams—were clear and focused. "You okay?"

She nodded, unable to spare breath for words. His hand remained on her elbow, grounding her in the chaos. For a suspended moment, the roar of the fire receded, and all she could feel was the press of his fingers against her skin, the solid reality of him beside her. Then a sudden gust whipped embers past them, snapping the moment in two.

"We need to move back farther," he said, voice hoarse from smoke. "The fire's jumping the breaks faster than we can dig them."

Together, they retreated toward the property line where other workers had gathered, watching helplessly as the fire consumed more of the vineyard. The smoke created a surreal atmosphere, the late-afternoon sun filtering through the haze in eerie orange light.

The firefighters arrived, hauling equipment, establishing a perimeter and taking command of the situation. Professionals with proper gear and training pushed the vineyard workers back, orchestrating a coordinated attack on the blaze.

"Was anyone hurt?" she asked Jules, who had materialized beside her once more.

"No." The vineyard manager's voice was rough from smoke. "But we're going to lose the entire northeast field. Those were the new plantings."

The financial loss registered with cold clarity—upwards of two hundred thousand dollars when factoring in future production. But at least she hadn't lost any humans. That was something.

A firefighter approached, his gaze shifting between Samantha and Jules. "Are you the owner?"

Samantha stepped forward. "I am."

"Chief wants to speak with you. We've got the fire contained, but he's found something you should see."

She followed him toward a cluster of firefighters near the edge of the burned area. Dean stayed right at her side, his presence both comforting and confusing. Here in crisis, he was solid, dependable, unwavering. Last night under the stars, he'd been all of those things too.

Until, suddenly, he wasn't.

The fire chief, a burly man with a deeply lined face, nodded as they approached. "Ms. Wagner? I'm Chief Renault. Follow me."

He led them to the far corner of the field, where the damage was most severe. Crouching down, he pointed to a scorched area where the vegetation pattern didn't match the surrounding burn. "See this? Accelerant. And here—" he moved a few feet to the right "—and here. Multiple points of origin. This was deliberate."

"Someone set this fire on purpose," Dean stated, voice hardening.

"No question," the chief confirmed. "This was arson."

The words landed like stones in Samantha's stomach. She'd known, of course—had suspected from the moment she saw the smoke. Too many "accidents" had accumulated for coincidence.

Her nails cut into her sooty palms.

"Mike has been conveniently absent this entire time," said

Jules, who had followed them, eyebrows drawing together. "Left the property right before the fire was spotted."

Dean and Samantha exchanged glances. She knew he was thinking of the threatening notes they'd found, the suspicions they already shared about the handyman.

"I need to speak with the sheriff when they arrive," Dean said, but his eyes lingered on Samantha a heartbeat longer than necessary. "Will you be okay for a few minutes?"

How to answer that when the question had so many layers— was she physically okay, emotionally okay, okay with him leaving her side briefly?

Honestly, the answer to all of them was no. But this wasn't the time to be having epiphanies about how much she'd come to depend on him.

"I'll be fine," she assured him. "Do what you need to do."

He nodded, eyes still searching hers before he turned away. The absence of his presence felt like a physical thing, a space that hadn't existed until he'd filled it and then emptied it again.

Jules watched him walk off, then shot Samantha a look. "Security consulting, huh?"

Samantha shut her eyes, tired of the cover story, tired of keeping up with the lies. "He also has an overprotective streak that he has a really hard time suppressing. I find it's best to step back and let him do his thing."

Thankfully, Jules didn't comment, but it seemed like Samantha might need to come clean with her staff sooner rather than later.

Hours passed in a blur of smoke and statements. The fire department eventually contained the blaze, leaving a charred wasteland where neat rows of young vines had stood that morning. The pungent smell of burnt vegetation hung heavy in the air as Samantha walked the perimeter of the damage with the fire chief and Carlos, assessing what had been lost.

The sight was devastating. What had been vibrant green

growth hours ago was charred beyond recognition. The metal trellises remained standing, blackened but intact, while the wooden stakes had been reduced to charcoal stubs jutting from the ground. The young vines themselves had been consumed almost entirely—their tender leaves and shoots destroyed, thicker stems left as charred, twisted fingers reaching from the scorched earth. The ground was covered in a layer of gray and black ash.

Actually, the black might be scorched earth. The sight nearly made her cry.

Her bare feet ached. Her eyes burned from smoke. But beneath the physical discomfort lay a bone-deep certainty that someone wanted to destroy not just her vineyard, but her.

And now, she wanted to punch something too.

"You should be resting."

Dean's voice behind her sent a flutter through her chest despite her exhaustion. She turned to find him watching her, his expression softer than she'd ever seen it.

"Says the man who looks like he went ten rounds with a chimney sweep," she replied, the attempt at humor falling flat as her voice cracked.

He smiled anyway, a small but genuine curve of lips that reached his eyes. "You were amazing today."

"I dug half a firebreak before the professionals arrived. Hardly heroic."

"That's not—" He stopped, seeming to gather his thoughts. "You stepped up. Jumped in without hesitation. Worked alongside your staff instead of directing from a distance."

The simple observation, delivered without flourish, touched something tender inside her. "They all did the same. Carlos, Jules, the field workers."

"They noticed," Dean said, "that you were there with them, getting your hands dirty. It matters."

A small connection forged in crisis. It wasn't much, but it was something. A step toward belonging.

The moment stretched between them, charged with unspoken words. There wasn't anyone else she'd rather be with though.

Samantha found herself staring at his mouth, remembering the pressure of his lips against hers last night, the sudden absence that followed. The emotional whiplash of his retreat after the best kiss of her life.

The weight of everything—the fire, the fear, the exhaustion— crashed over her at once. Her body swayed slightly, the events of the day suddenly too much to bear. Her vineyard. Her future. Her safety. All threatened, all hanging by a thread.

"Hey, now." Dean's voice softened as he stepped closer, concern replacing the guarded expression he'd worn since their midnight kiss.

She swayed again, and all at once, he enveloped her in an embrace that became the only thing that could have possibly held her together, even as it ripped her apart at the same time.

She wanted to snap at him, to ask what the deal was, what was happening between them, why he was so hot and cold. But the smoke-scented air, the charred remains of her vines, his solid presence, it was all too much.

So she just…melted, her cheek against his chest. His heartbeat thundered beneath her ear, strong and steady. Dean. He wrapped around her, holding her, keeping her on her feet.

"I've got you," he murmured, one hand moving to cradle the back of her head, fingers tangling in her smoke-dried hair.

"This isn't part of your job description," she managed, the words muffled against his shirt.

His chest rose and fell with a deep breath. "I know."

The simple acknowledgment carried more weight than a thousand explanations. This wasn't faking it for the audience, though there were plenty of people milling around. Either of them could have hauled out the fake boyfriend excuse, but it felt like a huge step that they hadn't.

"What are we doing then?" She needed to understand, to analyze, to get her head wrapped around—

"Don't ask me that question right now, Samantha," he murmured, his voice rough with emotion and exhaustion. "All I know is that I can't walk away from you."

She pulled back enough to look up at him, finding his blue eyes darkened with conflict and something else, something that mirrored the ache in her own chest.

All at once, she got it. He was wrestling with something huge and didn't need her angst added to the mix.

"Then don't walk away," she said softly. "I just need you to be here."

The lines in his face softened, even as his gaze remained troubled. "I'm here."

Two simple words. A promise and a confession wrapped into one.

Samantha let her head fall back down against his chest, too overwhelmed to navigate the complexity of what lay between them. For now, this was enough. His heartbeat beneath her ear, his arms around her, his presence steady as the ground beneath her feet crumbled.

And maybe she'd played a part in holding him together too.

When Dean finally spoke, his voice was low, barely audible above the distant sounds of the cleanup crew. "Let me take you back to the house."

She nodded against his chest, not trusting herself to speak. As they turned toward the main house, Dean's arm remained around her shoulders, a silent promise of protection and something deeper that neither of them was ready to name.

The burned field lay behind them. She'd deal with that tomorrow along with everything else. Get her difficult questions answered so she knew where she and Dean stood.

Because unlike the vineyard, her heart couldn't be rebuilt if it burned to the ground.

Chapter 16

Dean's scar throbbed like a jackhammer as he paced Samantha's bedroom for the third time in an hour, cataloging vulnerabilities with growing unease. The window latches were a joke. Easily compromised by someone halfway determined. French doors to the balcony had decorative glass panels that would shatter with minimal effort. Even the antique lock on the main door was more decorative than functional.

None of it was remotely good enough. Not after yesterday, when smoke had billowed across the vineyard in thick black columns, when he'd watched Samantha dig a firebreak with her own two hands and a shovel, face streaked with soot and determination.

Not when someone had proven they were willing to destroy a quarter of her property to get to her.

The arson changed everything.

A wrecking ball had demolished the wall between *investigation* and *protection*, leaving Dean trapped under the rubble of his own principles. He should be analyzing evidence, interviewing suspects, pushing forward on Greta's murder. Not mentally reinforcing Samantha's bedroom like it was the last bunker in a zombie apocalypse.

Yet here he was, fingers hovering over the contact for Maddox Security, run by a former Ranger who owed him from a case in Galveston.

Alfred, sensing his agitation, whined softly from his position near the door.

"It's okay, buddy," Dean assured him without conviction.

Nothing was okay. His fingers hovered over the call button, then froze. What was he doing? Since when did he prioritize security measures over the investigation? The *assignment*?

Since Samantha Wagner.

The realization settled like lead in his gut. He was in so deep he couldn't even see over the top of the pile of compromises he'd made. Strickland would have his head if he knew.

But all Dean could think about was how Samantha had felt like a sapling in a hurricane in his arms yesterday, how her ashen complexion matched her vineyard. But she'd waited to fall apart until she knew he had her. Because she trusted him.

And whoever had done these things was still out there, plotting their next move. Which might involve bloodshed. Samantha's blood, specifically.

He hit the call button.

After arranging the details, he ended the call. That had been the easy part. Now for the really difficult part. He pulled up the group text chat with Strickland's team.

Tanner Callahan and Beckett Granger.
I need you both here tomorrow.

He hit Send. The mandate might seem innocent enough, but it carried nuclear payload levels of significance. Working independently had been his entire approach since joining Strickland's team. Keep everyone at arm's length. Trust only himself.

And he'd voluntarily called in the team. He stared at his phone, the bullet scar on his side pulsing in time with his heart.

This wasn't just crossing a line; it was obliterating it.

But the alternative was leaving Samantha vulnerable, and that option had taken exactly zero seconds to dismiss.

Both Granger and Callahan responded immediately with thumbs-up emojis.

Be here 0900, he texted back. Fill Strickland in on the details. This is bigger than I thought.

Callahan's reply came immediately: Got it. See you then.

Dean dropped the phone on the bed, rubbing his palm over his face. The stubble rasped against his hand, reminding him he hadn't slept more than three hours combined since the fire. All he could see when he closed his eyes was Samantha surrounded by flames. Samantha trapped in a burning building. Samantha gone.

"I never should have kissed her," he told Alfred, who gave him a skeptical look that cut right through him. "You're right. It doesn't matter. That was just icing on the cake."

He was royally screwed either way.

Was this how Jake had felt? This crushing weight of competing priorities? This impossible choice between duty and… whatever this was that made his chest feel like it was caving in whenever he thought about the what-ifs of yesterday's fire?

For the first time since waking up in that hospital bed, Dean considered that his former partner might have made the only choice he could.

And that was a gut punch he hadn't seen coming.

"What are you doing in my bedroom?"

Samantha's voice hit him between the shoulder blades. He bobbled his phone, nearly dropped it, but caught it in time. Bad sign when someone could sneak up on him. Even worse when that someone wore four-inch heels that announced her arrival like a percussion section.

She stood framed in the doorway, arms crossed over her chest, one eyebrow raised questioningly. Even with the faint smudges of exhaustion beneath her eyes, she was breathtaking— all sleek lines and sharp angles softened by something vulnerable in her expression that she couldn't quite hide.

"Security assessment," he answered, slipping his phone into his pocket. "Your current setup is inadequate."

"I wasn't aware I'd requested one." Her tone was wry but carried a chill. Because of how he'd botched things after kissing her, probably. He'd been the king of whiplash since then.

He couldn't blame her for whatever kind of mood she felt like being in.

"The fire changed things."

"I get it." She stepped fully into the room, closing the door behind her. The click of the latch reverberated in his chest.

They were alone in her bedroom. Not the best place to be at the moment when all he wanted to do was yank her into his arms and—better not finish that thought.

"I've called in a security team," he told her, forcing his voice to remain steady. "They'll be here in a few hours to install upgraded systems. Motion sensors, cameras, reinforced locks."

All things I should have done days ago, before someone tried to burn down your vineyard.

"That's a lot of hardware for a boyfriend to take an interest in," she said with a quirked brow. "How are we going to explain that to the staff?"

Dean's shoulders tightened at the reminder of the elaborate charade that had somehow become more honest than half the truths he told himself.

"Forget the staff," he growled. "Forget the cover story for a minute. Someone deliberately set fire to your vineyard. They knew the property layout, the staff schedules, the vulnerabilities. Next time, the fire might not be limited to the northeast field."

The image flashed through his mind of flames engulfing the main house while Samantha slept. He would let her be an unprotected target over his own dead body.

Samantha's expression narrowed and she watched him carefully, as if evaluating something.

"This is about more than the investigation," she murmured.

Yeah, that was what he got when he tried to tangle with a smart woman. The Dean Carter who'd shown up here a few weeks ago would have said no. Denied it and meant it because nothing would have ever come between that Dean Carter and the truth about Greta Wagner's death.

But this version of himself, the one who'd held Samantha while smoke still billowed from her burning vineyard? The one who'd spent hours mapping vulnerabilities in her bedroom instead of focusing on the case? Yeah. This version had priorities that would have been unthinkable six weeks ago.

"I'm being thorough," he corrected, fooling neither one of them.

A small smile touched her lips. "Of course. Thorough."

Standing in this room was like being stripped bare in the middle of a war zone, all his tactical armor suddenly made of tissue paper.

"The security team is still coming," he deflected. Poorly. "Nonnegotiable."

"Fine." She moved toward the window, gazing out at the vineyard beyond. "But I want to be involved in the decisions. Where cameras go, which areas need priority coverage."

"Done."

She turned back to him, surprise flickering across her features. "Just like that?"

Despite everything, a smile tugged at his mouth. "Don't worry, I'll be insufferably authoritative about the recommendations."

Her genuine laugh loosened something in his chest, easing the weight of everything left unsaid between them. But the momentary levity faded as he recalled the other line he'd crossed.

"I'm also bringing in additional personnel," he continued, forcing the words out before they could become bitter in his mouth. "Professional security detail and…my team."

Her brows lifted. "Armed guards patrolling the vineyard? Is that what you're saying? The staff will love that."

"Just until we identify who's behind this," he insisted. "And they'll be discreet. Plainclothes, blending with the workers."

"You make it sound like I'm a high-value target."

"You are." The words emerged with more intensity than he'd intended, layered with meaning he couldn't afford to examine but wouldn't take back at gunpoint.

Because it was the truth.

Something flickered in her eyes. She sashayed close enough that he could detect the faint scent of her perfume beneath the lingering smell of smoke that seemed to permeate everything now.

"Is this the investigator talking?" she asked softly. "Or something else?"

Direct hit. And he took it like a man. There was no point in denying he'd developed a bone-deep need to be sure she stayed safe.

But with the admission came another truth. He'd crossed the biggest, most important line of all, one he wasn't sure he could retreat from. One that might cost him everything he'd been working toward: his place on Strickland's team, his shot at Ruiz, the vengeance he'd built his entire recovery around.

"Both," he finally answered. "The security is necessary for the investigation. Maybe next time we catch whoever is sabotaging you before they succeed. The team is—" he swallowed hard "—for me. So I can sleep at night knowing you're safe."

She nodded, her gaze sharp and missing nothing. "So, what happens next?"

She wasn't going to call him on his BS. She knew better than anyone that he already didn't sleep at night. No team could change that.

"Security upgrades, increased surveillance. My team will be

assisting with tracking Mike Thompson and investigating connections to the threats against Greta. They'll be here tomorrow."

My team. Not Strickland's. Because Dean had asked them to come and he'd be directing them. He was no longer operating solo, no longer shirking any kind of leadership role. Protecting Samantha had become more important than handling everything alone.

"Is that wise? Having more people here might compromise the cover story." She gestured between them. "The whole fake dating arrangement."

Since she'd been the one to insist on that plan, he had zero issue with crushing it under the feet of this new strategy. "I know it's important to you—"

"It's not, Dean." She stopped him with a well-placed hand to his chest, and the contact sang straight to his gut, lighting him up. "Just tell me. This isn't about solving a case for you anymore, is it?"

The question held layers, cutting straight to the heart of what neither of them had been willing to name. She wasn't asking about the escalating danger or complications; she was asking about him. About them.

"No," he admitted, thoroughly unable to deny her the answer she deserved. "It's not."

The bullet scar throbbed again, a physical reminder of what happened when emotions clouded judgment.

Yet he couldn't stop. Couldn't pull back. Couldn't rebuild the walls that had crumbled to dust and ashes under her steady gaze.

"I never wanted any of this," she said. "The sabotage, the danger, dragging you deeper into something that's becoming more complicated by the day."

"You didn't drag me anywhere," he corrected. "I'm here because I choose to be."

And that was the painful truth of it—every line he'd crossed had been his choice. Bringing in his team. Prioritizing her safety. Opening himself to the possibility that Jake had been right all along, that some things mattered more than the mission.

Something shifted in her expression, vulnerability naked on her face for a brief moment. "Why?"

"Because it's my job," he said automatically, falling back on the explanation that wore thinner each day. That she surely saw as an excuse. He could do better, and should. "And because you matter. None of this is fake anymore. I didn't mean for it to happen, but here we are."

Her expression softened, bloomed. "I'm not pretending either," she said quietly.

The atmosphere rippled as they stared at each other. Another line crossed, another boundary dissolved. But this crossing felt different—deliberate rather than accidental, chosen rather than stumbled into.

"Where does that leave us?" he asked.

"I don't know," she answered honestly. "But I think we've both been drawing lines in the sand only to step over them as soon as they're made."

The accuracy of her assessment tugged a reluctant smile from him. "You're not wrong."

And that was the truth at the core of everything. His carefully constructed boundaries, his sworn approach to justice, his vow to never make Jake's mistake—all of it had been swept away like lines in the sand once Samantha Wagner walked into his life.

Not because she'd pushed or manipulated or demanded. But because, faced with the choice between his principles and her safety, there'd been no choice at all.

Samantha stared at the marketing strategy documents spread across her desk until the words blurred into indecipherable smudges. It was almost midnight, and she'd been reviewing the same wine club proposal for three hours straight. Her brain had officially called it quits about an hour ago, but her stubborn streak insisted she push through.

Post-fire cleanup had consumed her entire day. The acrid smell of smoke still clung to her hair despite a thorough shower, a constant reminder of the destruction. The northeast field—gone. Two hundred thousand dollars in future production—gone. Her sense of security—definitely gone.

She massaged her temples, willing away the headache that had been building since dawn. The wine club proposal needed to be perfect before she presented it to Jules and Carlos tomorrow. It was the first step in her plan to rebuild Wagner Wines as something different from Greta's legacy, something ethical, sustainable.

Something worthy.

But her usual laser focus had abandoned her, leaving her mind to wander toward dangerous territory. Territory with broad shoulders and impossibly blue eyes and a habit of saying exactly what she needed to hear when she most needed it.

Dean had been in full protective mode since the fire, sweeping through the property like a human hurricane, demanding reinforced locks and security cameras and professional patrols. Normally guys like that, who took over and threw their weight around, irritated her. Instead, she'd found it comforting. And a little bit delicious. Which was irritating in an entirely different way.

She'd spent her entire career proving she could handle anything alone. So, why did Dean's steady presence make her feel more secure rather than less?

Her indie rock playlist shifted to a Lainey Wilson song—one of Dean's additions that had mysteriously appeared among her carefully curated tracks. Yet another change that had crept into her life since his arrival: the French press coffee waiting for her each morning, Alfred's now permanent indent on her office couch, the way her daily schedule now naturally accommodated their midnight walks.

Their lives had merged in a hundred little ways, and she didn't hate it.

She had someone in her life who knew how to make her a cup of coffee.

The realization should have sent her running for the sanctuary of spreadsheets and strategic projections. Instead, it felt unbelievably amazing.

Ugh, she couldn't pretend to work any longer. The vineyard, the fire, the constant tension between independence and need—it was all too much tonight. The diamond shell she'd always kept in place against the rest of the world had developed hairline fractures.

Before she could talk herself out of it, she grabbed her phone and typed a quick message to Dean: Still up?

Ugh, what a dumb thing to ask. Of course he was—it was almost time for his nightly walk. She should have just waited until he left and followed him, like she always did.

Except that wasn't going to work tonight.

Three dots appeared instantly, then: Always. Everything OK?

She stared at the reply, fingers hovering over the keyboard. She couldn't exactly say, *No, I'm drowning, and for once in my life I don't want to be alone.* That level of vulnerability wasn't in her professional skill set.

Found something interesting in the wine club analytics. Could use your perspective.

A flimsy excuse, but it would do. Three minutes passed before his reply came through—three minutes during which she contemplated throwing her phone into the vineyard and pretending she'd been hacked.

On my way.

She changed quickly into sleep shorts and a tank top, then immediately second-guessed herself. Too much? Too little? What message was she trying to send here? She just needed… what exactly? She wasn't even sure.

Okay, yes, she was. She wanted Dean. The steadiness he brought to every situation, whether he was inspecting sabotaged equipment or holding her together after a fire.

When the soft knock came at her door, she'd worked herself into a state of near panic.

"It's open," she called, her voice jumpier than corn in the popper.

Dean entered, looking rumpled and somehow far sexier than his daytime self in a worn Graceland T-shirt and flannel pants. The fabric stretched across his shoulders in a way that made her mouth go momentarily dry. Alfred padded in beside him, immediately claiming a spot at the foot of her bed as if he'd been sleeping there for years.

"So, what's this analytics breakthrough?" Dean asked, his voice carrying that slight rasp that always seemed more pronounced in the evening hours.

"Oh, right." She shifted, suddenly fascinated by the imaginary lint on her shorts. "I was looking at regional demographics and noticed some interesting patterns that could indicate—"

"Samantha." The gentle interruption stopped her mid-ramble. She looked up to find him watching her with a hooded gaze that made her feel like she'd turned to glass.

She sighed, deflating like a sales projection after a disastrous quarter. "Am I that obvious?"

"Only to someone who's been watching you face down crises without flinching for the past three weeks." The corner of his mouth lifted in that half smile that set her pulse on simmer. "Something's different tonight."

Samantha crossed to the window, needing distance from the intensity blanketing the room. Outside, the vineyard stretched into darkness, the moon highlighting a charred strip of the northeast field. A stark reminder she couldn't avoid.

"I keep thinking about everything that needs to be done tomorrow," she admitted. "The insurance claim, the staff reassignments, the replanting schedule. My to-do list keeps scrolling through my brain on repeat."

Dean didn't offer platitudes or easy solutions. He nodded, standing there in her bedroom looking far too solid and real. And *necessary*.

"You should get some rest then," he said after a moment, already turning toward the door.

"Wait."

He paused, one eyebrow lifted in question.

"Could you just—" She gestured vaguely toward the chair in the corner. "Could you stay for a bit? Until I fall asleep?" She forced a light laugh that sounded hollow even to her own ears. "The analytics can wait until morning."

Understanding flickered across his face, so quick she might have missed it if she hadn't been watching so closely. "Sure."

He wasn't going to bust her chops about it. Instant relief liquefied her insides.

Dean actually headed toward the chair, apparently on board with hanging out and watching her like a hired hand while she tossed and turned.

That wasn't what she wanted at all.

"Actually," she croaked, "you look exhausted too. We both need rest. We're adults. We can share a bed for one night."

She slipped beneath the covers and slapped a bright smile on her face, praying he wouldn't make a big thing out of it.

He didn't move, something cautious and questioning in his expression. "Samantha—"

"I'm not propositioning you, Carter." She rolled her eyes, deflecting with humor to hide the vulnerability crawling up her throat. "We've both had a long day. You're here. The bed is huge. It's practical."

"Practical," he repeated, and she couldn't tell if the amusement in his voice was directed at her or himself.

"Five minutes," she said. "Just…lie down for five minutes, cowboy. If it's weird, you can go back to your room and then jet off for your normal nocturnal rounds."

After a moment's hesitation that felt like it stretched into eternity, Dean moved to the other side of the bed. The mattress dipped under his weight as he settled beside her, careful to maintain a respectful distance. Not touching, but close enough that she could feel the warmth radiating from him. Alfred repositioned himself between their feet, apparently unbothered by the unusual sleeping arrangement.

She snapped off the light.

The room fell silent except for their breathing and Alfred's occasional contented sigh. This should be totally awkward, but instead she relaxed for the first time all day.

"You certainly know how to surprise a guy," Dean murmured into the dark.

"Having second thoughts?" She kept her tone light, though something in her chest constricted at the possibility.

"Not even close." He turned his head to look at her, the moonlight from the window catching the blue of his eyes and the slight stubble along his jaw that she suddenly, inexplicably wanted to brush her fingers against. "Just processing the fact that Samantha Wagner, the poster child for handling everything herself, asked me to stay."

And there it was—the truth she'd been dancing around. What had started as "just five minutes" and "it's practical" was really about needing him here. With her. Tonight. Maybe holding her hand, but if nothing else, giving off that vibe that made her feel like everything would be okay.

"I'm tired of being alone," she admitted in what felt like a surrender. "I want to sleep, and I can't seem to do that on my own tonight."

Something shifted in Dean's expression, a softening around the edges that drove straight into her heart and took up residence.

"Just sleep?" he asked, voice rough.

"I mean, yeah. It's my first adult coed sleepover, so there are probably some rules I should lay out, but I'm pretty sure you're already making up your own." She attempted a smile that felt shakier than she'd like. "You're the most honorable person I've ever met. Sometimes annoyingly so."

Dean's mouth quirked. "And here I thought you only noticed my 'reasonable muscles.'"

That lightened the moment, letting her breathe again. "Those didn't escape my notice either."

They lay in silence, the quiet punctuated only by Alfred's soft breathing and the distant sounds of the vineyard at night. This was what peace felt like. It was awesome.

"Dean?" she said softly, already drifting toward sleep.

"Hmm?"

"Thank you."

His hand found hers on top of the covers, fingers intertwining with a gentle squeeze. "Get some sleep, Samantha."

As shocking as it sounded, she actually thought she could now that she had an impossibly sexy former Ranger and his adorable dog in her bed.

None of it made sense according to her carefully constructed life plan. But for the first time since inheriting Wagner Wines, she felt like she was exactly where she needed to be.

Chapter 17

Dean's eyes felt gritty from lack of sleep, though not for the usual reasons.

Samantha had slept in his arms the night before.

He hadn't meant to stay, had planned to leave her bed once she drifted off, but something about her vulnerability had anchored him to the spot.

After she'd fallen asleep, he'd maintained a careful distance for about thirty minutes, wide-awake as he mapped out his escape. Then she'd turned, seeking his warmth even in unconsciousness, and something inside him had crumbled. He'd gathered her close, her head nestled against his chest, and held her through the night.

He'd slept better than he had since the hospital.

This morning, he'd slipped out before she woke, leaving her curled around his pillow. The image had stayed with him all morning like a brand seared into his retinas.

Now he stared at the evidence board in the makeshift command center he'd set up in one of Greta Wagner's unused offices. Photos of the vineyard, the fire damage, personnel files, and a timeline of sabotage incidents covered the wall. In the corner, Tanner and Beckett were already setting up, exactly as he'd requested yesterday after the fire.

When he'd finally admitted he couldn't handle this alone.

The reality of their presence still chafed like wearing someone else's clothes—technically functional but wrong in all the ways that mattered.

"Impressive setup," Tanner commented, surveying the evidence wall with a low whistle. "Very CSI: Vineyard. Though I'm pretty sure that show got canceled after the first episode."

Dean ignored the quip. "Any progress tracking Mike Thompson?"

"Working on it," Beckett replied, not looking up from his laptop. His fingers flew across the keyboard with surgical precision. "His digital footprint is surprisingly minimal for someone his age."

"Means he knows how to hide," Tanner added, unhooking a camera bag from his shoulder. "Smart guy."

"Or guilty," Dean said.

"I need better tools to go deeper," Beckett explained, opening a sleek carbon-fiber case he'd pulled from a black backpack.

Dean watched, impressed despite himself, as Beckett unfolded what looked like a standard laptop but clearly wasn't. The casing was military-grade composite, the screen resolution far beyond consumer tech, and the processor hummed with barely audible efficiency that screamed classified technology.

"What is that?" Dean asked before he could stop himself.

"NSA-grade quantum processing with proprietary software," Tanner replied with a grin. "Price tag would make your eyes water. Strickland wasn't kidding about resources."

"You get used to the toys," Beckett said, his fingers flying across the custom keyboard. "Wait until you see what we've got in the armory."

Dean's phone chimed with Strickland's ringtone. He'd been expecting the call since requesting additional security resources after the fire. The expenses must have finally come through, and Strickland had noticed.

"I need to take this," Dean said, stepping out of the office and onto the adjacent patio before he accepted the call. "Carter."

"How are things?" Strickland asked with his trademark warmth.

It was such a loaded question that Dean froze for a moment, wholly unable to figure out how to answer. Neutrally, of course. "Going well."

"Great. Glad to hear it. I approved the additional security you requested," Strickland said, "but I'm curious why you think it's necessary. Is Wagner in immediate danger?"

There it was. Dean scrubbed the back of his neck. Samantha *was* in danger and he'd made a call to protect her. The right call.

"The sabotage incidents are escalating," he said carefully. "First the ladder, then the equipment, now arson. Whoever's behind this is getting bolder. Until we identify the perpetrator, additional security seems wise."

"Wise," Strickland repeated, the word carrying unspoken nuances Dean absolutely didn't plan to press. "Just make sure you're keeping your eye on the ball, son. This is an investigation, not a protection detail."

An echo of the conversation he'd had with Strickland once before. *People would kill to protect their interests.* People like Mike Thompson, who'd vanished right before the fire.

People. Not Samantha Wagner.

The woman he'd kissed. The woman who'd trusted him with her vulnerability in ways he suspected she hadn't with anyone else ever.

The woman who was effectively destroying his objectivity with every smile, every touch, every moment between them that wasn't strictly professional. Which was all of them, honestly.

Dean's jaw tightened. "I'm aware of my priorities."

"Good. Because I need clear heads on this. Evidence gathering first, then arrest. That's your mission."

The subtle reminder stung more than it should have. Because Dean knew exactly why he was here—to get a shot at Ruiz.

So, why did everything feel upside down?

"I see you've called in the team," Strickland said, changing tactics. "Good. About time you used the resources available to you."

Dean glanced through the window, where Tanner and Beckett were examining the evidence board with laser focus.

"I requested their help, yes," Dean admitted, shoving back the knowledge that it had been a last resort because he didn't want to compromise Samantha's safety over his own pride.

"Smart move. They're the best at what they do. Different approaches than yours, but effective." There was a smile in Strickland's voice now. "Might be good for you to see how other people operate. Not everything has to be by the book to be right."

"The book exists for a reason," Dean countered, probably a lot less mildly than the situation warranted.

"True. But sometimes justice requires a more flexible approach. I've seen you struggle with that." Strickland's tone took on that mentoring quality Dean remembered from his early Ranger days. "Not everyone's as black and white as you, Dean. Results matter too, not just methods."

Dean didn't respond. Couldn't. The wisdom of his mentor warred with the principles that had defined his career.

"Anyway," Strickland continued into the silence, "keep me updated. And remember the stakes. Don't get distracted by side issues."

Side issues. Like Samantha. Like the way his body went into free fall when she walked into a room. Like the peace he'd found holding her last night.

"Understood," Dean said, ending the call with a headache forming at the base of his skull.

When he reentered the office, Tanner and Beckett had already transformed the space. Beckett had set up three monitors connected to his laptop, while Tanner was organizing what looked like surveillance equipment on the table.

"Good chat with the boss?" Tanner asked, not looking up from his task.

"Fine," Dean said. "What have you found so far?"

"Granger's the real MVP here," Tanner replied, jerking a thumb toward the third team member. "Ten minutes into examining the property's security system, and he's already found something interesting."

Beckett's expression remained impassive as he turned one of the monitors toward Dean. "Ghost folder in the surveillance archives. Set to auto-delete, but the program glitched. Someone wasn't as thorough as they thought."

Dean stepped closer, his pulse quickening as a video began to play. The footage showed Greta Wagner in what appeared to be a heated argument with a well-dressed woman in her fifties. Dean recognized her from the town website.

"Mayor Brooks," he murmured, leaning in for a closer look.

The time stamp showed the recording was from just days before Greta's death. Though there was no audio, the body language told a clear story—accusatory gestures from Brooks, defensive posture from Greta. Then Brooks slammed a folder on the desk between them.

"Can we enhance this?" Dean asked, focusing on the folder. "See what she put down?"

"Already working on it," Beckett replied. "Extracting still frames now."

"This is huge," Tanner said, abandoning his equipment to join them. "Proves Brooks had direct conflict with Greta right before she died."

"It proves they argued," Dean said cautiously, though his instincts were firing on all cylinders. "Not that she killed her."

"True, but it's a solid lead connecting her to Greta," Tanner said. "Brooks is a stellar addition to the threat list we've been compiling since Samantha found the messages."

"Speaking of which," Beckett said, fingers still flying across his keyboard, "I ran Mike Thompson's background. He has connections to Brooks going back years. Worked private security for her husband before showing up here."

Dean felt the familiar surge of energy that came when an investigation finally gained momentum. This was tangible evidence. Not conclusive, but solid leads connecting Brooks and Thompson to Greta right before her death.

"How did you find that connection?" Dean asked, since he'd run Thompson's background himself three times.

Beckett's expression remained stone cold, the only mode he seemed to have. "I have methods."

"He means illegal database access," Tanner translated cheerfully.

"Not illegal," Beckett corrected. "Unconventional. And not expressly authorized."

Dean stared at them both, waiting for the punchline, which did not come. "You hacked into government records?"

"I accessed information through nontraditional channels," Beckett said. "Information that was publicly available, just not conveniently assembled."

"Gray area," Tanner added with a shrug. "But nothing that would compromise a case. Beckett's careful that way."

Dean felt something twist in his gut. This was exactly the kind of approach he'd spent his career avoiding—the murky territory between legal and illegal, where results mattered more than methods.

Yet he couldn't deny the effectiveness. In mere hours, they'd uncovered connections he would have had to spend weeks slogging through official channels to find.

"And now for the pièce de résistance," Beckett said, turning his laptop toward Dean again. "Another video from the same system. Three days after the Brooks confrontation."

The footage showed Mike Thompson in Greta's office, receiving what appeared to be an envelope. His expression was grim as Greta spoke to him, her finger jabbing toward him accusingly.

"No audio on this one either," Beckett said. "But the body language suggests a payment and instructions. Or a threat."

"Was he working for Greta or against her?" Dean murmured, studying Thompson's posture.

"Both maybe," Tanner said, dropping the humor entirely as he shifted into investigative mode. "Double agent. Taking money from Greta while reporting to Brooks."

"And now that Greta's gone, he's targeting Samantha under Brooks's direction," Beckett added, the theory crystallizing between them with cold precision.

They still didn't have proof. But Dean had a lot more confidence in the possibility of its existence than he had this morning.

"We need to bring Thompson in," Dean decided. "He's the key to this whole thing."

"That's the problem," Beckett said. "He's gone dark. No digital trail since before the fire."

"But," Tanner interjected, "I've got informants in San Antonio who might be able to help. People who owe me favors."

"What kind of favors?" Dean asked, instantly wary.

Tanner smiled enigmatically. "The kind you don't ask too many questions about. Let's just say I've helped some people out of tight spots, and they're grateful."

Another gray area. Dean was beginning to see a pattern in how these two operated, always on the edge of proper procedure but never quite crossing into outright prosecutable offense territory.

"And if your informants find him?" Dean asked.

"Then we have a conversation," Beckett replied, his voice dropping to a register that sent a chill down Dean's spine.

"What kind of conversation?" Dean pressed, already suspecting the answer.

Beckett met his gaze, dropping the temperature a few degrees—exhibit A on how he'd earned the name Mr. Freeze. "The persuasive kind that encourages cooperation."

"We're not using coercion," Dean said firmly.

"Not coercion," Beckett clarified. "Pressure. Psychological leverage. There's a difference."

"A thin line," Dean countered.

"But an important one," Tanner noted. "Look, no one's talking about breaking kneecaps here. Beckett has a gift for finding people's weak spots and pressing on them until they talk. It's actually impressive to watch."

"It's effective," Beckett said, neither pride nor apology in his tone, just statement of fact. "And given what's at stake, effectiveness matters."

An echo of Strickland's words. Results matter. Not just methods.

Dean felt like he was standing on a precipice, the solid ground of his ethical certainty crumbling beneath his feet. These men operated in ways he'd always avoided, but they got results. They found evidence. They closed cases.

And they were his partners, for better or worse, if he wanted into the Shadow Rangers.

And with Samantha's safety on the line, wasn't that what mattered most?

Dean cracked his neck. Once again, everything came back to Samantha. Whatever this was between them had started to override his focus on the case. Started to? He could see "started to" in his rearview mirror.

Strickland's warning threaded through his mind—*Don't get distracted by side issues.*

But was her safety really a side issue? Or was it becoming the central focus of his entire mission? A good operative should know the difference, know when to shift. That was his excuse and he was sticking to it.

"Let's work the evidence we have," Dean said, blowing out a breath. "I want to know everything about Brooks's connection to Greta and Thompson before we start alternative approaches."

Beckett and Tanner exchanged a glance that Dean couldn't interpret.

"Your call, boss," Tanner said easily, though something in his tone suggested he disagreed. "We're just the hired help."

"We work together," Dean corrected. "But we do it my way. Clear?"

"Crystal," Beckett replied, turning back to his monitors. "Though if Thompson makes another move against Wagner, don't expect me to ask for permission before doing what's necessary."

The statement hung in the air like a gauntlet thrown at Dean's feet. A challenge to his leadership, yes, but more than that, a challenge to his principles. To the lines he'd drawn and maintained throughout his career.

The question was no longer whether he could work with a team. It was whether he could adapt his black-and-white worldview to include their shades of gray.

Whether he could bend his rules for the sake of results. For justice. For Samantha.

He wasn't sure he liked his instant gut feeling on how that was going to go down if it came to it.

"I have to update Strickland," Dean said, and pulled out his phone, keying in a quick text to their actual boss about the connection between Mayor Vivian Brooks and Greta Wagner.

Strickland: Excellent work, Carter. The governor's office has suspicions about her but didn't want to tip their hand. Keep me informed.

Before Dean could process that, his phone buzzed again with another incoming text, but this one was from Samantha.

Have dinner with me. 7 okay?

The words bled off the screen as he stared at them. *Dinner.* Just the two of them. Just like last night, which had led to her falling asleep in his arms. Midnight walks led to kisses he couldn't stop thinking about. Or take back.

His thumb hovered over the screen as Strickland's warning echoed in his mind. *Don't get distracted. Keep your eye on the ball.*

His priorities needed to be crystal clear. Find out who killed Greta. Secure his place on the team. Get a shot at Ruiz.

Not fall for the woman he was supposed to be investigating. Though that was a little like closing the barn door after the horse had already hightailed it for Houston.

With a resolve that felt like tearing out a piece of himself, Dean tapped out a response:

Can't tonight. Working with the team.

Short. Impersonal. How he should have been doing things this whole time.

He hit Send before he could change his mind, ignoring the hollow feeling in his chest. This was necessary. Professional. The right call. He was carving out his escape route and using it.

So why did it feel like he'd made the biggest mistake of his life?

Chapter 18

Samantha stared at the ceiling, sleep a distant concept that had packed its bags and taken off for parts unknown. Her mind cycled through the day's events like a particularly aggressive PowerPoint presentation stuck on a loop.

Can't tonight. Working with the team.

Six words, each one a tiny dagger. She'd been around the dating block a few times and could sense a brush off when it happened. Dean had shut her down with all the warmth of an automated customer service response.

Plus she hadn't seen him once today. Normally, he sought her out several times, and they almost always accidentally on purpose ran into each other on the balcony after most of the vineyard employees had left for the day.

"Absolutely unacceptable," she informed her ceiling, which had the good sense not to argue.

She'd faced down corporate competitors, hostile clients and Caitlyn's betrayal without flinching. She'd navigated vineyard sabotage, arson and a staff that viewed her as a walking disaster in designer shoes.

She was not about to be ghosted by a cowboy with emotional constipation.

Her phone screen lit up when she palmed it—12:17 a.m. Dean would be starting his nightly patrol right about now, circling the property with Alfred trailing behind him, both of them alert for threats that could materialize from the darkness. But really, he'd be in pain and pretending to be working to cover it up.

Perfect time to chat.

Samantha slipped from her bed and grabbed a cardigan to throw over her sleep shorts and tank top. Dean Carter had some explaining to do, and he was going to do it tonight.

The hallway was quiet as she padded barefoot toward the stairs. Upgraded security cameras—Dean's latest protective measure—tracked her progress, but she didn't care. Let him see her coming. Let him prepare his excuses. She'd been crafting persuasive ad campaigns since she was twenty-three; she could handle one former Ranger.

Outside, the night wrapped around her like a velvet cloak, warm and close and alive with cricket song. The moon hung overhead, nearly full, casting enough light to navigate the path toward the vineyard's southern edge, Dean's usual starting point for his midnight patrols.

She spotted him almost immediately, a shadow among shadows, standing motionless beneath the sprawling oak that marked the line between the fields and the house. Alfred wasn't with him tonight, which was unusual. Dean stood with his back to her, silhouette stark against the silver-painted landscape, shoulders rigid with tension she immediately wanted to soothe.

He carried a lot of burdens. She knew that. Because he'd shared some of them with her. End result—she wanted to be the one he turned to when it got to be too much. She'd thought they were getting closer to that. Instead, they were in this precarious place that didn't sit right.

In advertising, timing was everything. This wasn't a marketing strategy though. This was something else. Something she didn't have a prepared pitch for, despite the various scenarios she'd mentally rehearsed on her way out here.

Too late for second thoughts. Commit to the play.

She approached with enough fanfare that he would hear her

coming. Dean didn't turn, but a minute shift of his shoulders told her he knew exactly who was approaching and had chosen to keep up his statue impersonation.

"Your security measures need work," she called when she was still several yards away. "I walked right out of the house without any alarms sounding."

"The system isn't designed to keep you in." His voice skated across her skin, gravel and whiskey, rough around the edges. "Just others out."

"Semantics." She stepped into his line of sight, forcing him to look at her. "We need to talk."

"It's after midnight."

"Yes, and you're out here walking the perimeter instead of sleeping, same as you've been doing every night since you arrived." *Except for one.* The night he'd slept in her bed. She crossed her arms over her chest. "Don't pretend this is an unusual time for a conversation between us."

His expression remained frustratingly neutral, but something flickered in his eyes, a flash of emotion quickly contained. "I'm working."

"And I'm harvesting grapes in my sleep shorts," she retorted. "Try again."

A muscle jumped in his jaw. "What do you want, Samantha?"

What did she want? World peace, a successful vineyard and for Dean to stop looking at her like she was a problem to solve instead of a woman he had the power to hurt.

When had that *happened*?

"An explanation would be a good start." She kept her voice level, professional, controlled. "What's going on? You spend the night in my bed, then immediately rejected a perfectly innocent dinner invitation. I could have blown that off, but all afternoon, you treated me like I'm radioactive. Like you're doing now. That doesn't track."

"It's complicated."

"Uncomplicate it."

His mouth tightened. "I lost focus. Crossed lines I shouldn't have. I'm here to do a job, not—" he gestured vaguely between them "—whatever this is."

"Whatever this is," she repeated, something cracking open in her chest that worked its way into her throat. "That's what you're going with? We've been living as a couple for weeks. You held me all night after the fire. We've spent every midnight since you arrived having conversations most people reserve for their therapists. And your explanation is 'I'm on the job'?"

"I never claimed to be good with words."

"Then try actions. Those have been speaking loudly enough." She took a step closer, heart hammering against her ribs as if she'd mainlined an energy drink in anticipation of an all-nighter. "You slept in my bed. All night. It meant something, Dean. To both of us."

"It was comfort after a traumatic event. Psychological response. Adrenaline comedown." He rattled off the explanations like he'd rehearsed them, each one more clinical than the last.

"Wow." She couldn't keep the bite from her tone. "Did you get those from a first responder handbook, or are you naturally gifted at emotional deflection?"

His eyes narrowed. "I'm being practical."

"No, you're being a coward." The words escaped before she could filter them through her usual diplomatic sieve. "You're hiding behind your job because it's safer than admitting what's happening between us."

"Nothing is happening between us," he said, his voice hardening. "We work together. That's it."

"Is that why you keep showing up on my balcony every morning? Why you make enough coffee for both of us? Why your dog sleeps in my office instead of yours?" She crowded into his space, craving his touch but wholly unable to figure out how to break through this barrier he'd erected. "Work colleagues don't do those things, Dean."

"We're supposed to be a couple. Maintaining the cover story." His jaw set in a stubborn line she was beginning to know too well.

"Oh please." She rolled her eyes. "That excuse expired a long time ago. No one's watching when you walk with me at midnight. No one cares if Alfred follows me around. No one's monitoring whether you spend the night in my room."

"You're mistaking the things I have to do to play a part with reality."

The accusation landed like a slap. Samantha took an instinctive step back, her corporate armor failing rapidly as her chest flooded with something that hurt so badly, she could barely breathe. This was her heart breaking in real time under a Texas moon.

She wrapped her arms around herself, suddenly aware of the night's chill against her exposed skin as she replayed every single interaction they'd had. Every soft look. Every gentle touch. Every private conversation under starlight.

All an act, according to him.

But was it, really?

"You're lying." The words emerged soft but certain.

Dean's head snapped up. "What?"

"You're lying," she repeated, one hundred percent convinced of it. "To me. To yourself. About us being fake."

Something flashed across his face—panic maybe. Or recognition.

"Samantha—"

"No, it's my turn to talk." She took a deep breath, steeling herself in case she was wrong. But she wasn't, there was no way. "I know what fake feels like. I worked in sales. I sold *fake* for a living. Created illusions and packaged them as reality. I know the difference between performance and truth."

Her voice wavered but she pushed on. "What happened between us is not a product of the fake relationship I manufactured. The quiet conversations on the balcony weren't for an audience. Neither was the way you kissed me and *told* me it wasn't fake. Or the way you held me after the fire."

Dean stood motionless, his expression unreadable in the moonlight.

She took a step toward him, closing the distance he'd put between them. "I know you feel it too. I see it in how you look at me when you think I won't notice. In how your breathing changes when I'm close. In how your hand finds mine in the dark like it belongs there."

His jaw clenched. "Stop."

"Why? Because I'm right?" Another step closer. "Because it's easier to hide behind your mission than admit you have feelings for me?"

"It doesn't matter what I feel," he said, his voice rough. "I have a job to do."

"It matters to me." The admission cost her something—a piece of the diamond-hard shell she'd built around herself since Caitlyn's betrayal. Since all the disappointments before that. "Because I have feelings for you too. Real ones."

The night seemed to hold its breath. Samantha's heart pounded so loudly she was certain he could hear it, a terrified drumbeat keeping time with her racing thoughts.

So what if he did. This was Samantha Wagner laying it all on the line. Daring him to step over it.

"I don't do this," she said, gesturing vaguely. "I don't date men who show up. I don't prioritize time together with anyone unless it's work-related. I don't put myself in positions where I could get hurt. But here I am, doing all of those things *with you*, because what's happening between us is worth it, Dean."

His expression shifted, something raw emerging from beneath the stoic facade. Raw and honest, finally. Emotions spilled into the space between them, and she scrambled to sort them all: longing, fear, hunger, discord.

This was tearing him apart too.

"I can't do both," he croaked. "I can't focus on the case and…you. Not at the same time. Not without compromising one or the other."

"So you chose the case." It wasn't a question.

"I have to." He ripped the admission from somewhere deep. "I've spent months working toward this opportunity. If I succeed here, I get a shot at Ruiz. At justice. At the thing that's driven me since I woke up in that hospital bed."

"At vengeance, you mean." She said it softly, without judgment.

His eyes locked with hers. "Yes."

The simple honesty of his response caught her off guard. She'd expected more deflection, more evasion. Instead, he'd handed her a truth so raw it almost burned to touch.

"And me?" she asked, her voice barely audible. "Where do I fit in this mission of yours?"

"You don't." He huffed out a sigh. "That's the problem."

Okay then, they were going for brutal honesty here. "Why is that a problem?"

"You were supposed to be a suspect. Then a witness. Then an assignment." His hands clenched at his sides. "Not…this. Not someone who matters more than I want to admit. Not someone I think about when I should be focusing on the case. Not someone who makes me question every line I've drawn."

The confession wrapped around her like a sweater, hugging her doubts away.

"That sounds a lot like feelings to me," she said quietly.

A shadow of a smile touched his mouth and exploded in his gaze. "I never said I didn't have them. Just that I can't act on them."

And the doubts were back. "Why not?"

"Because I made a promise to myself. After Jake chose Aubrey over the mission. After I took a bullet and Ruiz walked free." The vibe between them grew some teeth, intent and serious. "I promised I'd never let personal feelings compromise justice. Never let anyone matter more than getting the job done right."

Everything clicked into place. His hot and cold routine wasn't due to lack of emotional stakes but because of an excess of them. "And you think I'm asking you to break that promise."

"No, the problem is that it's happening without any help from your end," he admitted. "Every minute I spend with you makes me want to do nothing but that. Every time I touch you, I question why I have to stop. All of it takes me further from my purpose. The fire made it worse. I've been wholly unable to concentrate on anything except making sure no one can get to you. Which means I'm failing the mission."

The brokenness in his voice cracked something inside. Her heart probably, though there wasn't much of it left that wasn't already grabbing onto whatever pieces of him he planned to give her.

This wasn't rejection; it was confession. Vulnerability from a man who valued control above all else.

In that moment, seeing him laid bare beneath the stars, Samantha did the only thing that made sense. The only thing that worked between them when words couldn't.

She kissed him.

Not the tentative brush of lips they'd shared on the vineyard path nights ago. Not the careful exploration of new territory. This was demand and declaration both—her fingers curling into the fabric of his shirt, pulling him down to meet her as she rose on tiptoes to claim his mouth.

For a heart-stopping moment, he froze. Then his hands were in her hair, at her waist, pulling her against him with a desperation that matched her own. The kiss deepened, evolved from challenge to surrender, from question to answer.

Her world narrowed to points of contact: his fingers threading through her hair, his chest solid beneath her palms, his heartbeat thundering in time with hers. Everything else fell away. The vineyard, the investigation, the careful lines they'd both drawn and redrawn.

In this kiss, there was no pretense. No cover story. Just the electric truth of what had been building between them since the first time he'd caught her when she fell.

When they finally broke apart, reality came crashing back like a cold wave. She saw it in his eyes, the moment clarity returned. The moment duty reasserted itself.

"That was—" his voice sounded wrecked.

"Real," she finished for him. "That's what *real* feels like."

His hand came up to touch her cheek, so gently it made her chest ache. "I know."

But even as he said it, she could see the fortress behind his skin rebuilding itself, brick by mental brick. She was losing him to his mission. Because she hadn't earned a place in his world.

"Ruiz is still out there," he said, the words heavy between them. "There's still justice that needs to be served. People who need to be protected. Lines I can't cross, no matter how much I want to."

Understanding bloomed, bittersweet and undeniable. Dean's world was black and white, right and wrong, justice and injustice. No room for gray areas. No space for compromise.

And she couldn't change that. Couldn't compete with a quest carved into his bones.

She'd fallen in love with a man who had more in common with Batman than she'd credited. It was like a terrible joke that wasn't funny.

"I understand," she said, her throat so raw she couldn't get any more words out.

She'd spent her entire life trying to prove herself worthy. Earn approval. Gain validation through achievement. But this was a line he wasn't willing to cross. Not even for her.

The realization cut deeper than she wanted to admit. If she had been enough, he would have found a way to choose her despite his principles. That he couldn't only confirmed what she'd always feared—that no amount of effort or accomplishment would ever make her truly worth choosing when measured against something that mattered more.

She had zero clue how to navigate that.

"I'm sorry," he rasped, and she could tell he meant it. "I wish—"

"Don't." She stopped him with a finger to his lips. "Don't say what you can't deliver."

They stood together in the moonlight, the moment stretching between them. Both recognizing the impossibility of moving forward but still mired in the ache of stepping back.

Dean pulled her into his arms and she went willingly, desperate for some piece of him to hold on to. She memorized the solid warmth of his chest, the steady thump of his heart, the citrus scent that had become as familiar as her own.

When they finally pulled apart, Samantha felt the space between them expand. Solidify. But she straightened her shoulders, reclaiming her composure piece by piece. She was still Samantha Wagner. Still the Vineyard Slayer. She would be fine. Eventually.

"I should get back," she said, her voice conveying none of the turmoil chopping through her tender places. "Early meeting with Carlos tomorrow about replanting the northeast field."

Dean nodded, his expression shuttered once more. "I'll finish my patrol."

She took a step back, then another before her stinging eyes tipped him off that none of this was actually okay. "Goodnight, Dean."

"Goodnight, Samantha."

She turned away and walked back toward the house alone, the taste of him still on her lips. Behind her, Dean remained motionless beneath the oak tree, a sentinel between her and the dangers lurking in the darkness. Protecting her still, even as he denied himself what she'd freely offered.

The night wrapped around her, cool and indifferent to the ache in her chest. This was the price of laying everything out and insisting he admit their feelings for each other weren't fake. This was reality—and not the version where love conquered all, but the messy, complicated version where choices had consequences and some lines remained uncrossed.

Dean had chosen his mission. She would find a way to live with that, even as it broke something inside her.

Chapter 19

Worse things had happened to Dean in his career than being forced to work alongside a woman he wanted but couldn't have, though none came to mind. Except being shot. That one he didn't have any trouble keeping front and center, and as a bonus, these two terrible things were at war with each other.

An eternal conflict with no resolution.

Which pretty much explained his entire mental state as Samantha crowded up against his elbow as they peered into the recesses of the desk in Greta's former office at the house. Her proximity shoved spirals of awareness through his gut, along with waves of whatever she wore that smelled like an exotic garden.

"Is that what I think it is?" Samantha asked, eyeing the dusty container Dean had pulled from another hidden compartment in the desk, one inside the original secret compartment where Greta had hidden the death threats.

Dean set the cardboard box on the desk gingerly. Beckett had gone over this office with a fine-toothed comb, but he'd been looking for secret compartments in the walls and had come up empty. Dean still didn't know what had tripped his own epiphany to try the desk again, but his efforts had finally uncovered this second concealed space that revealed itself when you knew where to press.

"Only one way to find out." Dean lifted the lid, angling it

away from them both with caution born from years of tactical training.

Inside lay stacks of neatly organized folders, each labeled with precise handwriting. Property deeds. Financial records. Photographs. Dean spread the contents across the surface like puzzle pieces, his heart rate quickening as these individual pieces coalesced to create a whole picture.

Mayor Vivian Brooks stared back at him from several surveillance photos, caught in clandestine meetings with figures he didn't recognize. Bank statements showed suspicious transfers. Building permits bore stamps of approval with altered dates.

"This is blackmail material," Samantha said, flipping through a stack of documents. "Greta had dirt on the mayor."

Dean nodded, scanning a particularly incriminating financial record. "Looks that way to me too. Brooks was diverting city funds through a shell company. Probably not her first rodeo either."

Dean tried to focus on the documents, but every breath Samantha took seemed to pull at something in his chest. Every glance she cast his way made him want to forget the evidence, forget Strickland and his audition, forget everything except the warm weight of her in his arms.

It was a physical ache, this need to be near her, to protect her, to touch her. Telling her they couldn't be a thing hadn't diminished it at all. If anything, his need for her had gotten worse.

"So, Greta was blackmailing Brooks," Samantha continued, her fingertips tracing the edge of a property deed. "Leveraging the mayor's corruption for…what? More water rights?"

"Seems like. Brooks needed Greta gone because she knew too much."

Samantha's gaze met his across the table, sharp and unflinching, because *she* wasn't having any trouble being this close to him. "And Mike worked for Brooks before coming here."

"Making him the perfect plant." Dean gathered the documents, careful not to let his hands brush against hers. He'd redrawn the lines and now he had to stay on this side of it. Even if it felt like walking barefoot on broken glass.

A faint sound caught his attention—the distinctive crunch of gravel under tires. His body went rigid, years of training focusing his senses.

"What is it?" Samantha asked, immediately alert to his change in posture.

Dean moved to the window, keeping to the side of the frame as he peered outside.

"Car. Headlights off." His senses heightened as he surveyed the dark driveway. "Two men getting out. Not staff."

No staff would arrive at 11:30 p.m. with no lights, moving with the deliberate stealth of these guys.

"How did they get past the security system?" Samantha whispered, already gathering the documents.

"Someone gave them the codes." Dean's jaw clenched. Mike. Had to be. Though how he'd managed that when he still hadn't surfaced remained to be seen. "Get your shoes on. We need to move."

To her credit, Samantha didn't waste time with questions. She thrust the documents back into the box and sprinted to the mud room, where she kept a pair of old running shoes, shoving her feet into them as she hobbled back across the living room, box of documents under her arm. Dean patted his gun, grateful he'd opted to start carrying it in a shoulder holster for easy access.

A crash reverberated from the front of the house—the door hinges splintering.

"They're in," he said, grabbing Samantha's arm and steering her away from the sound of intruders who clearly meant business. "Back door. Now."

Another crash, closer this time. Heavy footsteps in the foyer.

"Give us the files and no one gets hurt!" a male voice called out, his bravado betrayed by the edge of desperation.

The files they'd *just* found? How could anyone be aware of them already?

Dean nearly groaned as everything fell into place. Mike again. He'd been paid to find the files, if Dean had his guess.

Which meant Brooks had known the blackmail folder existed this whole time. He and Samantha had gotten lucky—for once—to have secured this box of evidence in the nick of time.

Dean rushed Samantha toward the back of the house, his body between her and the approaching threat. The security team should have responded to the breach, but something had gone wrong.

And his team had taken off for San Antonio. Tanner had insisted they needed to push his leads on Mike's connections, and Beckett had gone along to provide technical support. The timing couldn't have been worse.

They were on their own. His mind clicked through options.

"Where are you taking us?" Samantha whispered as they slipped through the back door onto the patio.

"The vineyard. Cover of darkness. We know it better than they do."

The night air hit them as they stepped outside, warm and thick with the scent of grapevines. Dean scanned the property, mapping their best route in his head. The security lights had been disabled, no doubt by the intruders.

Dean slipped on the thermal imaging glasses Strickland had insisted he take. The world instantly transformed into heat signatures—blue-green backgrounds with yellow-red human forms moving through the darkness. He tapped the frame, cycling the lenses to night vision, giving him perfect visibility despite the blackout.

"Stay close. Step where I step," he told her.

He felt her nod against his shoulder, her body glued to his

back, her fingers curled around his arm. She couldn't see what he could—the crystal clear outlines of every obstacle, the green outlines of their pursuers, the tactical advantages and escape routes all enhanced and highlighted by technology worth a small fortune. This was what Strickland had meant about resources. Equipment that gave his team every possible edge.

Even so, Samantha shouldn't be here, shouldn't be in danger, and yet, she trusted him to keep her safe despite everything else going on between them.

She was the reason he was doing all of this. The reason his heart slammed against his ribs with each passing second. It was doing a number on him, making him rethink every blessed choice he'd made thus far.

They moved quickly along the edge of the house, keeping to the shadows. Dean stretched his senses to the limit, cataloging each sound, each movement in the darkness. The box of documents sat tucked into Samantha's arms, physical proof that could bring down Brooks and whoever else was involved in Greta's death.

He should be the one carrying it, but opted to let her so he could keep his hands free. Lesser of two evils, but he hated that it made her a target.

"There!" A shout from behind them shattered the night. "By the patio!"

Dean grabbed Samantha's free hand. "Run."

They sprinted toward the vineyard, the neat rows of grapevines offering a labyrinth of cover. Behind them, flashlight beams cut through the darkness, bouncing wildly as their pursuers gave chase.

"Left here," Dean directed, pulling her into a row of Cabernet vines that would shield them from direct sight.

They wove through the vineyard, the vines scratching at their arms as they pushed forward. Dean calculated distances, angles, possible routes. The vineyard gift shop was too far. The processing facility was likely being watched. Their best option was to circle back toward the access road, where they might find help—if they could lose their pursuers first.

A gunshot cracked the air. Samantha flinched but kept moving.

"They're shooting at us," she hissed.

"Warning shots," Dean corrected, ducking lower between the rows. "They want the documents, not bodies. Bodies complicate things."

Another shot, closer this time. The bullet splintered a wooden trellis inches from Samantha's head.

"That didn't feel like a warning," she muttered.

Dean altered their course, pulling her down a perpendicular row to break the line of sight. The dense foliage provided momentary cover as they crouched low and caught their breath. Well, she might be able to. He wasn't sure he'd ever breathe right again after that close of a call.

"The maintenance shed is about forty yards ahead," he whispered. "We can shelter there, reassess."

Samantha nodded, clutching the evidence box tighter against her chest. Her face was composed but pale in the moonlight, her jaw set. Something fierce surged through him in a wave that threatened to consume him entirely.

He'd promised her that no one would harm her. That they'd have to go through him. He'd meant every word and still did, even if this ended with him taking another bullet, which didn't need a lot of fancy psychoanalysis for him to know that meant he'd handed her a much bigger chunk of his heart than he'd admitted even to himself.

"Ready?" he asked. "Go."

They moved again, faster now, breaking cover and sprinting toward the shadowy outline of the maintenance shed. Dean's pulse slammed into his throat. Normally, he could handle tense scenes like this, but he'd never done it with Samantha by his side.

She mattered.

The shed door yielded to his shoulder, and they stumbled inside. Dean secured the door behind them while Samantha set the box down, her breathing ragged but controlled.

"They're going to find us here," she whispered, scanning the dark interior, likely looking for something useful.

"Not our final destination. Just a place to take a breather."

Dean moved to the small window, peering through the grime-covered glass. Flashlight beams swept across the vineyard, weaving erratically as their pursuers sought them out. Two men, maybe three. Armed, but not professional mercenaries based on their movements. Brooks had hired muscle, not trained killers.

Small mercies.

"We need to split up," Samantha said out of nowhere.

Did she have a screw loose? "We absolutely do not."

As if he'd even entertain the idea of allowing her to fend for herself with armed men hunting through the darkness.

"I can create a diversion. You get the evidence to safety."

"No," he bit out. "Not happening. We stay together."

She crowded up into his space, her crossed arms bumping his chest. "This isn't up for debate, Dean. The evidence matters more than either of us."

"Not to me." His jaw flexed as they stared at each other.

She blinked first and heaved a sigh. "We don't have time for this. I know the property as well as you do. I'll head east while you go west toward the access road."

"Samantha—"

A crash against the shed door interrupted his rejection of that ridiculous idea.

They'd been found.

Dean reacted instinctively, grabbing a shovel from the wall as the door splintered inward. A large man filled the doorway, gun raised. Dean swung the shovel in a tight arc, connecting with the man's wrist. Incapacitate when possible, kill only as a last resort. The gun clattered to the floor as the man howled in pain.

"Climb!" Dean shouted, pushing Samantha toward the back window.

She scrambled through the opening, evidence box clutched against her chest. Dean fended off another lunge from their attacker, driving the shovel handle into the man's stomach before following Samantha through the window.

They hit the ground running, abandoning stealth for speed. The hillside sloped steeply ahead, offering an escape route that would be difficult to follow in the dark.

"There!" A shout from behind. Flashlight beams converging.

Another shot rang out. Dean felt something hot graze his upper arm, and his body registered the pain a half second later. Just a scratch. *Keep moving.*

The slope became steeper, treacherous in the darkness. Dean's boots slid on loose soil as he half ran, half slid down the incline. Samantha kept pace beside him, radiating determination and strength, the box awkward in her arms.

At the bottom of the hill, they found themselves in a small clearing, cornered against a rocky outcropping. Dean scanned their surroundings, looking for an escape route, but the sound of pursuit was already closing in from above.

"Give me the box," he said, turning to Samantha. "Find cover behind those rocks."

Her expression was mutinous. "I'm not leaving you."

"I'm not asking." He reached for the box, but she pulled back. "Neither am I."

The first pursuer appeared at the top of the hill, silhouetted against the night sky. They didn't have time to argue about this. Dean positioned himself between the man and Samantha, calculating angles, options.

The man descended as if he had zero experience with inclines, his focus on the box in Samantha's arms. Dean waited, timing his move. As the man reached the bottom of the hill, Dean charged, tackling him in a controlled takedown that sent them both rolling across the dirt.

The man was beefier but untrained. Dean found leverage, flipping their positions so he had the advantage. The goon struggled beneath him, a meaty fist connecting with Dean's jaw in a lucky shot that scattered stars across his vision.

Dean shook it off, pinning the man with practiced efficiency. Years of training took over as he delivered a precise strike that rendered the attacker unconscious without causing permanent damage. Clean. Professional. By the book. No bullets discharged, always his preference.

As he rose to his feet, a second man—larger than the first—appeared at the top of the hill, gun drawn. Dean evaluated distance, terrain, his options dwindling rapidly.

"Stay behind me," he told Samantha, moving to position himself between her and the new threat.

The second goon descended the slope with more caution than his partner had shown, keeping his weapon trained on Dean the entire time. Dean waited, watching for any opening, any mistake he could exploit.

"Hand over the box," the man said, voice steady. "Nobody needs to get hurt."

"Too late for that," Dean replied, nodding toward the unconscious man at his feet.

The goon's expression hardened. "Last chance."

Dean tensed, preparing to attack. The guy was too far away for a direct charge. Dean needed a distraction, something to throw off the gunman's aim for the split second he needed.

Before he could act, the man lunged forward with surprising speed—possibly under orders to leave Dean breathing, not bleeding. Dean shifted to intercept him, but his boot slipped on loose gravel. The momentary loss of balance created the advantage the goon needed.

The man's shoulder drove into Dean's midsection, sending them both crashing to the ground. Dean felt the impact jar through his bones, the wind knocked from his lungs. He twisted, seeking leverage, but the man was heavier, stronger than he'd anticipated.

A fist slammed into Dean's jaw, snapping his head back. Another blow followed, catching him in the temple. The world tilted and spun as Dean fought to maintain consciousness. He blocked the next punch, countering with a strike to the man's throat that should have ended the fight.

But the goon was either too amped up or too well trained to go down easily. He shook off the blow, wrapping massive hands around Dean's throat. Spots danced at the edges of Dean's vision as his airway constricted.

This was bad. Very bad. Dean clawed at the man's hands, trying to break his grip, but the lack of oxygen was inhibiting his movements, rendering them ineffective, less coordinated.

Then suddenly, the pressure was gone. The hands released his throat as the man's body went rigid, then collapsed to the side. Dean gasped, drawing precious air into his lungs, blinking to clear his vision.

Samantha stood over them both, a metal vineyard stake in her hands still vibrating from impact. Her expression was fierce, determined, not a trace of fear in her eyes as her gaze tracked from the unconscious goon to Dean.

"That was oddly satisfying," she said, extending her hand. "Too bad more of them haven't shown up yet. You okay?"

Dean took it, pulling himself to a sitting position as he continued to gulp air. "Been better," he managed, voice raw. "You shouldn't have done that."

Samantha's expression shifted from concern to indignation. "Oh, you're welcome, Dean. No problem, Dean. I'm happy to help knock out the bad guy who had his hands around your throat, Dean."

"You should have run. Gotten to safety." Dean pushed himself to his feet, ignoring the throbbing in his head and the burning in his throat. "He could have killed you."

"Back atcha, cowboy," she barked, her tone sharp enough to cut glass. "Or did you miss that part while you were busy being choked out?"

"I had it under control."

"Right." Samantha's eyebrow lifted in a perfect arch of skepticism. "That's why you were turning purple. My mistake."

Dean's jaw tightened. "You put yourself at risk. Unnecessarily."

"Pot, meet kettle." Samantha stepped closer, shovel still in hand, eyes blazing. "Now you know how it feels when someone you care about throws themselves into danger."

Scowling, he shook his head. "That's different. This is my job."

"Is it? Because from where I'm standing, you're far more obsessed with your mission, with Ruiz, with justice at all costs than you care about who gets hurt in the process. Including yourself." Her voice cracked slightly on the last words, revealing the raw emotion beneath her anger. "So don't lecture me about unnecessary risks when you're too busy playing Batman to see what's right in front of you."

Dean stared at her. The moonlight caught in her hair, silvered the edges of her silhouette. Even furious, even covered in dirt and holding a garden tool like a weapon, she was magnificent.

And wrong. So very wrong.

He could see clearly what was in front of him, and it was the equivalent of drowning while watching a life preserver float by that you were prohibited from grabbing.

"It doesn't matter," he muttered. "We're not dating."

"Oh yeah, right." Her expression glittered, diamond hard.

"Then that means you have even less of a right to tell me what to do. We're not a couple. I can do whatever I want."

Which was true. And made him want to punch a wall. He drew a shaky breath. "We should secure these two and get the evidence somewhere safe."

Samantha held his gaze for a long moment before nodding. "Fine."

They worked in tense silence, using zip ties from Dean's pocket to secure the unconscious men.

"You're bleeding," Samantha said, breaking the silence. She nodded toward his arm where blood had soaked through his sleeve.

"It's nothing." Dean secured the last zip tie, avoiding her gaze. "We should get moving. There could be more of them out there."

Samantha gathered the evidence box, which she'd stashed behind a rock during the confrontation. "This is your circus. I'm following you."

They moved cautiously through the vineyard, using the rows for cover as they doubled back toward the main property. Dean stayed slightly ahead, every sense hyperalert for threats. The pain in his arm had settled into a steady throb, easy to ignore. What wasn't easy to ignore was Samantha's presence at his side, the weight of her words still hanging in the air between them.

She was right about the risks he took, the single-minded focus on his mission that blinded him to everything else. But she was wrong if she thought he didn't care who got hurt. He cared. Too much. About her. About what could have happened if that goon had gotten his hands on her.

The thought made his blood run cold, and he instinctively moved closer to her, scanning the darkness for threats.

The sound of approaching sirens cut through his thoughts, red and blue lights becoming visible through the trees. Dean slowed, pointing toward the lights.

"Looks like the security system monitoring protocols finally kicked in," he said.

"Your boss," Samantha guessed, her expression lightening. "If the security system goes dark, automatic alerts go out."

"Smart woman." Dean allowed himself a small smile despite the circumstances. "Let's go meet them."

The police cars pulled up along the access road, officers spilling out with weapons drawn. Dean raised his hands slowly, positioning himself slightly in front of Samantha out of habit—a habit he should admit he'd formed because he cared what happened to her.

"Dean Carter," he called out. "And Samantha Wagner. She's the homeowner."

The officers approached cautiously. "Got a call about a breach at this address." the lead officer asked, lowering his weapon. "What happened?"

"Intruders," Dean explained, skirting the reasons why since he was still in the middle of an active investigation. "Two unconscious suspects down by the rocks. Armed. Dangerous."

As the officers took their statements and secured the scene, Dean found himself watching Samantha and the composed way she handled the questioning, the subtle strength in how she carried herself despite the ordeal. She caught him looking once, raising an eyebrow in challenge.

Look but don't touch.

He knew. He'd made his choice. It didn't stop him from being frustrated by it.

"You need stitches," she said once the officers turned their attention elsewhere, nodding toward his arm.

"It's fine."

"It's not fine. None of this is fine." She crossed her arms, irritation evident in the set of her shoulders. "Whenever you're ready to talk about how not fine it is, you let me know. Until then, I'm picking up as many metal trellis stakes as necessary. And you have no say in it."

Chapter 20

Dean's phone vibrated with Tanner's ringtone at 4:37 a.m., which normally would have earned his teammate an earful. But since sleep wouldn't be on Dean's agenda for the foreseeable future, he answered on the first ring.

"Talk to me."

"Brooks is making a move," Tanner said without preamble. "Her security detail just left her house with a convoy headed your way. Armed. Three vehicles minimum."

Dean's pulse scattered. "ETA?"

"Twenty minutes. Maybe less."

"You sure about this intel?"

"Beckett hacked her phone. She's coming for the blackmail files."

Okay, they'd have to have a conversation later about the ethics of such a thing, but for now, he needed his team. "Get back here. Now."

"Already on our way from San Antonio. Ten minutes out."

Dean ended the call and sprinted toward Samantha's bedroom, ignoring the pain radiating from the new bullet wound on his arm.

I'm picking up as many metal stakes as necessary. And you have no say in it.

He'd given up that right when he'd chosen the mission over her. When he'd told her he couldn't do both. This investigation might have been wrapped up sooner if he'd kept his focus, a sin he'd never forgive himself for.

The blackmail evidence had been right under Dean's nose this entire time.

And now he had to disrupt Samantha and her life once again because he'd crossed lines he shouldn't have. But he'd do anything in his power to keep her safe from a woman who'd already killed once and wouldn't hesitate to do so again.

He knocked sharply, three times. No answer. He knocked again, louder. "Samantha!"

The door swung open. She stood there in sleep shorts and an oversized T-shirt, hair tousled, eyes instantly alert despite the early hour. His heart sucked up the sight of her, greedily gathering up bits of her to hold close, because this was all he got. This distance and the cold reality of the job.

"What's wrong?"

"Brooks is coming. Armed convoy. We have maybe fifteen minutes." The words came out clipped, professional. "I need to get you somewhere safe."

To his surprise, she nodded without argument. "Let me change."

"Two minutes."

She disappeared back into her room while Dean took up position in the hallway, already mapping defensive positions, exit routes, contingencies. His tactical mind clicked through options with cold precision even as another part of him ached with every breath.

Samantha emerged exactly ninety seconds later wearing jeans and a dark T-shirt, hair pulled back in a practical ponytail with sneakers on her feet. Ready, and under the wire too, as if she got that it mattered to him that she cooperated.

Emotions slammed up against the wall of his principles like a bird desperate to escape a cage. He was so far gone over this woman that he couldn't stave off the flood of his feelings when it counted. Or ever.

"What's the plan?" she asked, all business.

"Tanner and Beckett are inbound. Ten minutes. Local backup will take longer. The evidence is in the safe, but they don't know that, so we're going to establish defensive positions outside Greta's office."

She scurried along with him, doing her best to keep up as he strode toward the study where the blackmail files were locked in the safe. "You want to set up an ambush."

"I want to control the engagement," he corrected. "On our terms."

Their eyes met in the dim hallway, and she nodded once. Whatever personal complications existed outside this moment, within it, they were aligned.

She was utterly amazing. And she was it for him. How could any other woman ever compare?

"Where do you need me?" she asked.

"Safe room."

Her expression hardened. "I'm not hiding while you face off against Brooks and her thugs."

"Samantha—"

"No." She crossed her arms. "Not negotiable, Dean. This is my home. My aunt. My fight."

So fierce. Samantha was a fighter at her core. Like him. It was what he'd respected about her from the beginning, whether he'd admitted it or not. What had made him fall for her. Did he really expect her to morph into someone different?

"Fine," he conceded. "But you follow my lead. Stay behind cover at all times. If I say move, you move. No questions."

"Deal."

They reached the office as headlights swept across the windows from the driveway.

"They're early," he muttered. "We need to get into position."

The sound of vehicles pulling up outside spurred them into action. Dean led Samantha through the house toward the kitchen where the best defensive position offered both cover and clear sightlines to the approaching threat.

"Get down," he instructed, positioning her behind the granite island as he drew his weapon. "Stay there."

For once, she listened, crouching low as Dean took up a position by the doorway. The distant sound of car doors slamming echoed through the predawn silence.

The door connecting the house to the garage opened, revealing Tanner and Beckett, weapons drawn, moving with the silent efficiency of men who'd done this countless times before.

"Three vehicles," Tanner reported in a hushed tone. "Six hostiles minimum. Brooks is in the lead car."

She'd come herself. That was a wrinkle Dean hadn't seen coming, but he understood the mayor's logic. Don't leave the critical tasks to someone else. The evidence box contained life-ending materials—proof of embezzlement, altered building permits, misappropriated city funds. Enough to destroy the mayor's career and send her to prison for years.

And they'd had no time to make copies of anything.

"Heavily armed?" Dean asked.

"Poorly armed," Beckett corrected. "Hired muscle. Not professionals."

Dean nodded, plans crystallizing. "Tanner, take the east side. Beckett, west. I'll cover the main entrance. We contain them in the foyer, control the engagement."

They moved without question, each taking up their assigned positions with fluid precision. The sense of operating as a coordinated unit rather than three guys who happened to show up at the same time settled over Dean with surprising comfort.

Samantha watched from her position, eyes tracking his movements. "What about me?" she whispered.

"You stay behind cover," Dean replied firmly. "But—" he

pulled his backup weapon from his ankle holster and passed it to her. It was better than the alternative "—just in case."

She accepted the gun with steady hands. "I know how to use this."

"I figured." Something like a smile touched his lips despite the tension. "Goes with your warrior costume."

A crash from the front of the house cut the moment short. The distinctive sound of a door being forced open, which didn't take as much effort as it normally would, given that it was a temporary from the first round of goons.

"Defensive positions," Dean ordered through the comms. "Nonlethal takedowns if possible."

"Copy that," Tanner's voice registered in his ear.

"Understood," came Beckett's cool acknowledgment.

Heavy footsteps moved through the entry hall, accompanied by the metallic sounds of weapons being readied. Dean signaled for absolute silence as he tracked the intruders' movements by sound alone.

"Find the files," a woman's voice commanded—Mayor Brooks, no question. "And find Wagner. I want to look her in the eyes when she realizes she's lost."

Dean caught Samantha's gaze across the kitchen, saw her jaw tighten at the threat. He shook his head a fraction. The last thing he needed was Samantha forcing a confrontation.

The intruders split up, moving through the house with the awkward enthusiasm of amateurs playing at being professional. Dean counted footsteps—three heading toward the study, two toward the living room, Brooks and one guard remaining in the foyer.

Perfect.

Dean pressed his comm once, the signal to engage. In synchronized movements, the team sprang into action. Tanner neutralized the two men in the living room with controlled efficiency, evidenced by a muffled thud then the sound of zip ties being secured. Beckett intercepted the group heading for the study, his ice-cold precision making short work of opponents who'd never faced a true professional.

Dean moved toward the foyer, weapon drawn but controlled. This was about containment, not elimination. Justice, not vengeance.

He rounded the corner to find Brooks standing in the center of the grand entryway, her hired muscle nervously scanning for threats. Even in the predawn light, Dean could see the desperation etched into the mayor's features.

"That's far enough, Brooks," Dean called out, emerging from cover with his weapon trained.

The guard swung his gun around, reactionary and wild, while Brooks seized the moment of distraction. She knocked a heavy vase from a nearby table, sending it crashing toward Dean. He dodged, but the movement gave the guard time to get oriented, pointing his weapon at Dean.

Dean sprang low, surprising the other guy into dropping his gun. They grappled for it, which caused Dean to have to holster his own weapon or risk losing it. The goon was bigger, heavier, but moved with the uncoordinated aggression of someone who relied on size rather than technique.

Dean twisted, using the man's momentum against him. A precise strike to the solar plexus, followed by a sweeping leg maneuver, and the guard went down hard.

But Brooks hadn't stayed still. She'd retrieved the dropped gun and now aimed it with trembling hands.

"I'll take those files now," she hissed, fury distorting her features.

Dean raised his hands slowly, calculating angles, distances, risks. "It's over, Brooks. The files are secured in a place you can't get to them, and they tell a very damaging tale. The evidence on the water rights. Coercion. Thompson talking to the authorities."

"Lies," she spat, calculation flickering in her eyes. "You have nothing."

The guard groaned, trying to rise. Dean kicked him back down without taking his eyes off Brooks. Where were Tanner and Beckett? They should have heard the commotion.

"Put down the gun," Dean said, voice level despite the adrenaline coursing through him. "You're only making this worse."

"Worse?" Brooks's laugh held an edge of hysteria. "Wagner was going to destroy everything I'd built. Years of work. My legacy. She deserved what happened to her. No one can win against me. I have too much power."

Something dark and familiar unfurled in Dean's chest. This woman had killed Greta. Had ordered Samantha to be killed. Had sent armed men to terrorize her in her own home. And now she stood there, weapon in hand, the same smug certainty he'd seen on Ruiz's face in that courtroom.

The same certainty that the system would fail. That she'd walk free.

Time seemed to slow as Dean assessed his options. The guard was down but not out. Brooks was armed but untrained. One clean move and he could disarm her. But something else whispered in the back of his mind—a darker impulse, born of bullet scars and courtroom betrayals.

One wrong move from Brooks. One justifiable response from him. It would be so easy to ensure she never threatened Samantha again. To make certain that this time, justice wasn't bought off or buried in procedural technicalities.

His muscles coiled, ready to spring.

But then an image flashed through his mind—Samantha staring at him with disdain as she told him she'd thought he was better than this, that he'd certainly maintained his hard lines when it came to her, but not in this?

He wanted to do better. Be something beyond vengeance.

Emerge beyond the darkness that had driven him since the hospital.

Dean drew a deep breath. "Last chance, Brooks. Put it down."

She hesitated, desperation warring with self-preservation.

In that moment of indecision, Dean moved, not with lethal intent, but with controlled precision. He closed the distance in two swift strides, deflecting the weapon upward as it discharged harmlessly into the ceiling. His hand clamped around her wrist, applying pressure to the nerve cluster there until her fingers released their grip on the gun.

Brooks twisted, clawing at his face with her free hand, but Dean had already pivoted, using her momentum to bring her to the ground in a controlled takedown. Not excessive. Not vengeful. Clean. Professional. By the book. As it should be.

His conscience was clear.

As he secured her wrists behind her back, Tanner and Beckett burst into the foyer, weapons drawn.

"Took you long enough," Dean muttered, breathing hard from the exertion.

"Had our hands full," Tanner replied, surveying the scene with raised eyebrows. "Looks like you did too."

Dean rose to his feet, ignoring the throb in his arm where the wound oozed new blood. "Secure them both."

"Got it," Tanner acknowledged, taking custody of the still-dazed guard.

Beckett approached Brooks with cold efficiency. "Mayor Brooks. You and I are going to have a conversation."

Brooks glared up at him, defiance written across her features. "I have nothing to say to you."

The corner of Beckett's mouth lifted in what might have been a smile on anyone else. On him, it looked predatory. "You'd be surprised how much people say to me, Madam Mayor. Let's get started, shall we?"

As Beckett zip-tied Brooks to a chair, Tanner caught Dean's eye. "You okay? Looks like you took a hit."

Dean shook his head, dismissing the concern. "I'm fine."

But he wasn't. Not really. Not when he'd come so close to crossing a line he'd always sworn to respect. Justice, not vengeance. Law, not vigilantism. The very principles that had defined his career as a Ranger.

Principles he'd nearly abandoned in that moment when Brooks had stood before him, gun in hand, threatening everything—everyone—he cared about.

Movement behind him made him tense, but he recognized the light footsteps. Samantha, ignoring his direct order to stay put. Of course.

"I told you to stay back," he muttered as she approached, his backup weapon held at her side.

"And miss all this?" she replied quietly, surveying the aftermath of the confrontation. "Not a chance."

Her gaze swept over him, assessing, cataloging. "You're bleeding."

Dean glanced at the spreading stain on his sleeve. "It's nothing."

"It's not nothing," she countered, but didn't press further. Instead, her eyes held his, something unspoken passing between them. "Did she confess?"

"Not yet," Tanner replied. "But she will. Beckett has a way with interrogations."

That sounded like something else Dean might need to get in front of. Soon.

Beckett approached Brooks with a tablet in hand.

"I think you'll want to see this," he said to her, flashing the screen in her direction, voice so cool it could give Jack Frost a run for his money. "Security footage from City Hall. The night Greta died."

Dean glanced at the screen over Brooks's shoulder, where

grainy footage showed the mayor and Mike Thompson in what appeared to be an intense conversation. The time stamp matched the night of Greta's death.

"Where did you get this?" Dean asked.

"City Hall security archives," Beckett replied with a slight shrug. "Amazing what people forget to delete."

Dean turned to Brooks, who had gone pale at the sight of the footage. "Want to explain, Madam Mayor?"

Her composure cracked. "It wasn't supposed to happen like that," she whispered. "Mike was just supposed to scare her, get the files. But she fought back. Had a heart condition none of us knew about."

"So you covered it up," Dean concluded. "Made it look like natural causes."

Brooks said nothing, but her silence was confirmation enough.

"Get it all," Dean said to Beckett, who was already recording the confession on his tablet.

"Working on it," Beckett replied, his tone shifting to something colder, more intimidating as he stepped closer to Brooks. "Let's talk about Mike Thompson. Your relationship. The timeline. Every detail. Now."

Dean had never seen Beckett's interrogation techniques up close, but within minutes, the mayor was spilling everything— dates, times, accomplices, the entire conspiracy laid bare under the relentless pressure of Beckett's questioning. Precision and psychology and a unique blend of physical intimidation. Clinical and effective.

Tanner caught Dean's eye, an impressed expression on his face. "Clean operation," he murmured. "By the book. We don't do that too often in the Shadow Rangers."

"Maybe not," Dean said, "but it's who I am."

"Even if it costs you a spot on Strickland's team?" Tanner asked quietly.

The question hit home. Strickland had been clear from the beginning—this audition was Dean's shot at Ruiz, at vengeance for the bullet in his side and the justice system that had failed him. Strickland wanted operators who could work in gray areas, who would do whatever was necessary to get results.

"Some things matter more," Dean replied. Even if it meant he'd failed the test.

"That's no lie," Tanner said with a nod. "Living in the shadows is a tough life. We need someone to help us remember where the light is."

Local law enforcement arrived twenty minutes later, taking custody of Brooks and her hired muscle. The sun was breaking over the horizon as the convoy of police vehicles pulled away from Wagner Wines, carrying with them the woman responsible for Greta's death and the attacks on Samantha.

Dean found Samantha standing on the front porch watching the last cruiser disappear down the long driveway.

"Thank you," she said quietly, "for finding out the truth about Greta."

"I was just doing my job," he replied automatically, then winced at how hollow the words sounded.

Everything unsaid hung between them, and he wanted to draw her into his arms, to hold on with the knowledge that the mission was over and they could move on to something new and exciting between them.

But he didn't.

"We should get inside," he said instead. "The team will handle the rest of the processing."

Samantha studied him for a long moment before nodding. "If that's what needs to come next."

As they walked back into the house, dawn fully breaking over the Texas hills, Dean realized something profound had shifted within him during this operation. Without conscious intent, he'd stepped naturally into the role of leader. Made crucial decisions that reflected not just tactical necessity but moral clarity. Guided his team through a clean, by-the-book takedown when personal vengeance might have been easier.

And in the moment Brooks had threatened Samantha, he'd placed her safety above all else. Above the mission. Above procedure. Above everything.

The same choice Jake had made with Aubrey.

Dean's hand unconsciously moved to his side, to the bullet scar that had defined his existence for so long. The injury that had crystallized his resentment toward Jake, toward love, toward anything that compromised the mission.

But what if Jake hadn't been wrong? What if protecting someone you cared about wasn't weakness, but strength?

He'd told Strickland his audition was all about getting a shot at Ruiz. About justice at any cost. But standing here now, watching Samantha walk away from him because of the boundaries he'd insisted upon, Dean realized the cost wasn't just high. It was immeasurable.

And the lines he'd drawn so carefully—the ones that had kept him isolated, focused solely on vengeance—suddenly seemed to be in all the wrong places.

Chapter 21

Dean gripped the steering wheel of his truck and watched the Texas Hill Country blur past his window. The drive to Strickland's compound had never felt longer. Alfred sprawled in the passenger seat, head resting on his paws, occasionally glancing at Dean as if sensing his inner turmoil.

"It's fine," Dean told the dog, who responded with a skeptical ear twitch. "Worst case, we walk away. Not like we haven't done that before."

Alfred huffed, clearly unimpressed by the pep talk.

Truth was, Dean wasn't fine. The operation at Wagner Wines had wrapped up neatly—Brooks in custody, full confession secured, evidence boxed and cataloged. By all metrics, a successful mission.

Except for one detail: Dean hadn't played by Strickland's rules.

He'd chosen by-the-book procedure over gray-area tactics. Restrained Brooks rather than letting his desire for justice veer into vengeance. Operated within strict moral boundaries when crossing them might have been more expedient.

In short, he'd failed the audition.

Which meant no place on Strickland's team. No shot at Ruiz. No chance to finally close the chapter that had defined his existence since waking up in that hospital bed with a bullet in his side and betrayal burning in his gut.

Dean's fingers tightened on the wheel as he turned onto the unmarked road leading to Strickland's fortress. The security gate opened automatically, recognizing his truck. His stomach clenched as he pulled into the circular drive, rehearsing what to say.

Honestly, there was no point in that. He had no idea how to live inside his own skin right now, let alone how to explain that nothing made sense anymore, especially not the rest of his life.

The bullet scar on his side ached, a reminder of everything that had led him here. But for the first time since the shooting, the ache felt different. Less like an accusation. More like a marker of the man he'd been, not the man he'd become.

Alfred nudged his arm as he cut the engine. "All right, buddy. Wait here."

The dog settled back in the seat with a sigh that sounded suspiciously like judgment.

Strickland opened the door before Dean could knock, as if he'd been watching from the window. His silver hair caught the morning light, his gray eyes as sharp as they'd been during Dean's Ranger days.

"Carter." The older man's expression gave nothing away. "Come in."

Dean followed Strickland through the imposing house to his office, mentally cataloging the high-tech security measures, the subtle reinforcements, the strategic layout—all the things he'd been too overwhelmed to fully appreciate during his first visit.

When they reached the office, Strickland gestured to one of the leather chairs. This time, he took the seat behind his desk, establishing a clear power dynamic. Dean tried not to read too much into it.

"Report," Strickland said, leaning back.

Dean outlined the operation with clinical precision, walking through each decision point, each tactical choice, each outcome.

He didn't embellish or downplay. Just facts. When he reached the moment of Brooks's takedown, he paused.

"I had an opportunity for a more expedient conclusion," Dean said carefully. "I chose restraint. Clean arrest. By the book."

Strickland's expression remained unreadable. "And why is that?"

"Because crossing that line wouldn't have been justice. It would have been vengeance." Dean met his former mentor's gaze squarely. "I didn't join the Rangers to be a vigilante. I don't intend to become one now."

Silence stretched between them, broken only by the soft ticking of an antique clock on the bookshelf. Dean refused to look away first.

"You know," Strickland said finally, "most men who come through that door would be scrambling to justify every choice, spinning a narrative about how they did exactly what they thought I wanted."

"Not interested in mind-reading games," Dean replied. "I made my calls. I stand by them."

A slow smile spread across Strickland's face. "And that, Dean Carter, is exactly why you passed."

Dean blinked, his prepared response dying on his tongue. "What?"

"You think I'm building a team of trigger-happy cowboys who'll cross any line to get results?" Strickland shook his head. "I need leaders who know where the lines are. Who can operate in gray areas without losing sight of what separates us from the people we hunt."

Dean struggled to process the words as everything he thought he was doing here shifted. "But you said—"

"I said this team operates differently than traditional law enforcement. That sometimes effectiveness matters more than strict protocol." Strickland leaned forward. "I didn't say we abandon our principles. I'm not running the Avengers, son. I'm building something with accountability."

"So this was all...what? A test to see if I'd cross the line?"

"A test to see if you knew which lines couldn't be crossed," Strickland corrected. "And you passed with flying colors."

Dean's thoughts raced, reevaluating every conversation, every instruction from a completely different angle. "What about Beckett and Tanner? Their methods aren't exactly straight-arrow."

"Each member brings different strengths. Different perspectives." Strickland's expression grew serious. "Beckett's interrogation techniques might push boundaries, but he never crosses into territory that compromises a case. Tanner bends rules but doesn't break laws. You—" he pointed at Dean "—you're their moral compass. The one who keeps the operation anchored when waters get muddy."

"So, I didn't fail the audition," Dean said slowly.

Strickland shook his head. "Not only did you not fail, you exceeded every expectation. Taking down Brooks cleanly, securing admissible evidence, leading a coordinated team operation while maintaining clear ethical boundaries? That's exactly why I wanted you. And why you're the right leader for this team."

Dean couldn't quite wrap his head around this conversation. What it meant. "Ruiz isn't off the table, then."

"Ruiz will face justice," Strickland said with a decisive nod. "That's what I promised you. You'll get your shot, Dean."

It was everything he'd been working toward, handed to him on a silver platter. All he'd had to do was give up everything. Was that why this victory felt so...hollow?

What was *wrong* with him? Maybe he was just tired. The case had taken a lot out of him.

"I'll take that shot. When I'm healed up," Dean said, gesturing to his arm, still bandaged from the operation.

Strickland studied him. "You sure you're ready? You've been

carrying that vendetta a long time. Might be healthier to let another operative handle it."

"I'm sure." And he didn't even choke on it. The burning need for justice hadn't waned, but he could separate himself from the dispensation of it. Like he had with Brooks. Things would be different this time, and he was finally in a place where he could accept that. "But it needs to be later. Much later. After I've worked out a few more things."

It was step one of a thousand to get to a place where he could stand in front of Samantha as a man who deserved her.

Strickland nodded, apparently satisfied. "Welcome to the team, Carter."

Dean extended his hand, and Strickland clasped it firmly. As they shook, Dean felt as if he were stepping across a threshold. Not abandoning his past, but moving beyond it. Carrying forward the lessons instead of the burdens.

"There's one more thing," Strickland said as Dean turned to leave. "Your approach to the Wagner case. It was unorthodox."

Dean tensed. "Meaning?"

"Meaning most operatives don't fall for their suspects." Strickland's tone was neutral, but his eyes missed nothing. "Or move in with them. Or prioritize their safety above all else."

Heat flooded Dean's neck. "She wasn't the perpetrator."

"No, she wasn't. But she was a complication." Strickland leaned back, studying him. "In your report, you mentioned making certain choices to protect Ms. Wagner. That those choices sometimes delayed progress on the actual investigation."

There was no point denying it. "Yes."

"Yet you never mentioned a relationship in your updates."

Dean shifted his weight. "It's complicated."

"Most worthwhile things are." Strickland's expression softened into something Dean rarely saw—genuine concern. "You know, when Jake chose Aubrey, I thought you'd never forgive

him. Never understand why someone would prioritize a relationship over the mission."

The bullet scar throbbed again. "I didn't."

"And now?"

A flood of Samantha washed through his soul. The way she
looked at him first thing in the morning. At midnight. When
she was standing toe-to-toe with him, refusing to back down.
How she felt in his arms. The way she'd *seen* him from the
very beginning.

"I think," Dean murmured, "that I owe Jake an apology."

"You might owe yourself one too."

That hit him right between the eyes. He took it without
flinching and let the idea roll around a bit before he nodded
once. Maybe Strickland had a point.

"Think about it," Strickland said, turning back to his desk
in dismissal. "We'll talk soon about your official onboarding."

Dean left the office, his mind in a swirl. When he reached
his truck, Alfred greeted him with an expectant thump of his
tail against the seat.

"Change of plans, buddy," Dean said, sliding behind the
wheel. "We've got a stop to make."

The ranch house hadn't changed much in the year since Dean
had last seen it. White limestone exterior gleaming in the Texas
sun, oak trees providing dappled shade across the broad front
porch. The only new addition was a wooden swing that hung
from the thickest branch of the sprawling live oak in the yard.

Dean sat in his truck for a full five minutes, gripping the
steering wheel.

"This is stupid," he told Alfred, who offered no opinion beyond a slow blink. "What am I even going to say? 'Hey, Jake,
sorry I ghosted you after you got married to the woman you
risked everything for. My bad.'"

Alfred's ears twitched.

"Fine." Dean sighed. "But if this goes sideways, we're getting drive-through and you're not sharing my fries."

The threat appeared to have zero impact. Dean climbed out of the truck, his boots crunching on the gravel driveway. Alfred hopped down after him, immediately investigating the unfamiliar territory with his nose to the ground.

Dean had barely reached the porch steps when the front door swung open. Jake Dalton stood there quietly watching him. Jake—his former partner, his former best friend, the man he'd mentally labeled as traitor for the better part of a year.

Jake looked good. Rested. The permanent crease between his brows that came from years on the force had softened. His hair was longer, and he'd traded the uniform for worn jeans and a faded T-shirt.

For a long moment, they stared at each other. Then Jake's face broke into a grin that contained equal parts disbelief and welcome.

"Well, I'll be danged," Jake said. "Dean Carter on my front porch. Is the apocalypse happening and nobody told me?"

Dean's rehearsed speech evaporated.

"Got a dog," he said instead, gesturing to Alfred, who had abandoned his investigation to sit politely at Dean's side.

Jake's eyebrows shot up. "That's what brought you out of exile? Wanting to show off your dog?"

"No." Dean scrubbed a hand over the back of his neck. "I've been...working through some things."

"I gathered." Jake stepped back, holding the door open. "You want to work through them inside? Aubrey made iced tea."

The casual mention of her name sent a jolt through Dean's system, but not the anger he'd expected. Just a dull ache, like prodding a bruise that was nearly healed.

He nodded, following Jake into the house with Alfred trotting at his heels.

The interior was cozy, lived-in, with gleaming hardwood

floors and comfortable furniture. Photos lined the walls: Jake with his family, Jake and Aubrey on their wedding day, Jake kneeling next to a horse, his arm around the shoulders of a teenage boy.

"Aubrey's at the store," Jake said, leading Dean to the kitchen. "She'll be sorry she missed you."

Dean doubted that. The last time he'd seen Aubrey had been in the hospital after the shooting, and he hadn't exactly been charitable about Jake's divided focus.

Jake poured two glasses of tea, sliding one across the counter to Dean before settling onto a barstool.

"So," he said, studying Dean over the rim of his glass, "you going to tell me what brings you here after radio silence for a year? Or are we going to play twenty questions?"

Dean took a long swallow of tea, buying time. "I've been working a case. For Strickland."

Jake's surprise lifted his brows. "Joseph Strickland? Our former boss who disappeared into the sunset with no explanation? That Strickland?"

"He's formed a new unit. Special ops, but with...flexibility."

"Huh." Jake absorbed this. "And he recruited you. That tracks."

"I just finished my audition case."

"Did you pass?"

Dean met his former partner's gaze. "Yeah. But not how I thought I would."

Jake nodded, waiting. One of the things that had made them good partners was Jake's patience, his willingness to let Dean find his way to the words in his own time.

"The case involved a vineyard owner. A woman named Samantha." Dean rotated his glass, watching condensation trail down the sides. "I was supposed to be investigating her aunt's death. Ended up protecting her from the same threat."

"And?"

"And I realized something." Dean looked up, meeting Jake's steady gaze. "I owe you an apology."

Jake's face registered genuine surprise. "For?"

"For not understanding. About Aubrey. About choices." Dean's hand drifted to his side, to the bullet scar. "For blaming you when Ruiz shot me."

The words hung in the air between them, heavy with months of unspoken resentment.

"You had every right to be angry," Jake said quietly. "I wasn't there when you needed me."

"No, you weren't. Because you were protecting Aubrey." Dean drew a deep breath. "And I would have done the same thing if it had been Samantha."

Jake's eyebrows lifted at the admission. "Sounds like this vineyard owner made quite an impression."

"She's…" Dean searched for words that could possibly encapsulate Samantha Wagner. "Independent. Stubborn. Brilliant. Drives me absolutely crazy."

"And where is she now?"

"Back at the vineyard. Probably fighting with her staff or battling spreadsheets or planning world domination."

"But not with you."

"No." Dean's grip tightened on his glass. "I told her I couldn't do both. The job and whatever was happening between us."

"Ah." Jake's expression held familiar recognition. "Look, I get it. The job becomes your identity. The badge, the mission, the black-and-white clarity of it all. It's addictive. Safe, in its own way. Easier than dealing with the messy reality of caring about someone."

"It's not just that." Dean set his glass down. "I spent months hating you for choosing Aubrey over the job. For not being there."

"And that changed?"

"Now I understand. She was your line in the sand. The thing

that mattered more than procedures or protocols or even justice."

Jake nodded, a small smile playing at the corners of his mouth. "Guess we both learned something, then. Because after you got shot, I spent months hating myself for the same reason. For not being there. For letting my personal feelings affect my professional judgment."

"But you don't regret your choice."

"Not for a second." Jake's voice carried absolute certainty. "I regret that you got hurt. I hate that Ruiz walked. But choosing Aubrey? That was the right call. Always will be."

Dean absorbed this, turning the words over in his mind. "Strickland told me I passed the audition because I didn't cross certain lines. Because I knew where the boundaries were."

"Sounds like Strickland. And you."

"But I'm starting to think I've been drawing those lines in all the wrong places."

Jake's expression softened. "The job gives you a framework. Clear rules. Defined objectives. Life's messier. Relationships especially. No tactical manual for those."

"So, how do you know?" Dean asked, the question bubbling up from some deep well of uncertainty. "How do you know when it's worth the risk?"

"You don't." Jake shrugged. "You just ask yourself what you're more afraid of—taking the chance and maybe failing, or walking away and never knowing what might have been."

The second one. Definitely.

"I should get going," Dean said, glancing at his watch. "Long drive back."

"To the vineyard?" Jake asked, the question weighted with meaning beyond its simplicity.

Dean met his former partner's gaze. "Yeah. To the vineyard."

Dean whistled for Alfred, who had made himself comfortable on Jake's porch as if he belonged there. The dog trotted after him, tail wagging contentedly.

As Dean drove away from the ranch, the weight that had sat on his chest for months felt lighter. Not gone entirely—he still had a whole lot of groveling ahead of him, assuming Samantha would even let him through the door—but transformed into something manageable. Something that no longer defined him.

He glanced at Alfred, who looked supremely satisfied with the day's developments. "One stop down. One to go."

The dog's tail thumped against the seat in apparent approval as Dean pointed the truck toward Fredericksburg. Toward Wagner Wines. Toward Samantha.

To the woman who had redrawn all his lines.

Chapter 22

Samantha stared at the email draft on her screen, cursor blinking at the end of a sentence that had taken thirty minutes to craft.

I'm writing to ask if you'd consider taking back your previous position of General Manager at Wagner Wines, effective immediately.

Simple enough. Twenty words that shouldn't require multiple revisions and half an hour of overthinking. Yet here she was, mentally rewriting a job offer as if it were a multi-million-dollar proposal.

Because in many ways, it was.

Ben Hawthorne had been the backbone of Wagner Wines before her arrival. The man who'd walked out the door the moment she'd stepped in with her corporate buzzwords and designer heels. Bringing him back meant admitting something she'd spent her entire career trying to prove otherwise—that she couldn't do it all herself.

Her cursor hovered over the salary field. She'd already entered a figure double what the vineyard's financial records showed he'd been making. Corporate Strategy 101: when you need talent badly enough, overpay.

"This is ridiculous," she muttered to the empty office. "Send the email."

But her finger refused to click. Because this wasn't just about rehiring a competent GM. It was about stepping back herself. Admitting that running a vineyard wasn't her area of expertise after all.

It felt like failure.

Excellence equals worth. Period.

The old mantra whispered through her mind, unbidden and unwelcome. A relic from childhood that had driven her through college, through corporate ranks, through boardroom battles. Always pushing, striving, proving.

And where had it gotten her? Alone in an eight-thousand-square-foot house, pretending to know something about viticulture while her heart ached for a man who'd walked away because she didn't fit into his black-and-white worldview.

She hit Send before she could talk herself out of it again.

The ping of confirmation seemed to echo in the empty house. Done. No take-backs. Ben would either accept or laugh in her face, but the decision was made. Wagner Wines needed his expertise more than it needed her ego at the helm.

About an hour after sending the email, Ben appeared at her door, as if materializing out of thin air. Their conversation was brief but productive. He accepted the position with no hesitation and agreed to start the next morning. It felt a little like he'd been waiting in the wings for that inevitable moment when she hit rock bottom. Or possibly doubling his salary had been her ace in the hole. Either way, she could check off the first stage of her new strategy.

After he left, Samantha stood at the window overlooking the vineyard. The northeast field was still a charred wasteland, but Jules had already marked out areas for replanting. The vineyard would recover.

She needed to be more like those vines—adaptable, resilient, able to grow in difficult conditions.

Her phone buzzed with a text from Carlos.

Delivery of new barrels arrived. Wrong specs. Need approval for additional expenditure to get correct ones.

A week ago, she'd have marched down to the processing facility, demanded to see the purchase order, interrogated the delivery driver and micromanaged the reorder process. Today she simply replied: Defer to Jules. She knows what we need.

Three dots appeared, then disappeared, then reappeared. Finally, he sent a thumbs-up emoji.

Carlos was probably having a stroke at her hands-off approach. Good. Let him adjust to the new normal.

A distinctive rumble rose from the road, and her soul recognized it instantly—a Ford Raptor engine. Dean's truck.

Her stomach dropped like an elevator with cut cables. She wasn't prepared for this. Hadn't constructed the perfect speech about how completely fine she was without him. Hadn't built up enough scar tissue to face him without revealing how much his rejection had gutted her.

"Perfect timing as always, Carter," she muttered, automatically smoothing her hair and adjusting her posture to project confidence she didn't feel. "Catch me when I'm completely off-balance."

She'd spent the last three days mentally rehearsing different versions of this inevitable crossing of paths, but it would definitely go something like this: a dignified acknowledgment that their paths had diverged, then a coolly composed farewell appropriate for a brief professional entanglement.

But now that the moment had arrived, all of it drained from her head in favor of a chaos storm that gripped her heart and wouldn't let go.

Why was he here? The mayor was in custody. The case was closed. There was no professional reason for this visit.

Obviously, he'd come to pack whatever belongings he'd left behind. To sever the last tenuous threads connecting them. It was the kind of thing he'd do.

The truck rolled to a stop, dust billowing around the tires. She watched as Dean climbed out, followed by Alfred, who bounded across the gravel like he'd been cooped up too long. Dean, on the other hand, moved with purpose, a mission on his mind, that battered Stetson perched at an angle on his head.

She took a half a second to wallow in the way her soul leaped, straining toward the magnificence of Dean Carter in the flesh, instead of the poor substitute of her memory. She'd like to say she hadn't thought about him, that she was too busy slaying it to worry about some guy who'd been a flash in her pan.

But the cantata her pulse was currently playing said otherwise.

She should retreat to her office. Lock the door. Send Carlos or Jules to deal with whatever Dean needed. Protect the fragile armor she'd rebuilt around her heart.

Instead, she found herself flying toward the front door, pulled by some invisible force that overrode everything, including her own good sense. At the end of the day, she apparently couldn't resist the gravitational pull of Dean Carter.

She reached the porch as Dean approached the steps, Alfred racing ahead to greet her with joyful barks. The dog's simple affection was a knife-twist of irony—here was part of the Carter package, unreservedly happy to see her, while the man himself had drawn lines she evidently couldn't cross.

"Hi," Dean said, the single syllable vibrating against her rib cage.

"Hi." She crossed her arms, instinctively shielding her heart. Her voice emerged with the polished composure she'd perfected in a thousand high-stakes negotiations, betraying none of the turmoil beneath. "This is a surprise."

It wasn't entirely a lie. They were done. He'd made that clear enough that she'd assumed the next time she'd see him would be months later, maybe at some chance encounter in Fredericksburg, where they'd exchange polite nods before hurrying in opposite directions.

"How did it go with Strickland?" she asked, figuring that was safe enough conversational territory.

"Better than expected." Dean climbed the first step, Alfred circling his legs with exuberant energy. "I passed the audition."

"Congratulations." The word emerged with professional polish—cool, collected, appropriate. As if they were discussing a promotion rather than the mission that had defined his existence. As if her heart weren't splintering all over again at the confirmation that he had his path now, and it led away from her.

This *was* goodbye. He was taking himself and Alfred away from her, and it shouldn't sting as much as it did.

"Thanks." He looked up at her, something flickering in his eyes that made her pulse skip. "I also went to see Jake."

That caught her entirely off guard. "Your former partner? The one who—"

"Chose Aubrey over the job. Yeah." Dean took another step up. "I needed to apologize."

Apologize? "For?"

"For not understanding his choice." Another step closer. "For judging him when he prioritized someone he cared about over the mission."

He was so close now that Samantha's heartbeat stuttered. Faltered. Raced ahead. "And did he accept your apology?"

"He did." Dean reached the top step, close enough that she could smell the faint traces of sunshine clinging to his skin and something else that belonged wholly to this man. "He's happy, Samantha. With Aubrey. With the life they've built."

She nodded, a mechanical response while her brain scrambled to process what was happening. Why was he telling her this? Was he simply sharing a professional update? Tying up loose ends before his final departure?

All her corporate training, all her years of projecting confidence in executive meetings failed her in the face of Dean. How he commanded the space around him, compelled her to be drawn into his circle.

She backed up, a reflexive self-protection. This man had rejected her, and all she could think about was flinging herself into his arms, knowing he would catch her. Wanting him to catch her like he'd done so many times in the past.

But would he? He'd shattered her ability to believe that when he walked away. When he decided she didn't fit into his world.

"I'm glad Jake's doing well," she said, her voice deliberately neutral as she put another step of distance between them. "Is that what brought you back? You wanted me to know you reconciled? That's great, Dean. It's a huge step for you."

"That's not all," he said, watching her retreat but making no move to stop her. "I came to talk to you."

"About what? I think we said everything that needed saying." The edge in her voice didn't quaver, thankfully. "Your case is closed. You got your spot on Strickland's team. Mission accomplished."

Dean flinched, his eyes shutting for a beat. "It turns out that wasn't the only thing I wanted."

What was he saying? That he had his big meeting with Strickland and then realized everything wasn't peachy keen? "You made your choice, Dean. You chose your mission over the very real relationship that bloomed between us. You drew your line and I didn't make the cut. I get it."

"That's why I'm here," he said, reaching out, then stopping when she tensed. "Because I was wrong."

She lifted her chin, impressed that he at least led with the right sentiment—a man admitting he was wrong always earned lots of points. "Wrong about what? The case? Your mission? Or just your assessment of me?"

"All of it." His voice roughened. "I've been thinking about lines. About the ones worth keeping and the ones I drew for all the wrong reasons."

"And?" She wouldn't make this easy. Couldn't. Not when the memory of his rejection was still so fresh.

"And I think I've been an idiot."

The bluntness of it caught her off guard, puncturing her defensive posture. "That's…not going to earn you an argument from me."

"Glad to see we can both agree on something." A hint of that half smile tugged at his mouth. "Alfred used a much stronger word to describe how stupid I was being."

Despite herself, a smile threatened to surface. She ruthlessly suppressed it. "Sounds like a smart dog."

"The smartest." The playfulness receded, his expression turning serious. "He also mentioned that I should acknowledge I tried to hide behind my job instead of admitting what was really happening between us."

Her pulse raced, heart slamming against her ribs. "And what was that, exactly?"

"I fell for you." The words landed in the space between them, heavy with implication. "Completely. Against every rule I made for myself. Against every line I swore I wouldn't cross."

A tidal wave of emotion crashed over her—hope, fear, disbelief, longing—all battling beneath her carefully composed exterior. She'd spent a lifetime learning to hide vulnerability beneath polish and poise. That training served her well as she fought to keep her voice steady.

"You weren't the only one who fell." If he could be honest, so could she. "But that didn't stop you from walking away."

"I know." Remorse shadowed his features. "I told myself it

was about the mission. About justice. About the principles I've built my career around."

"And now?"

"Now I realize it was about being scared of out of my mind." Dean didn't move, but she felt something give between them. A lowering of an emotional barrier maybe. "Scared of caring too much. Scared of putting someone else before the job. Scared of becoming Jake."

A man who could admit when he was wrong and that something scared him? She crossed her arms so she could pinch herself on the sly. If Dean had come here to lobby for something... "So, what changed? Did Strickland give you permission to have feelings?"

The edge of sarcasm in her question made him flinch, but he didn't retreat. More points in his favor.

"No. Jake did," he said, his voice steady despite the emotion behind it. "Saw the life he and Aubrey built together. And for the first time, I understood that he didn't make the wrong choice. He made the only choice. The one I should have made too."

"What are you saying, Dean?" She couldn't afford to misunderstand. Not about this.

"I'm saying I love you." The declaration hung between them, unadorned and absolute. "Not because you're perfect. Not because you've earned it. Just because you're you."

Her breath caught. After a lifetime of achievement defining her worth, those words struck at her core. But years of conditioning couldn't be undone with a single declaration, no matter how sincere.

"I wasn't enough before," she said quietly, the whole thing raking her insides raw. "What's different now?"

"Everything." He moved closer, still giving her space. "I thought my principles were keeping me on the right path. Turns out they were just keeping me alone."

She shook her head, fighting the yearning to believe him. "I won't be the exception to your rules, Dean. I can't be the thing you tolerate despite your principles."

"You're not an exception. You're the reason I realized I'd drawn all my lines in the wrong place." His voice broke in the middle, which did a number on her heart. "I've spent months hating Jake for choosing Aubrey over the job. But after talking with him today, I understood that he didn't abandon his mission. He found a more important one."

What was Dean saying, that he'd figured out that *Samantha* was his new mission?

The earnestness in his expression tugged at something deep within her, and she wanted this to be real, to be the beginning of something big and lasting and fulfilling.

But Dean had done exactly what she'd expected. Left. As soon as he realized she wasn't enough.

She needed him to see that she'd failed, that she was a hot mess who'd made a muddle of her fresh start. He had no clue what he was getting into, and soon enough, he'd hightail it back to wherever he'd come from *again*.

There was no way she'd believe he'd stay this time.

"I hired Ben back today," she blurted out. "At double his salary. I'm stepping back from running the vineyard myself."

Confusion crossed Dean's face. "What?"

"I'm terrible at running a vineyard," she continued, the admission rushing out, feeling cathartic as much as it felt…awful. "Absolutely hopeless. I killed a batch of wine worth thousands. I can't tell grape varietals apart without a cheat sheet."

"Samantha—"

"I spent my whole life trying to excel at everything," she said, pressing on, needing him to understand. "Believing that achievement was the only path to acceptance. That perfection was the price of being valued."

Her voice cracked slightly. "And when you left, I thought it was because I hadn't been good enough. That if I'd been more worthy somehow, you would have chosen me despite your principles."

Understanding dawned in Dean's eyes, followed by raw pain. "That's not why I left."

"Isn't it?" Every last bolt of her corporate armor vanished as she stared at the ground. "It's all I've ever known."

Dean reached into his pocket, his movements deliberate. "Wait right here. Don't move."

She watched, puzzled, as he turned and jogged back to his truck. He returned moments later with something in his hand—a small bottle no bigger than her palm.

"What's this?" she asked as he held it out to her.

"The wine you ruined." His voice had gone soft around the edges. "I had Carlos salvage a small batch before they dumped it all. Had the label custom-made."

She took the bottle, something catching in her throat as she read it: *Samantha the Vineyard Slayer. First Attempt. Limited Release.*

"It's probably terrible," Dean said, a tender smile touching his lips. "Carlos said it's practically vinegar. Might strip paint if you're not careful."

A laugh bubbled up despite the boulder sitting on her rib cage. "So, you got me terrible wine?"

"I got you imperfect wine," he corrected gently. "Because it's not about the result, Samantha. It's about the attempt. The fact that you put yourself out there and tried something new, even though you knew you might fail. You made this. That's what makes it special. To me."

Something cracked open inside her—a lifetime of striving for perfection challenged by this small gesture that celebrated her failure. This wasn't just about wine. It was about seeing her—really seeing her—and valuing her, not for what she accomplished but for who she was. Flaws and all.

"You kept this?" she whispered, her fingers tracing the label.

"I did." Dean's voice roughened, which was saying something given its already smoky quality. "I saw how devastated you were. How hard you were on yourself. And all I could think was that you didn't see what I saw."

"What did you see?" Good grief. Now her own voice was scraping from her throat like she'd swallowed glass.

"Someone who refused to give up even when she was in over her head. Someone who faced down a staff that hated her, sabotage attempts, arson, and never once ran away."

His words wrapped around her like a warm blanket, soothing places that had been raw for so long she'd forgotten they could feel any other way.

"This isn't solely about saying I'm sorry," Dean continued, his eyes never leaving hers. "It's about showing you that I see you. All of you. Not just the achievements. Not just the successes."

The bottle felt impossibly weighty in her hands, carrying the significance of everything he was trying to convey. "I don't know how to be loved without earning it first."

"Then let me show you," he said, his voice dropping to that register that vibrated through her chest. "Every day, until you believe it."

The sincerity in his eyes broke through her last defenses.

They were just words. Phrases anyone could say using the same combination of letters. And yet, coming from Dean, they meant so much more than that.

He'd remembered her worst moment, recognized what it meant to her and transformed it into something precious. Something that spoke directly to the deepest parts of herself.

"I'm still mad at you," she whispered even as all of her ire drained away.

"You have every right to be." He reached out, his fingers hovering short of touching her face, asking permission. I walked away because I was scared. But I'm not anymore."

She didn't pull away, and his palm settled against her cheek, warm and solid and real.

His thumb brushed away a tear she hadn't realized had fallen. "I love you, Samantha. Not for what you achieve. Not for what you prove. Just for who you are."

The declaration broke something loose inside her. All the fear, all the doubt, all the desperate need to prove herself worthy of affection fought for purchase, but it slid away in the face of his certainty.

Because if there was one thing she knew, Dean always did and said exactly what he believed.

"I love you too," she whispered, shocked that she could speak at all. "And it terrifies me."

"Good." His half smile made her stomach flip, like always. "Means we're both stepping into unfamiliar territory. Together."

His lips found hers, and this time there was no hesitation, no pulling back, no lines being redrawn. Just the certainty of two people who had finally found their way to the same truth at the same time.

When the kiss wound down, she rested her forehead against his chest, listening to the steady beat of his heart. "What about your job? Strickland's team?"

"I'm still in," Dean said, his arms tightening around her waist. "But with modified parameters. Including a home base here instead of at the compound. I already cleared it with Strickland. It was one of two conditions I worked out with him."

She pulled back to look at him, one eyebrow cocked. "You're moving in? Just like that? No conversation, take it or leave it, here I am for better or worse?"

"How else will anyone believe that we're a couple? We don't want the staff talking." His expression carried a smug certainty but also a hint of vulnerability that made her heart swell. "Alfred and I come as a package deal though. Nonnegotiable."

"I think I can live with that." Samantha glanced down at the dog, who sat watching them with what looked suspiciously like satisfaction. "What was the other condition?"

Something in Dean's expression gave her pause, and her stomach swooped as he stared at her. "That my shot at Ruiz would come at some point in the future. After I had a chance to make things right with you. Because you're my number one priority."

Forget sonnets. That sounded like poetry to her. The small bottle of imperfect wine remained clutched in her hand. She'd probably sleep with it, honestly. For the first time in her life, the constant drive to achieve, to excel, to prove her worth, eased into something quieter. Something that felt, surprisingly, like peace.

"I'm not going to be running the vineyard day-to-day though," she told him. "So I might be underfoot a lot."

Dean laughed, the sound warming her from the inside out. "If you thought that was a detractor, sorry. I consider it a perk."

He kissed her again, and Samantha let herself sink into it—into him. Simply accepting what was freely given.

Maybe Greta had been right about one thing after all. Samantha did have the Wagner steel. But unlike her aunt, she would use that strength to build something different. Something that valued people over profits, relationships over results.

Alfred barked once, as if signaling his approval of this new arrangement. Dean laughed against her lips.

"I think that means he's hungry," he murmured.

"Or maybe he's happy to be home," Samantha replied, taking Dean's hand and leading him inside. "Same as his person."

Epilogue

Six months had transformed Wagner Wines from a charred battlefield to a renovated showcase. The Winter Wine Festival lights twinkled across the grounds, casting a warm glow over the northeast field, where new vines now stood in orderly rows, tiny promises of future harvests. Music drifted from the newly expanded tasting room, where Ben efficiently managed the event's logistics with the same precision that had earned him his doubled salary.

Samantha watched from the back patio, smiling at Carlos as he handed her a glass of Tempranillo, his award-winning vintage that had earned a gold medal at the Hill Country competition. A well-deserved victory, announced in the local news alongside a profile of Wagner Wines's new community-focused approach.

"I can't say enough how fabulous this is," Samantha commented and toasted her winemaker before taking a big sip.

Carlos accepted the compliment with his usual deference. They'd come a long way in their relationship, and she appreciated him more than she had words for.

"I can't say enough how nice it is that all the excitement around here is about wine," he said with a suggestive eyebrow lift. "Can we expect that Mr. Carter will be doing his *security consulting* someplace else from now on?"

She'd never fully explained the genesis of Dean's presence

at the vineyard, and frankly, the time had passed. Let the staff think what they liked. "Yup. He's only here for personal reasons. Mine."

Carlos mimed putting his hands over his ears. "I don't need any details about that. I have something to attend to."

He took himself away as she contemplated the many and varied aspects of the festival.

"You're plotting something," Dean said, appearing at her side with Alfred at his heels, as if the conversation with Carlos had summoned him. "I recognize that look."

Good grief, would she ever grow immune to the sight of him in a button-down with his sleeves rolled to the elbows? She sincerely hoped not. The man defined perfection. "I prefer to think of it as strategic vision."

"So, plotting." He grinned and kissed her cheek. "Only you could watch a successful event and immediately start planning how to make the next one better."

"It's my superpower," she agreed, leaning into him. "Just like your superpower is always knowing when I'm thinking too hard."

Dean's arm settled around her waist, comfortable and secure in a way she never could have imagined six months ago. Their relationship had been built on nights of holding each other through nightmares (hers about fires, his about bullets), mornings of coffee on their balcony, and an understanding that Alfred belonged to both of them, but mostly Samantha.

Dean cleared his throat. "Strickland called."

All at once, Samantha's lungs stopped working. "I can't tell from your expression if it's good news or bad."

A smile ghosted across his face. "It's good. Ruiz's bail was denied. Seems the judge correctly decided he might be a flight risk. It's over."

The name that had once haunted Dean now carried a different weight. Three weeks ago, Strickland's team had finally closed the case with Ruiz behind bars, facing airtight federal charges that would keep him locked away for decades. Dean had been there, had watched the man who'd put a bullet in his side finally face justice.

"Justice, not vengeance," Dean murmured, guessing her thoughts. "The right way."

"The Dean Carter way," she corrected, squeezing his hand. "I'm proud of you."

He was quieter for a moment, his gaze distant. "There was a time I would have crossed any line to get him. But when the moment came…"

"You chose to be better than him." Samantha tilted his hat at the angle she liked best on him. "That's why Strickland wanted you on the team. Why he still does."

"I'm glad he didn't mention a new assignment when we talked. I'd like to have a break."

But when the next call came, Dean would go, as he always did, and return to her, as he always promised. Their rhythm had become established over months of learning when to hold tight and when to let go.

The patio doors slid open, revealing Tanner Callahan in all his charming glory. He'd traded his usual tactical gear for dark jeans and a crisp shirt, looking more California surfer than operative.

"Sorry to interrupt the romance novel moment." Tanner's voice carried that edge of amusement that suggested he wasn't sorry at all. "We've got a situation in Austin that needs a strong dose of Knightfall."

Dean winced. "You're not supposed to say my code name in front of people."

"What?" Tanner lifted his hands. "Samantha's not people."

She couldn't stop grinning. "That's your code name?"

"Yeah. With a *K* because everyone is a comedian," Dean said.

It fit him in so many ways that she couldn't count them all.

But now she wondered if his team knew that she'd walked with Dean at midnight all those times and that so much of their relationship had formed on the shoulders of his honor.

He really was her black-and-white knight.

Tanner laughed at Dean's expression. "You should be glad Strickland didn't go with Pack Daddy. That was my suggesti— hello. What have we here?"

Samantha followed his gaze to where a woman stood at the edge of the festival grounds looking lost and as if she'd wandered into a maze with no map. She wore a simple black skirt and an ill-fitting blouse that did her no favors, which immediately made Samantha want to take her shopping so she'd fit in better among the wealthy wine enthusiasts and local dignitaries. The woman had dark hair swept into a severe knot, her enthralled gaze glinting in the festival lights.

"Is that who I think it is?" Dean asked, instantly alert.

"Haven Howard," Tanner confirmed, his expression growing sharp and thoughtful. "This is a fortuitous coincidence. I believe Ms. Howard could use a glass of wine supplied by *moi*."

"What am I missing?" Samantha asked. "Is she someone I should know?"

"A true crime author," Dean murmured as Tanner glided over to snag a flute from a passing waiter. "She wrote a book that exposed a criminal organization operating out of the Hill Country, which has made her a very popular subject of conversation amongst the shadier crowd. She's on Strickland's watch list."

"Is she in danger?" Samantha's eyes widened. "Should you go stand closer to her?"

Dean shot her an amused glance. "I'd clearly be in the way."

They watched as Tanner waltzed across the grounds, his entire demeanor transforming before their eyes. It was like watching a chameleon change colors. His posture subtly altered, shoulders curving forward to diminish his height. The easy confidence in his expression morphed into a seriousness that suggested he frequented tax seminars and libraries.

"Five bucks says he'll ask to be assigned to her case," Dean said as Tanner approached the author.

Tanner's transformation completed itself as he reached her. The confident operative had vanished entirely, replaced by an earnestness that seemed entirely genuine as he introduced himself. Even from a distance, Samantha could see a slight nervousness in his movements, the carefully calibrated impression of harmless enthusiasm.

"That's incredible," she said, not bothering to hide her fascination in watching Tanner in action. "He's completely different."

"Best undercover operative working in the field today," Dean agreed. "A new face for every situation. Sometimes I think even he doesn't know which version is the real Tanner anymore."

Haven Howard seemed cautious at first, then gradually engaged in conversation with Tanner, her guard lowering by degrees right before Samantha's eyes. It was actually impressive to see how easily Tanner drew the woman out of her shell, and when Ms. Howard laughed, Dean shook his head.

"Well, that mission's launched," he said, turning back to Samantha. "Now, where were we?"

"You were going to scope out the perimeter to ensure no baddies are about to crash my festival," she suggested with raised brows.

Dean captured her hand, pressing a kiss to her palm that sent electricity through her entire body. "Duty can wait a few minutes."

"That's not what you said six months ago," she teased gently.

His expression sobered. "Six months ago, I thought lines couldn't be redrawn. I thought protecting justice meant sacrificing everything else."

"And now?"

"Now I know that justice means nothing if I don't have you to come home to." He cupped her face in his hands, his touch reverent. "Everything else can wait. Right now, I want to dance with my fiancée under these ridiculous twinkle lights you insisted on hanging everywhere."

"Fiancée?" she repeated, her heart doing a pirouette in her chest.

Dean's slow smile spread across his face. Before she could process what was happening, he pulled a small velvet box from his pocket, one that had definitely not been there earlier in the evening, or she'd have felt it as often as she'd had her hands on him.

"Dean Carter," she whispered, voice catching. "Are you proposing at a wine festival while a new case unfolds?"

"I'm proposing to the woman who taught me that the most important lines are the ones we choose to cross together," he said, opening the box to reveal a ring with a diamond that caught the festival lights. "The timing is terrible, I know. But when has anything about us been conventional?"

Samantha couldn't help the laugh that bubbled up. "A fake relationship that became real. An investigation that became a partnership. A vineyard disaster that became a home."

"So?" Dean's eyes held hers, steady and certain. "One more line to cross together?"

The answer had been waiting inside her for months. She'd known he was the one probably from that first day when he'd caught her falling from a sabotaged ladder. "Yes."

As he slipped the ring onto her finger, Samantha caught sight of Beckett watching from the patio doors, wearing his usual stoic demeanor, though even he managed a slight nod.

"Mr. Freeze approves," Dean murmured, following her gaze. "That's practically a standing ovation from him."

"Maybe he's jealous," she mused. "I'll have to look through

my contacts and see if I can find a single friend who can thaw him out."

Dean laughed, pulling her close as the band shifted to a slower song.

As they swayed beneath the lights, Samantha felt the weight of the ring on her finger. A line crossed willingly, together. Around them, Wagner Wines hummed with new life and possibility. Somewhere in the crowd, Ben, Jules and Carlos were continuing the work of transforming Wagner Wines into something worthy—not of Greta's legacy, but of the new one they were building together.

"I love you," Dean murmured against her hair. "My Vineyard Slayer."

She smiled. "I love you too. Let's go see if Tanner needs any backup."

Some slaying, after all, was better done as a team.

* * * * *

Get up to 4 Free Books!

We'll send you 2 free books from each series you try
PLUS a free Mystery Gift.

FREE
Value Over
$25

Both the **Harlequin Intrigue®** and **Harlequin® Romantic Suspense** series
feature compelling novels filled with heart-racing action-packed romance
that will keep you on the edge of your seat.

YES! Please send me 2 FREE novels from the Harlequin Intrigue or Harlequin Romantic Suspense series and my FREE gift (gift is worth about $10 retail). I may cancel anytime by emailing ReaderServiceInfo@Harlequin.com or by calling 1-800-873-8635.If I don't cancel, I will receive 6 brand-new Harlequin Intrigue Larger-Print books every month and be billed just $7.19 each in the U.S. or $7.99 each in Canada, or 4 brand-new Harlequin Romantic Suspense books every month and be billed just $6.39 each in the U.S. or $7.19 each in Canada, a savings of 20% off the cover price. It's quite a bargain! Shipping and handling is just 75¢ per book in the U.S. and $1.75 per book in Canada.* I understand that accepting the free books and gift places me under no obligation to buy anything—they are mine to keep for free no matter what I decide.

Choose one: ☐ **Harlequin**
Intrigue
Larger-Print
(199/399 BPA G3CD)

☐ **Harlequin**
Romantic
Suspense
(240/340 BPA G3CD)

☐ **Or Try Both!**
(199/399 & 240/340 BPA G3CE)

Name (please print)

Address   Apt. #

City   State/Province   Zip/Postal Code

Email: Please check this box ☐ if you would like to receive newsletters and promotional emails from Harlequin Enterprises ULC and its affiliates. You can unsubscribe anytime.

> ### Mail to the **Harlequin Reader Service:**
> **IN U.S.A.:** P.O. Box 1341, Buffalo, NY 14240-8531
> **IN CANADA:** P.O. Box 603, Fort Erie, Ontario L2A 5X3

Want to explore our other series or interested in ebooks? Visit www.ReaderService.com or call 1-800-873-8635.

*Terms and prices subject to change without notice. Prices do not include sales taxes, which will be charged (if applicable) based on your state or country of residence. Canadian residents will be charged applicable taxes. Offer not valid in Quebec. This offer is limited to one order per household. Books received may not be as shown. Not valid for current subscribers to the Harlequin Intrigue or Harlequin Romantic Suspense series. All orders subject to approval. Credit or debit balances in a customer's account(s) may be offset by any other outstanding balance owed by or to the customer. Please allow 4 to 6 weeks for delivery. Offer available while quantities last.

Your Privacy — Your information is being collected by Harlequin Enterprises ULC, operating as Harlequin Reader Service. For a complete summary of the information we collect, how we use this information and to whom it is disclosed, please visit our privacy notice located at https://corporate.harlequin.com/privacy-notice. Notice to California Residents—Under California law, you have specific rights to control and access your data. For more information on these rights and how to exercise them, visit https://corporate.harlequin.com/california-privacy. For additional information for residents of other U.S. states that provide their residents with certain rights with respect to personal data, visit https://corporate.harlequin.com/other-state-residents-privacy-rights.

HIHRS2603